LOVE RADIO

Ebony LaDelle

USBORNE

*For that young person who might be from Detroit
and might say, "I could do this, I could write this story,
and I might do it better." Do it. I dare you.*

First published in the UK in 2022 by Usborne Publishing Ltd., Usborne House,
83-85 Saffron Hill, London EC1N 8RT, England. usborne.com

Usborne Verlag, Usborne Publishing Ltd., Prüfeninger Str. 20,
93049 Regensburg, Deutschland, VK Nr. 17560

Written by Ebony LaDelle. Text © Cake Creative LLC, 2022

Author photo © Taylor Baldwin

Cover illustration: Noa Denmon - http://noadenmon.com/illustration

Cover design: Krista Vossen © Simon & Schuster, Inc.

A CIP catalogue record for this book is available from the British Library.

Trade paperback ISBN 9781801313452

Waterstones exclusive paperback ISBN 9781803708133

07611/1   JFM MJJASOND/22

Printed and bound in Great Britain by CPI Group (UK) Ltd, Croydon, CR0 4YY

[LOVE RADIO TRANSCRIPT]

[CROSSFADE OF SONG HERE]

PRINCE JONES: Detroit, what up doe! I'm DJ LoveJones, the prince of love and your new host for the three to four p.m. hour, with DJ Mike coming in for rush hour from four to seven. Welcome to the LOVE RADIO! I can't thank you enough for the outpouring of love with my segment "Last Night a DJ Saved My Life." You kept emailing and DMing us with so many questions that 98.6 decided I needed my own show time! And even crazier, at fifteen I'm the youngest person to ever have a show here.

So, there you have it. Follow me online at @DJLoveJones or call me between three and four every day, and I'll answer any love questions you may have. But trust me, I ain't forgot what time it is – I'll still be spinning all the hits. So hit me up too for requests and with all your love problems. I know you got them...and I have all the solutions.

I'm your guy. Your certified high-school love coach.

[PRINCE PLAYS A SONG]

Chapter One
Broken Record

I've never met a person more drunk on love than my mom. She's got a list of old-school romance movies she's always been obsessed with and has the nerve to rate them in order of her favourites. Thing is, that order changes every month.

For September it's:

1. *Love Jones*
2. *Love & Basketball*
3. *Waiting to Exhale*
4. *How Stella Got Her Groove Back*
5. *Jason's Lyric*
6...the list goes on and on. But you get the point.

I'd be lying if I said I've never watched these movies with her...multiple times...maybe more like thousands of times. But the verdict is still out on how I feel about them.

"This is the best part, sweetie," Mom says, pointing at the screen. "Look!"

Every part is the best part, according to her.

I watch her as she's intensely focused on a movie she's seen over and over again, her feet tucked underneath her butt, her elbow perched on the couch's armrest, and her head resting in her hands. Everyone says my forehead scrunches just like hers when we're concentrating, the brown of it all creasing like the frosting on a caramel cake. "Camille spit you out," says every single relative.

I study her face as her bright, big eyes widen and take in the movie. I guess I have her laser-sharp cheekbones and thick, long hair. But besides that, I'm all Dad. Thank god he's not the constantly lovesick one.

She clasps her hands together as the hero and heroine kiss. "Isn't that everything, baby?"

I roll my eyes.

On the one hand, I appreciate Black artistry in all forms. But these movies always follow the same formula:

1. You got your main characters – the strong Black female lead who has had enough with life and needs to get rid of some sort of dead weight. Usually she does something drastic – like chopping off her long hair, taking a trip to a remote island, or just throwing herself into her work.

2. And then you got your supporting cast. Friends, colleagues, that one over-the-top person who brings comedic relief to the story.

2A. They fit into one of two categories as well. Either they are strongly encouraging the main character to go after the love interest…

2B. …or they're strongly discouraging them until the main character has some epiphany about their unhappiness or lack of love and manages to come around at the end.

The plotlines are predictable and *always* come to a lacklustre climax. Super stale. But everyone thinks that's just my cynical behind.

Take *Love Jones*. Within the first five minutes, the scene opens with a neon-red sign in the cut, illuminating the Sanctuary, a local, moody, smoke-filled poetry spot where the main characters, Darius and Nina, meet, all while listening to the sleek sounds of a woke brotha schooling Black people about how to talk to one another *basic*. Then smooth-ass Darius rolls up on the stage, reciting some poem that was inspired by Nina, speaking on blues and funk…and sex. Nina blows him off at first, but they eventually get together. Had that been me, I guess the movie would be over before it began, because there's no way he would have gotten a first date eroticizing me like that.

As the two characters profess their love for one another *again*, my mom glances over in my direction, expecting me to complain. But I don't – this time. She would just say that these romance tropes are everywhere, and with White Hollywood feeding us Black trauma porn, why not show more romances onscreen with Black leads?

And so, I'm conflicted. As a writer, I love watching for the cinematography, the banter, the showcase of a Black love story blossoming. But at my core, I'm not a rom-com type of girl. The tropes alone make me uneasy when you really think about them.

Childhood friends? I gag at the thought of dating anyone in the cesspool of boys from my childhood.

Falling in love with a bad boy? Let's examine the abusiveness of this trope.

Enemies to lovers? Funniest one yet.

Forbidden love? Mkay.

Just not feeling any of these. If we really want to go there, they're all problematic and simple. Give me writing with more conflict, more depth, something that's more nuanced and grips you, makes you question the world around you. Let's talk about real-life issues that affect us daily, and the traumas our community is untangling. At least, that's the type of writing I want to do.

I feel like the platform should be used to bring more meaning into this world than just a story about two people falling in love. Just my humble opinion.

Still, for some reason, every time I'm tasked with dusting the shelves of our basement entertainment centre and my mom's DVD collection – yeah, don't even get me started – I can't help but pull out *Love Jones* and look at the package. It's the scene of Darius and Nina passionately kissing, in the rain. When no Black girl with a silk press is really gonna want to stand out there and lock lips while getting their hair drenched. And yet? Sometimes I catch myself daydreaming it's me.

"We all deserve a big love story," Mom says as the love scene fades out. "There's nothing better."

"I guess, Ma." I take a deep sigh and exhale it into my blanket. I don't want a lecture today.

I know I sound pessimistic and all over the place. But the truth is, the concept of love just ain't that simple anymore. What people call love now is merely infatuation – more about themselves than trying to actually get to know a person. Whatever happened to someone actually asking you out to dinner, walking you up to your porch to make sure you get in safe, having picnics in the park or passing notes to profess your love? Whatever happened to love that isn't superficial?

I stare up at the family portrait still hanging beside the TV.

Take my parents. While climbing up the military ranks, my dad always said he was *searching for his "other rib"*. And he found her in my mother, a second-year student at University of Detroit Mercy, a private Catholic school in the city. My dad did it all; once he got to know my mom and what she liked, he prided himself on taking my mom places she didn't know about, even though she was born and bred in the Motor City. He wrote her love notes with lines from his favourite poems and her favourite songs, showered her with flowers because she had a budding interest in gardening. He *courted her*.

Meanwhile, most of the guys I know are way too shallow and self-absorbed. They send messages telling their new pursuits how sexy they are. Dudes hit you up depending on how valuable you are online; how many likes and comments you get from your most recent selfie. But the worst of it is, guys don't show respect. No matter how you "present" yourself, how you act, what you do or don't do, a guy will still push it to the limit. Make you feel uncomfortable. Won't respect your wishes when no means…*no*.

I start chuckling when Mom bursts into tears from all the fake movie emotions.

"You laugh now," she says, catching me looking at her. "But wait until it's your heart. It reminds me so much of me and your dad."

I think of my mom and wonder, *How did she create me?* A girl who's so disconnected from love it's frightening. My mom lets out a sigh and turns off the DVD player as the credits roll.

"If that ever happens," I tell her, getting up from the couch and heading to the kitchen.

I snap open a can of Vernors, listening to the pop hiss as I pour and my mom fuss in the background.

Mom follows me into the kitchen. "You'll find love one day. And stop drinking pop in my mugs! Use a glass like a civilized human being."

"Well, the cup's already dirty, so," I say, sipping on my drink with a pinky in the air like a refined woman. I love teasing her.

My mom rolls her eyes. "Sooo, any guys at school you've been eyeing?"

"Meh," I mumble, grabbing a bag of Better Made chips from above the fridge. I'm into the first week of senior year and already over it.

Mom opens the dishwasher and adds a few more plates to

the load. "There are like, what, five hundred students there? I don't understand how there hasn't been *one* boy who's piqued your interest."

I dig loudly into the bag and my mom turns around, inspecting me since we just ate dinner while watching the movie. I find myself slouching, so I stand up straighter and fix my face, trying to do anything to make my anxiety less apparent. But my mom can read me like an open book.

"Are you stressed, Dani? What's going on with you?"

She's asking me about boys. Again. Yes, Ma, I'm stressed as hell.

"I'm a teenager. This is what we do," I grumble, arm deep in the bag of chips. "College applications are a headache, I'm still struggling with this freakin' essay, and I know New York is expensive, but I'm going to be low-key devastated if I don't get into any schools there."

She runs the dishwasher and fixes her gaze intently on me. "I know, baby. You've been anxious about that essay for a while. But if it's too much to juggle right now, there's nothing wrong with staying here, either. Michigan has some great schools, and you can even live at home for a few years while you get yourself acclimated," she adds, smiling. "Plus, your old mama could always use the company."

I take a long look at my mom. At her silky smooth, dark brown face. At the few grey hairs leaping out of her scalp, the rest masked by her most recent colour touch-up. At the clear skin that hasn't even begun to grow crow's feet, or the other normal side effects of age I hear my classmates' mothers complaining about. Thirty-nine. That's how old she is. When my friends used to marvel at how young she looked, my mom would simply remind them about the benefits of being Black, of having melanin. Studying her face closely right now, she barely looks thirty.

We're both hitting pinnacles. That's what Dad calls them. Me heading to college and her turning another decade. I love the age gap between us; she's young enough where I feel like she's been open in telling me so much about herself and her life in ways my friends' mothers wouldn't dare.

But sometimes, I feel like she married my dad and settled into family before her life even began. This isn't the first conversation we've had about me applying for schools in-state while my dad's on the road. But as much as I love her, I know it's just as important for me to do my own thing. With all the love and support my parents have given me, I still feel like a caged bird. I gotta fly.

The hum of the dishwasher is the only sound we hear, which is clear – I've been quiet for too long – so she goes back to cleaning and pivots. "Plus, you'd probably be more interested in college boys anyway." Her statement causes me to jolt, and before I know it the mug slips out of my hand and shatters on the kitchen floor. We both jump.

"Dani, are you okay?" she asks.

I'm still standing there, watching the brown liquid fill up the spaces between each tile.

"Dani. Dani!" My mom touches me, and I recoil. Her soft gaze makes me want to curl in a ball and hide somewhere.

She stares for a moment too long. "Where did you go just now?"

Unsure of what to say next, I just shake my head.

"Baby, I know something is up. You've been acting like this for a while now." Her voice shakes a little. "Talk to me."

"It's nothing, Ma…" Her cell phone rings and my mom jerks.

She hesitates to answer the phone, but before she has time to challenge anything, I tap *accept* for her and my dad's face pops up on the screen.

"Hi, babyyyyy!" Dad says, gushing like a big kid and waving into the camera.

"Hey, Dad," I say, shooting him a head nod.

"How are my two beautiful ladies doing?"

"We're doing fine," Mom replies, still looking at me. I can tell she's trying to collect herself, and I use this time to quickly clean up the broken mug on the floor. She never likes to stress my dad out while he's away. "Just talking about Dani's college applications."

"And how is that going, Dani?"

"It's going fine, Dad," I say, throwing away the pieces, and then deflect, "And *Ma* was watching *Love & Basketball*. AGAIN! Getting all weepy over the part where Monica asked Quincy to play him for his heart."

My dad is cracking up and Mom gives me a playful push. "That scene gets me every time, had me wanting to learn how to hoop back in the day. Both of y'all can kiss my Black behind."

"Gladly," Dad says, and Mom giggles.

WHY.

I give them both a look of sheer horror. "Okay. Ew. Can y'all keep that to yourselves?" They both laugh again. "Dad, I'll talk to you later."

"Love you, sweetheart."

I blow him a kiss and leave, feeling my mom's stare burning the back of my neck.

I dart upstairs and dive onto my bed. I stare at the ceiling. I need to clear my mind, to think about something else. After taking a few deep breaths and waiting for my heart to slow, I take in my favourite place in the whole world – my bedroom. My safe haven.

Along with all things love, Mom is obsessed with DIY projects, so about a year ago, we overhauled my room and now the memory washes over me as I stare at my desk.

After we finished, Mom sat on my bed in awe of all we'd done together. Transformed my little-girl room into a place for this new version of myself.

"It needs one last thing," she said, before racing out of the room.

I sat there, waiting and wondering if she was going to try to have a talk with me about how I'd been reclusive and kept to myself. I prepared all the excuses. But when she returned, a large box sat in her arms. "Come. Sit at your desk. It's missing something and I have just the thing."

My heart thudded as I yanked the tape off the box. "Ma, oh my god, you've done enough!" I said. "What the heck is this?"

"Just open it." She beamed. "And don't try to pick it up. It's heavy."

I opened the lid, and inside was a mint-coloured Adler typewriter.

"I read somewhere that this collector bought Maya Angelou's electric Adler typewriter and said that he didn't care about how it looked or whether it still worked, but he cared that Maya Angelou had touched it. I wanted to get you something that inspired you just the same."

Together, we lifted the typewriter out. It was perfect. A vintage feel to it, with keys rich and black. The body was shiny and luminescent, like it had been buffed and waxed until it was made glossy and new.

"Did you restore this?" I asked.

"Yeah, sort of," she said. "There were a few online that looked like they went through it. But I found this one and it didn't need much, just a little TLC. I figured a few touch-up coats and some new keys would make it look brand-new. And it did."

I ran my fingers over the keys, over the slick body of the machine. And then I saw an emblem underneath the strikers that made me stop dead in my tracks. On closer inspection, I realized the lettering wasn't a logo, but an inscription: MAYA, ALICE, ZORA, TONI, ROXANE, JESMYN, DANI. A knot formed in my throat and I started shaking until I felt my mom's strong hands behind me, gripping me upright.

"It's powerful, isn't it? Seeing your name with the women you admire." I nodded, unable to form any words. Unable to draw in breath. I'd admired these writers for as long as I could remember, but in recent months their work was the only thing holding me together. To see my name next to theirs helped me see that one day I could be that voice for someone like me.

"I don't know if you'll ever use this typewriter to write, but if you do, I want you to see these names as you type *and* I want you to see your name next to them. They are strong, dynamic forces of nature. So are you. We come from a line of strong women, and this" – my mom pointed at the inscription – "is so you never forget that. You deserve to be next to each and every one of these women on this machine, you hear me?"

She'd given me an instrument to write my way through the gloom and toward my dream of being an author.

The same tears that stirred inside me then come back now. I try to use this as a reminder when I'm seated at my desk, tapping at my typewriter, frustrated that the words that used to spill out so easily no longer flow.

My phone buzzes, yanking me away from that memory.

DESTINY: You need to stop being antisocial
and hit up this party with me later

I grimace as I switch my phone to silent mode and pull myself up and to my desk. It's been over a year, and occasionally Destiny still randomly hits me up like everything is normal. I'm not ready to face her. I tried that already and she dismissed me, making me feel like I asked for it. So screw her.

And just like that, it's back. Everything from *that night* begins to repeat like a sports reel replaying on the news, and I'm panting. I try to shift my thoughts and recall an anxiety graphic I saw online. Ways to release the tension in your body:

Roll your head in a circle.

Drop your shoulders.

Take a deep, extended breath from your chest.

I repeat these exercises a few times, until the pressure in my chest begins to lessen and my breath slows.

After that night, my anxiety deepened, and it's been a struggle to write anything ever since. It started with the short stories I used to enjoy scribbling in my journal, and then spilled over into my college applications and the dreaded essay. *Think about an accomplishment, event, or realization that sparked a period of personal growth and a new understanding of yourself or others.* After weeks of staring at my computer screen, I decided to move on to my typewriter, hoping the names my mom had inscribed on this piece of metal would carry me out of the writer's block. But the only thing that's seemed to help me was typing letters to writers I may never meet, sharing how their stories seem to be the only thing helping me. I sit in front of my typewriter now.

High school is a time to grow, to evolve, and for me it feels like I've receded, still not being able to shake something that should be behind me. Maybe I shouldn't be so stuck in the past. Maybe I should get over it, but no matter what I try, nothing seems to work. Even in the privacy of my room, in my own damn thoughts, maybe there is *no* safe haven here. As much as I love this city, maybe I won't stop feeling like this until I'm out of Detroit, starting a new life with new people surrounding me. Building a new crew of people I can trust.

Sometimes it be the ones closest to you that hurt you the most.

Dear Maya,

I'm feeling what you felt growing up. A caged bird. I'm crying out to everyone and to no one at all. My mind is full of rage and hurt and…noise. I can't escape my shrieks and cries and yet I'm unable to sing a song to the people I love the most. My family. My friends.

I can tell my mom notices my retreat – I think she appreciates me being home more while my dad is away, but she knows my social life is at a standstill. She keeps asking about Rashida, and Esi, and Destiny. What do I tell her? That I have no trust in anyone? Even close friends? Because when they're supposed to have your back but don't, that pain is hard to shake. How do I tell her I need help, without her prying and asking what's wrong? Without her wanting to know every detail of that humiliating night? How do I tell my dad, who grew up only understanding to pray the pain away, that prayer won't be enough?

The most important question is, why do I feel so deeply ashamed? I felt like you did, Maya, in that courtroom. I felt strong in my convictions, that in the moment I didn't want it. But now I'm not so sure. I wish I knew, Maya, I wish I knew. How were you able to find your voice again? I keep rereading your words, looking for answers. Looking for closure.

In my darkest hour, thank you for continuing to give me what no one can. You are my remedy. You are my cure.

Dani

Chapter Two

Raising the Bar

PRINCE

It's only a week after Labor Day weekend, but you can already feel the cold coming. Detroit winters wait for no one, and the city gets a lot of flack for somehow never being ready. Sure, there are potholes the size of craters destroying people's tires, and we're always getting hit with some sort of arctic or polar vortex. But for me, I see the end of summer as the calm before the storm, which is the best time. There's just something about the leaves in our backyard turning all types of oranges and golds and browns and the playful breeze whizzing through my basement windows. I hate the stickiness of summer, so the promise of fall gets me hype. It's when I feel I'm most in my zone.

"My dude, you the only one that uses that shit," Malik says. "Stay on everything Hov is up to."

I'm in the basement (aka my bedroom) with my boys after school and we're nodding along to the latest Big Sean album, which just dropped last night on Jay-Z's streaming service, Tidal. Malik's lanky ass is trying to dance. Ant is still in the bathroom and Yaz is the only one actually taking this workout seriously, getting all flushed and shit while he's working on his biceps. "I mean, you and every Beyoncé fan," Malik adds.

"Man, whatever. Listen to this master quality. You not getting this on any of them other streaming platforms." The metal weight clinks as I place it back on the stand. I hoist myself up from the weight bench, vibing to the bass. "Throw me my towel."

Malik winds up like he's about to throw me a curveball and chucks the yellow rag right at my face. I snatch it mid-air, wipe down my neck, and toss it next to my phone, which is vibrating again.

"Malik sort of has a point," Yasin says, taking a plate off the bar. "All my playlists are on Spotify too, so…"

"What about supporting our own, though?" I reply.

"He right, though," Anthony says, coming out the bathroom, a big grin on his face. "If we don't support our own, who will? Dawg, this hand soap smells good. What brand is this?" The stench hits our nostrils at the same time.

"Ant, dude…" I blurt out, scrunching up my nose. "DID YOU LIGHT A MATCH?"

Everyone starts laughing. "Seriously," Malik chimes in, fanning the air. "You could bless us with some spray or something!"

I break to the bathroom and scoop up the air freshener. "It would be helpful for you not to funk up my room. Y'all already stinking it up with your body odour," I exclaim, spraying air freshener directly at Anthony's back.

"Chiiiilll," he whines, protecting himself from the aerosol.

"Here's the real question," I probe. "Ant, what streaming app do you use?" Anthony doesn't say a word and looks at me, like a dog who just got caught chewing his owner's favourite kicks.

"OH, C'MON!" I yell, as laughter ripples through the basement. I shake my head like a disappointed grandma. Another buzz from my phone. I check my messages. No one important.

"What? Spotify had a student deal with no commercials," Anthony argues. "I had to jump on that! Plus, Jay is like a billionaire, so as far as I'm concerned, he ain't missing my nine dollars. I'm just saying. I got a little mouth to feed."

That mouth is his one-year-old daughter, Kisha. The cutest little girl in the world and I will fight anyone who says otherwise.

Malik deflects real quick. "I'm so happy your uncle gave you this weight bench, 'cause we about to be here every day lifting. I'm trying to have every single girl at Mass Tech on me this year." He's checking out his caramel-brown biceps in the mirror hanging over my bathroom door. "I wish I had this before I went to Caribana."

"Try some lotion on them elbows," Anthony adds, making Malik inspect every inch of his arms.

"That's why you're in your current...predicament." Yasin teases.

"Huh?" I ask.

"Oh, you haven't heard?" Anthony replies.

Yasin and Anthony look at Malik on some, *you didn't tell him?* So I know it's bad.

"First week in and Malik had two girls cursing each other out in the hallway at school." Anthony spills the whole thing.

"Wait, WHAT?!" My neck snaps over to Malik. "Care to explain?"

"Listen. It wasn't even like that! So, Rashida is the one I hang with after school when I'm not with y'all, but Charte is my weekend jump-off," Malik says as I begin massaging my temples. "And Charte comes right up to my locker, while I'm hanging with Rashida, mind you, and goes off on me. Talking about, 'You didn't answer your phone this weekend. And by the way, WHO IS THIS!?'" He's imitating Charte as he's telling the story, rolling his neck and pointing his finger nowhere in particular.

"M, really?" I sigh.

Buzz, another phone sound. I quickly check my phone again, and this time put it on *do not disturb*.

"Wait, I'm not done. Then before I can even give an excuse, Rashida pushes me to the side and gets right up in Charte's face. Which is exactly why I'm into Rashida. She's a quiet one but will be quick to defend ya dude when necessary." Malik beams.

A choir-like groan fills the air.

Anthony interjects, "I'm walking up at this point, and all I hear is Rashida telling Charte, 'He's with me,' and Charte popping off, saying, 'You don't know me.' And meanwhile this one right here is beelining to the bathroom. By the time he's almost out of sight, both girls ask him where he's going and this fool replies…'I GOT CLASS!' Hits a corner and books it."

I'm shaking my head, trying my hardest not to laugh. Malik loves when folks are entertained by his foolery, so I can't give him the satisfaction today.

"What?" Malik replies slyly.

"Malik, you know better, that's what," I say. "If you're feeling Rashida, then why won't you let Charte go?"

"'Cause Charte is putting out on the regular! Rashida is ready and willing one minute and gets conflicted and needs to pray to Allah the next. It's too much."

"So, you don't want to be serious with Rashida because she isn't having sex?" I ask.

"Here he go! Mr Luva Luva with his lil radio show advice," Malik says. They all give me shit for it but are constantly listening to it and asking me to fix their relationship problems. The irony.

Yasin and Anthony stare at each other like, *Who is that?*

"Why you gotta be so diplomatic about it?" Malik asks, hopping on the bench and starting his reps.

I walk over to spot him and ignore his *lil* comment but make a mental note to check him about that later. "'Cause you make it sound like a game, M. It's nothing wrong with Rashida's beliefs. But you gotta respect them. And let that girl go if you don't want to be serious. She's really into you, bruh. Do you like Charte?"

Malik takes a beat before speaking. "I mean, I don't know. Charte is a wild ride, just like me."

"But do you *need* another *you* in your life?" Yasin chimes in.

We all shake our heads violently.

"Hell nah," Ant replies. "We can barely stand you!"

"You know what I think?" I let Malik get a few more reps in before I continue. "I think if you went to Charte tomorrow and told her what it is, she'd be fine with it, because she's not ready to really be committed to one person. But you really like Rashida. Just because she's quiet doesn't mean she ain't fun. If she wasn't, you wouldn't be so invested in hanging out with her five days out of the week."

"I mean, I didn't say I was hanging with her *all* five days…" I slap Malik's shoulder and he hops off the bench. I got next.

"You know who this is?" Anthony lowers his voice to sound like a late-night DJ host. "This is the prince of love, here to tell us *all* about our relationship woes. He'll give us advice…and then turn on the ratchet music right after. You feel me?"

Everyone laughs, but Malik is still in his feelings. "Man, whatever," he says, and walks away.

I throw my hands up. "So you not even gonna spot me?"

Malik grabs another towel for himself. "You so worried about me, what about you, Prince Jones?"

"What about me?" I say nervously. I motion for Yasin to come over and assist instead.

"We're gonna ignore that Mr Popular, DJ LoveJones here

keeps checking his phone, hoping it's a certain someone?" Malik sneers, and I tense up. "We're not gonna talk about what happened with you and your ex?"

I lie down and grab the bar. "It's nothing to talk about," I tell him, driving the metal bar hard in the air. My endorphins kick into high gear.

"Yeah, okay," Malik says. He can tell he hit a nerve, so I know some shit talking is about to commence. "I'm not the only one who feels that way, man. Ant and Yaz curious too."

Anthony speaks up immediately. "Man, Prince, it ain't even like that. You haven't said a word about the break-up, and now that Morgan went to college and is with that new dude..." The bar plummets onto my chest and knocks the wind out of me. Yasin struggles to grab the bar, and Anthony and Malik rush over to help. "Yooo, you didn't know??"

I slide off the bench and crouch to the ground, trying to catch my breath. All I can do is shake my head.

Out of nowhere, Yasin slaps Malik upside the head.

"What the fu..." Malik howls.

Somehow that does it for me, and I'm fighting a coughing fit from cracking up. "Yasin just smacked the shit out of you!" I manage to get out. Anthony is laughing so hard, he's holding his belly in pain.

"Yaz, you lucky I like you or you'd be on the floor with Prince," Malik replies, rubbing his head. "See? Always the quiet ones you gotta watch out for."

Yasin extends his hand out for me to latch on to. Yaz moved down the block from me when we were both six, and we've been cool ever since. He's Chaldean and his parents are pretty strict, so back in the day he'd pretend to be in his room studying and would sneak over to my crib, until I convinced his dad I could get his grades up in six months and came through on my promise. Now they assume every time Yaz is with me, we're deep in the books.

"I'm sorry, man," Yasin says after helping me up. "You okay?"

"You mean outside of you hurting everyone tonight?" We all laugh. "Nah, I unfollowed her." I'm still rubbing my chest, trying to push out the sensation. "So, who's the guy?"

Anthony is already on the case. "Some guy named Tyrone. I looked him up. The guy is swole as shit. He like, plays ball or something."

I feel myself getting light-headed. "Wait, wait, wait. Tyrone Jackson?"

Malik and Yasin nod slowly, scared of what might happen next.

"Oh, they said you might know him," replies Anthony, who at this point has given up on working out and is eating a bag of salt-and-vinegar Better Mades he pulled out his backpack.

I sigh. "Ant, if you ain't the most non-sport-watching dude I know. Everyone knows him. He's Michigan's top wide receiver." I throw my towel in the hamper and sit on my navy-blue futon (aka my bed). I look around at my room to try to centre myself – blue futon on one side of the basement, weight bench on the other, Marvel drawings by Yasin hung up on my wall. My boy's got talent.

Malik plops down next to me. "I feel like shit, man."

"You should," I spit back.

"But hey, now is a good time to get yourself back out there. You a lil rusty anyway, and since you all over Detroit's radio, you could bag anyone at school if you wanted to." This is his way of making me feel better. Typical Malik. A few girls have caught my attention, but there's one above them all who I've secretly crushed on since we were kids. They make fun of me every chance we get, reminding me she's unattainable, but they know the code. This secret stays between us.

I'm interrupted by a resounding *boom* upstairs, and the ceiling reverberates from the sound.

Mom.

Malik and I jump off the futon.

"Be right back. Wait down here!" I race up the stairs before anyone can question anything and frantically check every room.

"What happened?" My little brother, Mook, peeks out of his bedroom door, the sound of his video game buzzing in the background.

"It's nothing, lil man. Go back to playing your game." I try to play it as cool as possible so I don't freak him out. And it works. He slams his door and probably rushes back to what he's doing.

Where did that noise come from?...The bathroom.

I open the door, and my worst fears are right there laid out in front of me.

My mom in her birthday suit with her butt planted on the

floor, looking dazed. I mean, I thought I'd experienced it all with her.

I quickly shut the door and stand on the other side of it.

"Oh Lord!" I can hear her squeal, and it sounds like she's trying to use something to cover herself.

"It's okay, Ma," I say as I quickly open the door again and throw her a towel I grabbed from the hallway closet. She looks at me with those sorrowful hazel eyes. The same eyes each time. When she tries to be a little more careless than usual with her routine...no, when she tries to *normalize* her routine. Without restrictions, things turn quickly. Taking a bath is a struggle for her. So I tried to save money and install a grab bar myself, but of course I wouldn't call myself Mr Fixit. It lasted all of three weeks before it started raising up from our bathroom floor. I told my mom to wait for Uncle Jerome to come and fix it, but she's one of the most hard-headed people I know. And we can't afford to install a walk-in tub. So here we are. His schedule is crazy busy with his radio appearances and yet somehow, I'm the one who feels guilty for not being able to get him over sooner.

"Prince! Everything okay, man?!" I hear Ant yelling from the bottom of the basement stairs. God bless him for not trying to come up.

"Ma, how do you feel? You think you broke anything?" I ask through the cracked door.

"No, just my butt," she replies. Then chuckles.

"Okay, stay right here. Let me ask the guys to leave." I rush downstairs and let them know my mom needs my assistance, without giving them details, and head back up to tend to her. I knock this time.

"You covered?" I ask, still trying to unsee what I saw not even five minutes earlier.

"Prince!" she exclaims.

I peek in.

"Pass me my robe."

I lightly throw the robe hanging on the bathroom door and close it again. I listen closely to make sure she's okay and can hear her fussing on the other side.

"You need help?"

"Nah, baby."

My heart pounds as I wait until she tells me she's decent.

I open the bathroom door and she gives me a look of deep embarrassment as I walk in.

"Ma, it's okay," I whisper, and crouch down next to her.

"No, it's not. This is like the worst thing a mother can do to her son. All I was trying to do was do something on my own. But I never would have imagined...God! I scarred you for life!"

I shrug. "I mean..."

She flicks my shoulder. "Prince!"

"Look, I'm going to be messed up. That's what it is. I might need therapy."

We both laugh.

"PJ, I am *so* sorry. Your mom is just trying to be, well, a mom. The MS just..." Her voice breaks.

Multiple sclerosis is a tricky one. She was diagnosed after

my ninth birthday, so I was old enough to see her perfectly healthy, and old enough to notice her health's decline. I will never forget it. The day after my party, I found her on this very floor, her speech slurred. I thought I was going to lose her that day, but even in my fear I somehow managed to call my uncle Jerome, who drove like a maniac to the house while calling the ambulance. After many tests we found out she had relapsing-remitting MS, which meant she'd have periods of remission, with a relapse happening based on anything – high stress, a cold I caught at school, or just about anything that attacked her body. With each relapse, her body started to betray her. She went from being able to walk just fine, to suddenly having a fall and needing a cane. She could go months without having a flare-up, and then one would hit her with a vengeance, having her in and out of the hospital for weeks. Her muscle spasms began coming more frequently, and once Mook came into this world, her fatigue spells came more often than not. By ninth grade, I essentially stepped in as her caregiver.

"I'm going to be okay," she keeps muttering.

"Yes, Ma, you will." I get that tight feeling in my throat and suddenly feel flushed. I'd like to think it's from the steam of the bath, but deep down I know what it is.

Guilt.

Before the guys came over, I was online, browsing some of the extracurriculars CUNY has to offer, fantasizing about a dream internship at one of NYC's hottest satellite stations. But this is my reality. As much as I want to attend a school out of state, I can't imagine abandoning my family. Or leaving my mom. They need me.

"Ma, I know you don't want the help. I get it. You should be able to take a nice bubble bath and put those bath rocks and balls and all that other shit you want in there."

She smiles. "Bath salts, Prince. And watch your mouth."

I always get "in trouble" for dropping a curse word here or there, but my mom secretly enjoys it. The only thing she asks of me is to watch my language around her church friends. Which is pretty easy, since they're always helping moms out around the house when she's feeling especially sick, and usually stuffing my face with bomb soul food.

I shrug. "Rocks sound better." She touches my face endearingly. "But Ma, the biggest thing I need from you? Is to be *here*. Stop trying to be superwoman. That does me no good if something happens to you while you're trying to prove a point and I'm stuck trying to hold it down for me and Mook. Please. Promise me." She wipes a tear from my cheek, which catches me off guard. I didn't realize I was crying.

"Okay, PJ," she whimpers. "Okay."

An exhale escapes my mouth. "Grab on to my shoulders. Let's get you up."

[LOVE RADIO TRANSCRIPT]

[CROSSFADE OF SONG HERE]

PRINCE JONES: What up, Detroit, I'm DJ LoveJones, the prince of love, back today for another segment. Welcome to the LOVE RADIO! I'll keep the hits spinning and keep answering your questions.

Let's start with an email I got a few days ago from my homie Derrick. He says: "There's this girl in my school that is fine as hell. She seems cool but is always around her girls every time I see her, so there never seems like a good time to holla at her. But I finally did it. I approached this girl after months of trying to talk myself into it, and she curved me. Like *hard*. It ended with her and her girls laughing at me while I walked away. I'm still trying to recover from my hurt ego. How do I even step to any girl again after this?"

Damn. When one guy's soul gets crushed like this, it hits us all. All I can say is every guy probably has a similar rejection story, even me. A few years ago I stumbled on this video that was wild: some guy decided to overcome his fears and embrace rejection for a hundred days, so every day he came up with some new way to put himself out there and every day he got a little more comfortable getting shot down. But then one day he went to this donut shop and asked a woman to make Olympic-style donuts, fully expecting her to say no. But she ended up doing it! I started to look him up, and he had this lecture about not letting rejection define you, but letting your reaction to how you get rejected define you – to turn rejection into an opportunity. So you took an L, use this opportunity to take what happened with ole girl and change your approach a little for next time. I'm not saying step to every girl that comes your way, but there will be more you're feeling. Not everyone is for everyone. For every girl that is not feeling you, there are others who will be.

Now to get your ego going, here's a song I think you can appreciate. Don't let one bad moment mess up your game.

[PRINCE PLAYS A SONG]

Chapter Three
Sour Note
PRINCE

I'm in the Detroit Public Library on a Saturday morning, scrolling through these picture books and getting annoyed. Like damn, are all these books about animals? You got shit like *The Chicken and the Pig*, *The Snake and the Fish*, and all these other animal combinations that I swear would be enemies in the animal kingdom. But somehow they think it's cute to put all these random-ass animals together and call it a day.

I already know my lil bro will not be impressed. One, 'cause he isn't gonna feed into this fake peace-and-love bullshit, but two, 'cause he's gonna want some faces on the covers of these books that he can recognize. Boys with brown faces, doing boy things. Where's the books on riding your bike, or playing ball? Hell, I'll even take a book on Black boys gaming. Anything but this sorry selection.

"Can I help you?" the librarian asks, sneaking up behind

me. The lady approaching me is rocking a short, curly do, and her amber-brown skin is covered in freckles. She's wearing flashy red glasses, so based on her style I'd peg her as not a day over thirty-five. But you know, the way Black women age she could honestly be pushing fifty. "Looking for something in particular?"

"Yeah, I'm trying to find something for a seven-year-old whose attention span is…extremely short."

"Hmmm." She ponders for a bit before she picks up *The Snake and the Fish*. Goddamn it. "Well, this book has vivid illustrations, and the storyline is easy and fun to follow. It's—"

"May I?" She nods. I kindly take the book from her hands and read aloud one of the pages.

"'The snake is down to ride all day, when the fish comes out, he's ready to play.' For real?" The librarian snorts, and then quickly covers her mouth to keep quiet. "Like, who vetted this shit and said it was okay to put out?"

She clears her throat and gives me a stern look.

"Sorry," I quickly respond. "I'm just saying, this is wack. My brother would chuck this book at my face if I tried reading it to him."

She sighs. "You don't know how many librarian conferences I've been to, complaining about this very thing to publishers. In our community, this doesn't fly."

"Thank you, you feel me." I lean against the end of the bookcase. "So where are the Black books at?"

After she helps me check out a couple of books worthy to take home to Mook, I decide to glance around. It's been a while since I've stepped foot in any sort of library or bookstore. I'd love to one day fill my brother's bookshelves with all types of reads, but first, that would require me purchasing him a bookshelf, and second, that would require me to have extra funds to buy all those books. And the way my family's funds are set up right now, that's not really an option.

Now, walking through the row of cinnamon-coloured bookshelves, I'm realizing more and more how much my ass needs to read, and how surprisingly soothing this place is. I should bring Mook here. I spent the early morning at the station and decided to pop in after, since Ant has been telling me for months to come here and get some books for my brother. The main building is beautiful, and the architecture is dope, with its white marble and Renaissance vibe. Plus, they have free programming for kids, so it would definitely help to get Mook out the house when moms is feeling under the weather. I stumble into the non-fiction section and my eye catches a book on the history of radio. Mr Smith, my high school guidance counselor, has been telling me to look up some literature on music and deejaying, and I told him I'd check it out but I was just blowing smoke. Looking at this section, I feel bad for not listening. Dawg, where have I been?

I scoop it up and take a look at the description on the back when I hear shuffling. I glance up, and it feels like time slows down.

She's here.

The girl my homies have been clowning me about since middle school.

The crush I could never shake.

It sounds cheesy, but somehow her chestnut skin is still able to radiate under these abrasive-ass fluorescent lights. Usually she doesn't shy away from switching up her hair, but today, her long box braids pulled back by a colourful silk scarf let me see her clear skin even more so. She's wearing Chucks, and some semblance of a sweater that is also a dress. It's wild, 'cause I know this is probably her casual look, but I'm all the way into it.

She walks slowly down the aisle, tracing her fingertips along the spines of the books with one hand, a healthy stack of books nestled under her arm. In a split second something catches her eye, and she jerks like she just found gold and places her pile of books on the ground to take a closer look. Like, she's looking at every aspect of her new joy: scanning the cover, reading the summary that appears on the back of the book, and you can tell she's reading the intro shit on the first couple of pages before the book even starts. I'm intrigued. What is it about this book that has her so captivated?

Prince, man, just walk up to her and say hello. I've been wanting to do this for years, but it never seemed like the right time. In the earlier parts of high school she'd be with her girls, and then I stopped seeing her around them altogether. Now I'm lucky if I even spot her in the hallway between classes. She's usually got AirPods in and in a rush to get to her next destination. This is the only time she's alone and…approachable. But for some reason my feet are planted on this damn library floor like I'm Spider-Man. What is wrong with me?

My stomach flip-flops and sweat trickles down my back the closer I get. I force myself to continue walking until I'm right up to her. She looks up suddenly, her eyes in a state of panic. Doubt creeps in as I realize maybe in my attempt to approach her, before my nerves got the best of me, I might have been a little too…pressed. I'm so mad at myself. I'm right up on her and she probably thinks I'm a weirdo.

She blinks a few times. "Can I help you?"

"I'm sorry," I finally answer. "I'm so tall that sometimes I have a hard time recognizing how close I actually am to someone shorter than me."

Smooth, Prince.

C'mon.

"Well, I'm not above six feet, but from what I hear, five-six is still above average," she says.

"No, no, no, I didn't mean it that way. It's just…" She's giving me a look that I can't shake. It's obvious she's trying to figure out why I'm still standing here. I swallow hard and try my best to fix this train wreck. "So I noticed you were really into the first few pages of that book. What had you so…" *Use big words, man.* "Entranced?"

She smirks. "The dedication."

Huh?

"Oh yeah, those are cool," I say as if I've actually read a book dedication.

She sneers. "You have no idea what that is, do you?"

I nod, but my mouth betrays me. "Noooope." An expression that looks like…confusion, annoyance washes over her.

"It's exactly what it sounds like. Like when singers or actors dedicate an award to someone or something special. Authors do the same thing."

"But why are you reading it?" My diarrhoea of the mouth is going strong today. And yep, she definitely rolled her eyes at me.

"Because it's nice to see what headspace an author was in at the time. What they were feeling. Who they directed their love, admiration, or even their resentment to in that moment." She turns her body at me and gives me her full attention, as if suddenly she's had an epiphany. "I'm sorry, do I know you?"

"My bad, I'm not doing myself justice right now. I promise I'm normal. But you don't remember me?"

She gazes at me, perplexed. *Guess not.*

"We had a couple of classes together in middle school… but you also might know me as DJ LoveJones on WXRB 98.6." She blinks a few times, but nothing. "The Prince of Love? I'm Prince. That's me."

Dawg, what is happening to me?

"I have an Apple subscription. That's what I listen to when I'm driving."

Ouch. "You probably should be supporting Tidal, since they give their artists more of the profit share."

"Thanks, Dad, I'll keep that in mind." She rolls those divine eyes of hers. Again.

Damn, she just crushed my entire ego with that one. She glances at my arm, filled with children's books. I quickly hide them behind my back.

"Are those picture books?" she asks smugly.

I give an awkward smile. "Yeah, they are."

She sighs. "Look, I see what's happening here. But guys who have kids aren't really my thing, so sorry." She directs her attention back to the book she's holding, as if she's decided this conversation is over.

I shake my head slowly and bite my lip, a thing I tend to do when I'm pretty heated and trying to parse my words. But it doesn't work this time, and my verbal diarrhoea strikes again. "Damn, are you always this judgemental?"

"Excuse me?" she replies, slamming her book shut. "*You* approached *me*…"

"Yeah, I did. 'Cause you're in the library, with a stack of books by your side, completely enamoured with them. So it told me not only are you beautiful, you're also cultured. You can teach me a thing or two. I bet your conversations are fire. You respect the arts. Even if I'm not a big reader, or know what a dedication is, watching you makes me want to find out." She fidgets. "But I'm good now. 'Cause while I'm writing your story, you doing the same thing. My friend Ant has a one-year-old, and he's a bwwetter human and a better dad than anyone else I know. So if you judging people based on that, then I changed my mind, I don't need to get to know you." I hug the picture books close to my heart. "And just so you know, my brother was diagnosed with attention deficit hyperactivity disorder. I read to him every night to calm him down." I bounce and leave her standing there, stunned.

As I pass the front desk, I throw up the peace sign to the librarian. "Thank you for your help."

"I hope your brother enjoys," she calls back, as I walk out. I turn the corner in time to get one last peek at Danielle. With the book still in her hand, she looks shocked and downright dejected. And even though I didn't put my best foot forward when stepping to her, I've never felt more proud of myself.

[LOVE RADIO TRANSCRIPT]

[CROSSFADE OF SONG HERE]

JEROME WILLIAMS, HOST [a suave, soothing voice comes over the airways]: Back up a spot from number seven to number six is Sade's "Your Love Is King." I'm DJ Romes and you are listening to WXRB 98.6's *Quiet Storm*.

[JEROME PLAYS THUNDER RUMBLING SOUND EFFECT]

It's chilly out tonight, which means I'll be playing music that will make you want to hold that special person tight all night long. But before I do, I got a special treat for you.

To all my brothas out there looking for a special lady, or who already have one and are looking for advice, I'm introducing a new segment called "Last Night a DJ Saved My Life." So many people call or DM me for relationship advice, but I am just here to provide the jams for sweet lovemaking.

But I did call in a special someone to help me in that department. Tonight, I'm joined by my nephew DJ LoveJones, our newest DJ and Detroit's unofficial expert on love. Welcome.

PRINCE JONES: Thank you for having me, DJ Romes.

JEROME WILLIAMS: And what are you schooling us on today?

PRINCE JONES: We're going to talk about the art of trust.

JEROME WILLIAMS: Okay, I'm into it, go on.

PRINCE JONES: You got an email a few weeks ago from Jasmine, asking about monogamy and trust. She says, "I have never been one to get too jealous too fast, but lately my boyfriend has been hanging out with his co-worker a lot. They text all hours of the night, and I found out recently that he and her go on lunch dates twice a week. When I confronted him about it, he said they were just friends and I was acting jealous. My thing is, I wouldn't have tripped over any of this. But when I ask you about your day and for the past three weeks you've skipped your lunch plans, it makes me think there's a reason you're not telling me this. What should I do?"

JEROME WILLIAMS: Damn, DJ LoveJones, that's a tough one.

PRINCE JONES: It is. It's easy to point blame when there is blatant disrespect or infidelity, but what if the lines are murky? What do you do if you see something abnormal happening and your significant other is totally oblivious to it, or refuses to acknowledge it? What do you do if the trust is slowly chipping away?

JEROME WILLIAMS: Well...?

PRINCE JONES: You have to confront them. Any friendship done in secret isn't a friendship. It's generally an emotional affair. Ask your partner if their co-worker has ever given them relationship advice and if so, what type?

Ask them if they are sharing feelings and general life problems with them over you. And the biggest question – if your significant other and this person are so close, have you hung out with them? It seems trivial, but if that friendship is important to your partner, and you are important to your partner, it should be shared with you.

JEROME WILLIAMS: That's solid advice, DJ LoveJones. Would you ever advise this woman to confront the co-worker?

PRINCE JONES: Hell nah. That gets messy. The co-worker ain't gonna do nothing except deny. They both in this affair together, and the last thing the co-worker wants to do is jeopardize that.

JEROME WILLIAMS: But what happens if you get nothing from your partner when you confront them?

PRINCE JONES: It's rough, but at a certain point you have to decide how much you're going to take. If they still love you and you threaten to leave, they should fight for you. But you can't make idle threats, either, so don't just talk the talk. If they aren't committed to keeping you there, it's time to go. People fall in and out of love all the time. Either your partner will come to their senses, or you'll be back on the market and that will open you up for true love with someone else.

JEROME WILLIAMS: There you have it, lovebirds. Make sure whoever you're with tonight is always ready and willing to fight for you. And tune in every Friday night for another segment of "Last Night a DJ Saved My Life," where

DJ LoveJones will be answering your relationship questions. DM us on Facebook or Instagram or give us a call at 313-555-5113. DJ LoveJones, give the people something to snuggle to.

[PRINCE PLAYS KEITH SWEAT'S "TWISTED"]

Chapter Four
My Heart Skips a Beat
Danielle

"Shit, shit, shit!" I shove myself away from my desk and scowl at the typewriter. It's 7:02 a.m. and to spark some sort of creativity, I'm trying to rewrite a short story I drafted months ago, but now my essay-writing funk has turned into an I-can-no-longer-write-anything-anymore writing funk… and now to add to it, all I can think about is that terrible run-in with that boy from my school.

Prince.

But I can't focus. That whole thing keeps playing on repeat. I need to really figure out who this guy is. In order to keep a level head, I've completely detached myself from high school life so that my focus is on college…which means I have no idea what's going on at Mass Tech anymore. It took me a while of scrolling through some old yearbooks, but I found the guy from yesterday. In our middle school classroom pictures, he looks completely different, a scrawny little thing then, with his hair in cornrows. Now he's attractive by high school standards. And extremely tall, so you know girls are all over him. Initially I thought he was an athlete, which are the guys I adamantly stay away from.

But the radio?

I mostly listen to music on streaming sites or audiobooks. So what if I assumed he had a kid? I had every right to think so, based on the evidence. And I had every right not to want to date a guy with a kid, right? Plus, he came up to me extra pompous and practically everything he said was off-putting.

Then why do I feel so awful?

I do the thing I always made fun of my friends for doing: online stalking. I reactivate my social media accounts, find all his handles, and click through them. He's got several thousand followers, and most of his content is sessions of him showing music samples; him mixing songs and educating his followers on the sample versus the sampler. I watch a few and learn about some of my favourite artists and the old-school songs their work came from, watching him speed up or slow down a track, fiddling with his controller until you can hear the sampled song emerge. Other than that, his accounts are mostly flooded with photos of him at the radio station, with DJ Romes, the voice of Detroit. Trolling the comments, I find out DJ Romes is in fact his uncle. So that's how he got this gig. His uncle is like the city's most beloved DJ. Interesting.

I scroll through his Instagram page some more until I see a picture of Prince with the most adorable mini version of him. The little boy has Prince in a fake chokehold, and Prince has the most ridiculous look on his face, like he's surrendering to his little brother's strength. His brother is giving him everything he's got, too, I mean tongue sticking out while he's attempting to keep him pinned down, his mini locs all in his face, his little muscles flexing. I can't help but be amused by this picture. The joy on his brother's face…the way he's looking at Prince.

Ugh. I feel like the worst person in the entire world. This little guy clearly sees his brother as the most important person on the planet. And the way Prince roasted me in the library, it's clear the feeling is mutual.

The caption reads: *My forever ace. Happy birthday to my favourite little man Mook. I got you always.*

I click back to my main feed, and a selfie of Rashida and Esi pops up. Rashida's rocking a tan hijab with a matching trench, giving me Halima Aden vibes all the way. Of course, Esi is looking radiant as ever, her perfect chocolate skin popping with zero blemishes, her cat eyes creeping out of the sharp bangs of her weekend wig she named Donna. The picture was posted from Rashida's account, with the caption, *Girls' night out…high heels with higher standards.*

I chuckle. Anytime that caption pops up, it usually involves rebounding from a crush. Last time I hung out with them, Esi was trying to get over Kayla. Esi is our Ghanaian queen, always dolled up, with the confidence of someone twice her age. She was always the one coming over, trying new hairstyles on my mane, me happily obliging for a chance to get free, at-home salon service. And she never disappointed. Esi started taking "clients" to earn some extra cash and was so popular we began to joke about her pencilling in our friendship when she had time. Even my mom was in awe of her self-assuredness, so to see her cave under Kayla's trap was a shock to both Rashida and me.

I can't fake, I miss them. It was so much easier for me to be around them when I didn't have this secret looming, eating me up. And they know me too well, so faking like everything is all right wouldn't work around them. I'm just not the same person I used to be.

I can only imagine what they would tell me in this situation. I miss them piling up in my room. I look around, thinking about how they'd claim their spots as we'd all be hanging, preparing for midterms. I daydream about what they might say if they were with me right now.

"I don't blame you," Esi would say, filing her nails. "A kid? I would make the same assumption."

Rashida would throw a pillow at Esi. "Both of you are something else. Dani, you're foul for that one."

My mouth would be agape. "Damn, Rashida, don't hold back!"

"What?! This guy comes up to you…in like your favourite place in the *world*. And asks you what you're reading?" She'd huff. "I wish a guy our age would show interest in any of my hobbies."

"You might have a chance, if you let a certain someone go," Esi says, rummaging through my nail polish collection. Rashida rolls her eyes.

"What's his name?" I ask.

"Malik. It's just…" Rashida plops on my bed and folds her arms. "When it's good, it's good. He can be flaky, but it's hard when you're into someone."

"Is he messing with other girls, Rashida?" I would ask, sitting beside her.

"I mean, we haven't made it official…" she'd reply.

"Plus, Shida hasn't given him none," Esi would butt in. "She knows what she's doing."

Rashida sighs. "I want to…I just don't trust him yet."

I'd give her a side hug. "I think it's a smart decision. Be sure of his intentions first."

"Personally, hon, I think you could absolutely do better." Esi throws the pillow back at Rashida and sighs, finally giving us her full attention. "But back to you, Dani, let me be clear. Yes, I would have assumed he had a kid, but afterward I would have apologized. Family is everything, and my dad always said the way a man treats his family shows you how he'll treat you."

My phone vibrates in my hand and snaps me back to reality. I tap accept.

"Heeey, beautiful!" My phone screen is taken over by my dad's chiselled face and rich brown complexion. I've never known him with facial hair, but anytime my dad is home for more than a few days, his five o'clock shadow always lingers, waiting to emerge after years of pruning. He still has on his army fatigue hat, but he's wearing a fitted tee with his head leaning against a cement wall somewhere, currently in North

Carolina. I can't see the rest of his body, but I can tell he's sitting on the floor, one leg probably propped up and the other lying flat on the cold ground. Dad says when you've been in the army as long as he has, you learn to get comfy anywhere. He's been gone for a few months now but will finally return home next week. As much as FaceTime keeps us connected, I can't wait to have him home long enough to see his five o'clock shadow again.

He typically calls me at the oddest hours, usually early in the morning, while my mom is asleep and I'm up doing everything and nothing. My mom is a night owl, and I'm an early riser like him.

"How's it going, babygirl?"

"I'm good, Dad. Did you get my email?"

He pauses. Which isn't a good sign. "I did…"

"And…?" I enquire.

"I gotta be honest, Dani baby, I don't know if this is the one."

I dramatically throw my head back and let out a loud sigh. "This college essay will be the death of me," I say.

My dad quickly tries to reassure me. "There's something there, though. It just feels like…how do I put this…" he responds, caressing his chin. "It still feels like you're holding back a little."

If only he knew how much. I nod. "I think I get it, Dad. Thanks for looking at it."

"Anytime," he says. "Was that too much? You look extra pensive."

I shrug my shoulders. "Can I get your advice on something?"

"Shoot," he says, and for a brief moment nods at someone who passes by him. Then he's right back to giving me his undivided attention.

"I was at the library yesterday…"

"Oh, what did you get?"

I roll my eyes. "Ummm, the only thing I think you'd appreciate is Nikki Giovanni's latest collection. Everything else is new authors you haven't been put onto yet."

He nods in approval. "Niiice."

I point my two fingers to the phone. "Focus! So anyway, this guy from school comes up to me and is trying to get at me. He's annoying." Dad lets out a hearty laugh. He's absolutely smitten with his little girl not being boy-crazy. "He has these picture books in his hand and I flat-out tell him I'm not interested in a guy with kids."

"What did he say?"

"That's the thing, Dad. He went off on me. Told me that the books were for his brother and not his child, but even if he had a child, so what, and he thought I was interesting but now he just sees me as some stuck-up girl…"

Dad holds his hand up to the phone. "Wait, wait, wait. Did he say all that?"

I take a beat. "Well…not exactly."

"Well, what exactly did he say?" Dad asks.

It wasn't just the way he curved me, but the sweet things he said before he did it. He mentioned my love of books and me being cultured and the narrative he had already made of me…before I shattered it. "I mean, it wasn't that bad, but I don't remember," I lie.

"You know I love you, right?"

Uh-oh.

"Dani baby, what you said was messed up."

My guilt settles in, so I turn my whining dial all the way up. "But Daddyyyyy…"

"I don't want to hear it," he tells me, voice stern. "You complain about going to stores in Farmington Hills and being watched or followed, and you and me both know our people are stigmatized all the time. You can't complain about being vilified and then turn around and do the same thing. 'But she looked suspicious.' 'But he's wearing a hoodie, officer, how else am I supposed to feel?' 'But he reached into his pocket – what else was I supposed to do?'"

Damn, okay, Dad.

I don't have anything to say, so I'm giving Dad the serious pout face. He chuckles and says, "Remember how you felt when you visited your aunt Dorothy for two weeks in Alabama?"

I know what story he's getting at, because I remember every damn detail. I went down south and stayed with his baby sister, Dorothy. She's my favourite of the bunch, and just had my cousin, who was the chunkiest little baby I had ever laid eyes on. I mean rolls for days. I was a scrawny little twelve-year-old, but that didn't stop me from placing Katelyn on my hip and carrying her around everywhere we went.

Katelyn couldn't get enough of me either, so once when we were shopping in Walmart, we both ventured off while Aunt Dorothy went to purchase things for the house. A Waspy White woman approached me as I was browsing the books section.

So yeah, I remember. But instead I mumble, "Kind of."

"Well, I do," Dad exclaims. "I remember you describing some crotchety White woman coming up to you, asking you what size does your daughter wear." She had on a floral dress, white gloves…the quintessential White woman church attire starter pack.

"You called me, livid," Dad continues. "Said, 'Daddy, I told that woman I'm twelve years old, and this is not my offspring. Now if you'll excuse me, I'm off to take her to her actual mother.' And stormed off. 'Offspring'?" Dad is laughing even more at this point, and so am I.

"I *did* channel my best, 'May I speak to your supervisor?' voice, just like Mom taught me," I reply, and then sigh heavily. I walk over to my bedroom window and let my mind drift a bit, looking at the multicoloured Tudor-style homes with bay windows and manicured lawns lining my block, watching a fireball of colours caress the landscape, the sun rising to its full glory.

We live in a two-storey redbrick home in Palmer Woods, what most would call one of the most upscale neighbourhoods in the city. My dad bought into this neighbourhood a few years after joining the army – he was a man who said going into the military saved his life, and his pockets, too. He grew up poor and in the South, and used it as an opportunity to attend school for free. But my dad always bought into the idea of family, even before he had one. I think growing up in a shack with too many brothers and sisters to count, his dreams manifested into caring for his own and stability. By my mom's senior year of college they were engaged. They got married right after graduation, and a year later they settled into the home we live in today, with me cooking in the oven.

While the architecture and curved streets have stayed the same, the community has changed a lot since I was born – first as the place to live for auto executives and politicians, then a haven for the Black upper class, and when the audio industry collapsed and left many out of a job, it changed again. Now it's full of families from different backgrounds – people who either moved out of the city for college and came back to establish a life for themselves, or people who are benefitting off the new tech boom in the city and coming here for jobs. To be honest, it's all still weird and new for me.

"Hey, sweetie, you okay?" I come to with Daddy's worry lines covering the screen. "I don't mean to be so hard on you."

I shake my head. "No, I absolutely deserved it." I huff. "I just don't know how to make it right."

"You know," Dad says, smiling. "You're a smart cookie, Dani. Something will come to you. It always does."

A knock jolts me out of my sleep. "Come in," I grumble, rubbing the haziness from my eyes.

"I'm sorry, baby, I didn't know you were sleeping."

"I didn't know I was either," I mutter, still trying to get my bearings. I guess the sleepiness hit after talking to Dad, because last I remember, I was lying on my bed, rereading *Sula*. "What time is it?"

"One thirty," Mom replies.

"Oh, shoot. I didn't mean to sleep that late." So much for trying to read to draw some inspiration for this college essay.

"Destiny is downstairs."

"Wait, what?" She has the nerve to show up to my house, unannounced. "Tell her I'm not home. I have nothing to say to her."

Mom looks worried, and sighs. "What happened between you two, Dani? You haven't hung out with her or even mentioned her for months. I can't remember the last time you had any of your friends over. I don't understand."

I say nothing, trying to prevent myself from tearing up. Mom sighs, and with each sigh I can sense her defeat, her failure to connect with me. And I hate myself for putting her through this. I just can't say this thing out loud. I ball my fists. The anger coils inside me.

"Look, I already told her you're here. She pleaded with me to ask you to talk to her. She said you've been ignoring her."

I snap. "So what, you're on her side?"

Mom is shocked and hurt. "How am I supposed to know about sides when you won't even tell me what happened, baby?"

I don't answer, so she begins scanning the room, searching for the answers I won't give her.

"Do you want me to ask her to leave? Because I'll do it."

I don't know what to do. But I don't feel right leaving Mom to do my dirty work. If anyone should be telling Destiny she's no longer welcome here, it's me. "No, Mom. Let me throw some clothes on and I'll be downstairs."

I reach the bottom of the steps and see her in the family room, chit-chatting with my mom about who knows what. She looks different than the thirteen-year-old I first met in dance class. She's wearing her hair short and has more make-up on now, her brown skin dusted with golden powder with a touch of red lipstick. Mom was never the biggest fan of Destiny from jump, which of course made me feel some type of way. I questioned her constantly about it. Was it because we didn't grow up in the same neighbourhood? Or was it because three of Destiny's siblings had different daddies? I grilled her because I assumed she was being judgy. "No," Mom always said. "It's just that she's extremely insecure. Be careful. Insecurity breeds jealousy."

I should've listened. When moms know, they know. She was right: Destiny's insecurity ruined our friendship. And I think she's still totally oblivious as to why.

"Hi," she says as I walk past the couch toward her.

"Hey," I say coldly. "Let's chat out front." I turn to my mom and say as softly as possible, "No offence. We just want some privacy."

"None taken." Mom has a cup of tea in her hand, and I watch as the steam travels up to her face, her eyes watching me like a cheetah looking at her prey. I know she'll pounce on me when I come back in the house, so I need to prepare myself to tell her *something*.

"Thanks, Mrs Ford," Destiny says, putting on her most respectable voice.

Mom nods. "Of course. You take care."

We're outside and Destiny is already talking like nothing has happened. "So I was thinking tonight we could go to this party…"

I stop her short. "What do you want, Destiny?"

She gets defensive immediately. "Damn, what's your deal? You haven't been hitting me back, so I figured I'd come over to invite you out tonight."

This is the shit I'm talking about. This girl is impossible to get through to. I realize already this conversation is a waste of my time.

"I don't have time for this," I say, turning back to the door.

"See, I knew I shouldn't have hung out with your bougie ass. You think you're better than me 'cause you live in this fancy house and all, but you're not."

I spin around. The hairs on my arm rise all the way up and I feel my whole body warm. "Excuse me? So *that's* why you think I'm not talking to you? I have always been a good friend to you, Destiny. Did you ever stop and consider there might be a legitimate reason I haven't answered your texts or DMs in *months*?"

She stares at me with the blankest look on her face.

"Let me spell it out for you. I told you what happened to me, you blew it off like it was nothing, and now you try to just carry on with our friendship like everything is normal?"

She shrugs. "You knew what it was when we stepped foot in that apartment."

"No, Destiny, I didn't!" I hiss. My voice is getting louder and louder at this point. It's like every word that comes out of her mouth feeds my rage.

"Chill out," she mutters. "Look, you were down to hang when I mentioned college boys. I thought you'd be over all that shit by now. You're still holding on to it?"

Every little thing she says infuriates me to no end, and I find myself counting backward to one. Trying to use any mechanism to calm myself down, to keep from shutting this chick up with one jab to the mouth. But I know if I do that, there's no way I'll get away with not explaining myself to my mom. I can't risk it.

"Well, hit me up if you change your mind about tonight," she replies nonchalantly. She steps off my porch and walks away.

I sit down on the porch, not prepared to face my mama just yet, and bury my face in my hands as the memories wash over me again.

I *was* excited to hang out with college boys. I imagined going to a dorm room, with freshman boys sipping on hard seltzer and having intense and intellectual conversations about Langston Hughes and James Baldwin and Zora Neale Hurston. Having them introduce me to something new I should be reading, stuff they'd had to dissect in their freshman symposium. Or if I was lucky, I'd meet a dude who'd signed up for a critical race theory course and would indulge me on his thoughts.

I didn't get that. What I got was quite different.

"Destiny, we're passing all the dorms," I said as I drove. My parents had surprised me with a Ford Escape, just in time for summer joyrides. My mom complained it was too much for a first car, but Dad wanted something he knew was dependable while he was away. He wanted a car that I could easily drive through the snow, and as far as he was concerned, Ford was a company to trust, though it probably had more to do with the hook-up he got from a friend working at the plant. "You sure we're going in the right direction?"

She double-checked her phone and cross-referenced it with my screen's directions. "Yep, this is it. We must be going to student housing."

That should have been sign number one. Student housing is essentially...apartments. No supervision. More intimate setting. Not that I was opposed to it, but there was a level of comfort I felt knowing that a staff member was always around to monitor activity. This just seemed...unexpected.

We pulled up to the address, slightly off-campus and extremely residential.

I began strategizing how I'd find the courage to leave my car when Destiny pulled me away from my thoughts.

"You ready?" she asked. I slowly nodded and we hopped out of the car.

She banged on the apartment door, like she'd done it a thousand times. These were college boys, so how was she so confident?

"Ayyyye, the party's here," a cute guy in a plaid shirt announced. Destiny went in for a big bear hug and grabbed the red cup in his hand. "Damn, girl, you ain't wasting no time!"

Destiny smirked and took a hearty sample of whatever was inside. "Nope."

"Well, I'm glad you came. It's been a minute," he replied, pulling her in and nibbling at her neck. I watched her cave into him, giggling. Why was he rolling up on her like they were...familiar? How *well* did she know him?

"You comin' in, cutie?" I sort of stood at the entryway, frozen. I did a quick scan of the living room, realizing five boys were there total.

And two girls. Us.

Destiny saw my hesitation. "What are you doing?" she whispered, her tone short.

"I don't feel comfortable," I whispered back. "We should go."

"Oh my god, D, stop trippin'! It's fine. Come inside." She grabbed my hand and slammed the door behind me.

"Desstinyyyy!" another boy called out. "Welcome back, gorgeous."

An angry knot churned in my stomach; my uneasiness turned into outrage. She didn't have a car and they obviously weren't picking her up, so she used me to be her chauffeur and sidekick. Again. I'd been to a few gatherings with Destiny throughout the school year, and some of her decisions made me question if I should continue hanging with her, but none like this. This felt like a set-up.

This was the Destiny show.

She ran over to one of the other boys and sat on his lap. The dude who'd answered the door gave a fake look of disapproval.

"What about me?" he said, hands to heart like he was devastated.

"Don't worry, there's enough of me to go around," she shot back.

I felt sick to my stomach, and all I could think about was that I wished Esi and Rashida were here. Our freshman year of high school I introduced Destiny to Rashida and Esi and we all got along…for a period. But Destiny seemed to be in competition with Esi anytime we went out, and by sophomore year, Esi grew tired quickly. She politely told me whoever I chose to hang out with was my business, but Destiny was too messy and they clashed too much for her taste. So I began separating my time between two groups – Esi and Rashida, and Destiny and whoever she chose at the time to be part of her crew, until they also got tired of her and moved on to another friend circle.

Destiny had a "reputation" at school, first as a girl who grew up in a household full of kids, having to take care of them by herself. And then as a girl who over the summer grew hips and a butt and big boobs and suddenly became this girl everyone needed to have, a sexual conquest. And Destiny wore that title as a badge of honour. I also never bought into the rumours. A girl goes after what she wants just as much as a dude...and? Why should we subscribe to these heteronormative rules that allow men to be men, but make women a hoe? Every body is one's own, and every choice a person makes should be one's own also. Jury was out on if I was waiting for the one. But what I did know was I definitely wasn't ready. And I definitely wasn't ready tonight. Destiny came here knowing what she wanted for herself, and subsequently what she wanted for me. I had no choice in the matter.

I walked over to the kitchen. "You wanna drink?" a guy with the deepest voice I had ever heard said. All I could do was nod. I watched him start to dunk another red cup in a punch bowl.

"No!" I grabbed his wrist. He gave me the side eye, and realizing I looked suspect, I changed my tune and softened my expression. "Do you have a beer?"

"Ooh, yeah, I got you, lil mama." He smiled. Ugh, now he thought I was flirting. I eyed his movements like a hawk, watching him pull the bottle from the fridge and pop open the top with his belt buckle/beer opener. I felt way more comfortable with this than drinking some suspect punch that could be spiked. He passed it along to me. "So, you go to school with Destiny?"

"Yeah," I said, sipping my bottle and attempting to casually observe Destiny in the living room. I asked the guy how he was liking college, hoping to strike up some conversation.

But I swear, he wasn't concerned about nothing but flirting. He talked briefly about his classes, and more about the party scene, pledging and girls. Meanwhile, Destiny was the life of the party at this point, hopping from one lap to another, snatching drinks from everyone's hand, and at one point she started twerking while all the guys watched. One of them walked right up to her and started grinding on her, and not long after, they were kissing. It was enough to make the beer taste increasingly sour.

"Did you hear what I said?" Deep Voice asked me.

"Oh! Sorry, I didn't."

"I said I thought girls would be prettier in college, but you shitting on all these girls on campus." He smiled and licked his full lips. That was the dumbest compliment I'd ever heard, and a blatant lie. I knew I was nice to look at, but college women were refined in a way I was not. This dude just couldn't pull a decent woman, if he was even looking for one. "You want to show me what you got?"

"Huh?" I spoke. He nodded at Destiny, who was mid-grind.

"Nah, I'm good," I said. "Where's the bathroom?"

"Down the hall, second door to your left."

I couldn't remember this boy's name, but I could tell he wasn't happy he'd just spent however long talking, only to realize I wasn't putting out tonight. I was just ready to GO. I quickly walked to the bathroom and took my time collecting myself and washing my hands. When I came back to the living room, Destiny and three of the boys were gone.

"Where did Destiny go?"

Deep Voice rolled his eyes. "She went in the room with Darius, Jay and Matt."

What?! So she leaves me with two guys by myself?

"Destiny is always down for anything," he added.

I stared him down, waiting for him to say something about what he thought he'd get from me tonight. "Just so you know, Destiny and I are nothing alike," I replied.

"I can see that now." He shrugged and parked himself on a barstool nearby, messaging whatever college girl he could, I was sure, to salvage his night. I sat on the couch, trying to figure out how long I planned on waiting before I left her ass. The betrayal I felt was inconceivable.

All those memories are still flooding through me as I drive through a neighbourhood right off 6 Mile and Wyoming, watching the sugar maple and dawn redwood trees and rusty-coloured brick homes pass my rear-view mirror while I try to find the address my phone is feeding me.

Tree-lined streets are a thing in Detroit neighbourhoods, and for some reason they've been an obsession of mine since I was little. I asked my dad once what type of trees were standing tall on our lawn, and he did what he always did: took me into our home office, pulled my mom's desk chair beside his, and helped me look it up. We determined that a man by the name of Judge Augustus Woodward had planted the trees alongside the city's broad avenues himself, wanting to give Detroit a Parisian flair. There are so many species of trees in Detroit that while my navigation skills are pretty useless, I tend to be able to tell where I am based on the trees in the area.

The fragrance of the air is crisp and earthy, with slight notes of winter looming ahead. That's what I'm smelling right now, with the windows down and the autumn breeze tousling my braids. Soon enough the heavy snow will cover the white pine trees in the area, giving me the white Christmas I look forward to. I can't wait to experience the holidays in New York City – taking pictures at the Rockefeller Center tree, throwing snowballs in Central Park – all the things that make New York seem so magical.

And for a brief moment that thought soothes me and I can put that night in the back of my mind.

Just in time, too. My phone tells me I've arrived at my destination.

I park in front of a redbrick and white-aluminum bungalow-style home with a black gated security door. I hope this boy doesn't think I'm weird stopping by like this. But I need to apologize and make this right, and for some reason walking up to him at school with a bag of kids' books seems even weirder to me. I hear Dad's voice in my head, the disappointment breaking it. I grab my gift bag out the passenger seat and head to the porch.

The doorbell doesn't seem to work, so I slip my hand through the steel bars and knock for what feels like for ever, until the door opens and a little face peeps through.

"Hi," I say, waving. The little boy on the other side just looks at me with those same big eyes I saw from Prince's social media accounts, staring between strands of locs covering his face. "Is your brother here? I wanted to give him someth—"

"Mook!! What I tell you about opening the door without an adult!" a powerful, yet warm voice from the inside booms. My heart skips a beat.

Prince.

"But I can't open it without a key anyway!" he whines. "And there's a girl at the door!"

"I don't care how pretty she is, you still can't—"

The door opens wide and Prince stops in his tracks. He drops the keys to the metal screen door, and I'm starting to think this is a bad idea. His brother picks them up and places them back in his hand, and it snaps Prince out of his shock. "Oh, thanks, little man," he says, rubbing Mook's head. "How about you take the ground beef out the fridge so we can get started on burgers? I'll be there in a sec."

Mook wastes no time and jolts to the kitchen.

I clear my throat. "I'm sorry if this is a bad time," I say, nerves making my stomach squeeze. "I just wanted to come over and bring this." I lift the bag in my hand and Prince realizes he still hasn't opened the metal door.

"My bad." He unlocks it and almost jumps outside. "Wanna sit?"

We both find spots on his porch steps and I watch him attempt to wipe the wrinkles out his sweatpants. I'm trying not to notice, but he doesn't look bad for someone in grey sweats and a faded black tee that's probably been worn far too many times at home. I pass him the bag and when he looks inside, a smile spreads across his face. He looks at me with genuine glee.

"You didn't have to do this."

"Yes, I did. I went back to the library today and talked to Ms Thompson. She told me how you were going in at the book selection, and even did a dramatic reading in front of her."

"Maaaan." His smile turns into a chuckle. He pulls a book out of the bag and starts flipping the pages. It's then I notice his dimples, mischievously creeping out as his smile grows. There's something charming about the way he's admiring the books I brought him, something that makes me feel…at ease. If Mom were here, she'd try to say this whole thing was a meet-cute or whatever, but I'm here to make things right and *that's* it. "Yoooo, who is this?"

"Oh." I say, coming to. "Kadir Nelson. You've seen his work before." I watch him as he's in a trance, trying to put his finger on it. "You're the music head. Where have you seen this style of art before?"

A light bulb goes on. "Oh shit! Drake's *Nothing Was the Same*!"

"Yep! He also did the artwork for a Michael Jackson album. My dad told me about that one." I give Prince space as he carefully reads each page of *I Promise*. I knew he'd be a LeBron James fan, and I wanted to give him something he'd enjoy reading just as much as his brother would enjoy listening to.

While he takes in the story, I take in the scenery; we are approaching the golden hour and I watch the crimson-hued leaves shimmy to the ground. Across the street are two older women, sitting on their porches and probably gossiping about the latest neighbourhood drama. And I can smell freshly cut grass thanks to the gentleman a few houses down, who's finishing up the last bit of details on his well-groomed lawn.

"Danielle, thank you."

I put my hand up. "No need. I'm sorry, Prince. I shouldn't have come at you like that." I notice not all the books have been taken out of the bag. "There's one more book in there."

He pulls out the last book in the bag. "*Crown*," he reads aloud. "A book on getting a lineup? That's dope!" He turns it over and looks at the book description. "Are there any picture books about little boys with locs?"

I'm stumped. "I don't know if I've seen any, to be honest. But I'll look out for some."

"I'd like that." Prince eyes me, his expression wistful.

I feel myself beginning to panic.

I start to get up and walk to my car, which catches Prince by surprise. He scrambles to get up and follow me.

"Wait, are you leaving?!" I don't stop until I'm right at my car, hitting the unlock button on my fob. "I…I thought we were having a good time."

"Yeah, no…this was cool," I say, refusing to look at him while I fiddle with my keys. "I just lost track of time and I have some homework to get done." I don't know why I'm acting so strange right now.

"Well, can…can I see you again? Maybe you could recommend some more books? I feel like these books are ones I'm actually gonna enjoy reading to him. And I have you to thank for that."

"I don't think that's a good idea," I mutter.

It's time to go.

Right.

Now.

"Hey, Danielle, can you look at me?" I slowly turn around and look up. He *does* tower over me, and I feel exposed.

I glance up at him.

"Why don't you think it's a good idea?" he asks simply.

I go to open my mouth, but nothing comes out. I don't have an answer for him that makes sense.

"Look, if I did anything on the porch to make you uncomfortable, I'm sorry. I was so excited you showed an interest in someone I care about so much. I…I just want to thank you." He looks nervous, like he can't take the rejection I'm about to give him. "Can I do that, please?"

I sigh. For some reason, everything he says feels right, and yet that feels so wrong. I don't talk to guys. I don't date. I don't like any of this. But screw it. Just a thank-you, right?

"Next weekend?" I say. "Hanging out?"

He heaves a huge sigh of relief, and that damn dimple makes another appearance. "Next weekend it is."

Chapter Five

On the Right (Sound)Track

Danielle

My nervous fingers type, delete, and retype a thousand iterations of a message to Prince. They're all clammy and weird and I can't figure out what's wrong with me. Technically I had a whole week to cancel on him, yet here I am texting him on Friday, the day we're supposed to hang. I need to just cancel this whole thing and get it over with.

> DANI: Hey, sorry to do this, but can we hang some other time? I have to take out my braids and it's gonna take for ever. I won't be ready in time for tonight.

I quickly press send before I change my mind. Technically, I *do* have to take my hair down. And technically, taking my hair down will take some time. But I honestly could do this today or tomorrow if I wanted to. I just think I acted prematurely by thinking I was ready for any sort of interaction with a boy, when I barely interact with anyone else.

Okay, phew, it's done. But he starts responding. My heart thuds. I turn the phone facedown and count to ten. Maybe if I don't look, then I can just ignore whatever he says.

The phone pings.

I bite my lower lip.

I can't *not* look.

Ugh.

I turn the phone over.

PRINCE: How about I come over and help you?
I'll bring snacks.

I scream. Did he *really* just say that? My fingers fly across the tiny keyboard.

DANI: I don't know how my father will feel about
a boy up in my room.

The audacity of him to think he can just chill in my room.

PRINCE: I understand…def don't want to disrespect
you or pops. You got a basement, right?

"Crap!" I yell out into the void, staring at the message. He's a smart one. Of course, the one boy that I'm nice to is a sweet talker.

PRINCE: And your dad can drill sergeant the shit outta me. Whatever I gotta do to make him feel comfortable.

PRINCE: Tell him don't be fooled by the DJ gig. I'm nothing but a gentleman. A Renaissance man. Bet he'll love that.

Why is he making it so hard to say no? I throw my phone on the bed, deciding what to do next.

My nerves are on ten right now and I've shocked even myself. I'm bringing a boy to my house. And not just any boy, but a boy I barely even know. I've completely disconnected from my social circle. Like seriously, if we want to talk about ghosting, I got that down to a science at this point, so this is totally unlike me.

But what surprised me most was my dad. I told my parents Prince wanted to come over and help me take out my hair, and of course Mom was ecstatic. One, because she didn't have to help take them out, but two, because I was bringing home a boy for the first time. Dad, who's been home since Wednesday, needed some convincing until I explained it was Prince's idea to help me in the basement and showed him Prince's message. He took the phone and nodded with approval. He was happy I fixed what happened at the library.

I was sort of hoping Dad would shut it down, though how

could he if I was defending Prince at the same time? I should have told my dad that Prince wanted to go up to my room and help me "take down my braids." I bet he would have swiftly said no. But while I might be suspicious of Prince's motives, I gave my parents every reason to believe this is a respectable boy. Why would they respond any differently?

I spend an hour picking an outfit – which inevitably becomes my favourite boyfriend jeans and a vintage Aaliyah tee. I don't want to look too desperate, but I still want to show I made *some* effort.

But why am I doing this? He's just a guy. I'm *not* interested in him. I'm not interested in anyone. I can't let anything distract me from becoming the writer I've always wanted to be.

I tidy up obsessively downstairs, while still trying to look like it's no big deal to my parents. But my mom knows. She comes down to wash clothes and offers to help and when I say no, I catch her casually eyeing me between loads, with a smirk on her face. She's loving all this. "You deserve a great love story, Dani," she says to me.

"It's not like that, Ma," I reply, trying to squash all the wild ideas she has blooming in her mind. My eyes find her extensive collection of DVDs again. All those Black love stories stare back at me.

The pressure.

Ping!

I grab my phone.

PRINCE: Out front.

Oh my god. It's 7:02 and he's right on time.

The doorbell rings. I count to five and head to the door. My parents are in the family room and have already made it clear they need to be introduced before we venture downstairs.

More pressure. I open the front door.

"Hi," he says.

Heat crawls to my cheeks. "Hey," I manage to get out.

Prince also looks like he's made very little effort, but in a different way. He's wearing a Mass Tech hoodie and jeans, but this time neither his jeans nor his sweatshirt have a single wrinkle.

"Can I come in?" he asks, and I realize I've left him standing on the doorstep.

"Yeah, yeah, sorry." I grimace.

He lifts up a *Frozen* gift bag and I can't help but laugh. "What is this?"

"Well, last time you saw me, you gave me a fancy gift bag with goodies, so I wanted to return the favour. But this was all the dollar store had left."

I take the bag out of his hands and notice it's surprisingly heavy. I look inside to find every snack and candy bar ever manufactured.

"Are you trying to give me type two diabetes? Look at all these snacks!"

"Did you forget how long it takes to take out braids?" he says. "Don't worry, I'm going to need to replenish after all the work I gotta do and don't want to eat you outta house and home. I'll help with these."

"'Cause you're so tall, right?"

He blushes.

I catch myself. Am I actually flirting?

Nope. Just being nice. He's a guest, right? That's what I'm supposed to do.

"And I'm only seventeen...for all we know, I might still be growing. Zion Williamson grew six inches in one year." He begins staring at the family pictures hung up on the entryway wall and stops at a picture of me at the roller-skating rink, holding my mom's hand. "You still skate?" He points to the picture.

"I think the last time I went was...ninth grade?"

"Ninth grade!" he shouts. "So basically, you're an amateur."

"It's only been three years, relax." I try to swallow a giggle.

He looks at me and smiles. A nice one.

Get it together, Dani, I tell myself.

"Dani, is your friend here?!" Mom's voice echoes through the whole house.

I jump.

"Sorry, Mom," I yell back. "We're coming now."

I motion for him to follow me. We enter the family room and both my parents are already standing.

"Mom, Dad. This is Prince Jones."

Prince steps right up to them, addressing my mom first.

"Pleasure to meet you, Mrs Ford." He smiles and bows to her hand and for a moment I think he's going to kiss it. A chuckle comes out of my mom that I've never heard before.

I roll my eyes. She's already mush. I'm sure she's planning my wedding in her head.

"The pleasure is all mine," she replies with a big grin.

Prince immediately looks to my dad. Prince is taller by an inch or two, but my dad's bruteness dominates Prince, making him almost look like a pit bull: overpowering, extremely intimidating, and ready to attack if necessary. I know Dad is the biggest softie, but Prince doesn't know that and right now I feel nervous for him.

"Mr Ford, it's very nice to meet you." He extends his hand for my dad to shake. "Thank you for letting me come over."

Dad accepts and grips Prince's hand, and I can tell he's squeezing it hard. "No problem, son. Although, taking down my daughter's braids is a rather unconventional activity for a date, isn't it?"

"Is it a date?" Prince looks back at me.

I gulp. "Hanging out, right?"

He grins back.

"Is that what you kids call it?" Dad teases.

I want to legit die right here.

Prince chuckles and glances at me. "Yes, it is. But I can sense your daughter doesn't trust me...yet." He steals a glance at me.

I look away, trying to avoid showing my cheeks, which are starting to burn.

"So if this is the only way I can spend time with her and prove my intentions, I'm willing to do it."

His words surprise me. Startle me. He's so honest and clear and decisive, so different from the other boys at school... maybe the other boys, period.

"Plus, my mom has MS and gets her hair braided, so she doesn't have to worry about doing it, and I help her take them out all the time. It's sort of like a bonding moment for us."

My mouth drops open. I didn't know this about Prince's mom, but why would I?

Dad and I lock eyes, and he's flabbergasted. That wrinkle of surprise mars the deep brown of his forehead. I know that look. Prince hasn't gained my dad's trust completely, but he definitely permeated a layer with that comment.

"Well, can't argue with that, can we? It's very nice to meet you, Prince. My wife and I will be down periodically to check in on you two, but for the most part we'll leave you be. I trust you will show my Dani nothing but respect."

"The utmost, sir." Prince nods, and Dad pats his back, happy with his response. Prince turns to me. "You got the essentials? Plastic bag, scissors…that little rat-tail comb?"

Everyone in the room cracks up. "That's not what it's called!" I protest.

"Yes, it is!" Prince walks toward me. Oh, he's turned his charisma up to one hundred with my family and knows it's working. "I buy them on Amazon for my mom all the time."

"I didn't even know that! But I guess it's 'cause I just buy them at any beauty supply store."

"These beauty supply stores be like the size of a mall. I'm good."

I gesture for him to follow me downstairs.

"Thanks again, Mr and Mrs Ford," he says.

"Nice to meet you, Prince!" Mom shouts back.

"And make sure to leave the door open!" Dad calls out.

Jesus, Dad.

We walk down the hallway. Prince freezes, eyeing my family photos again.

"What?" I ask.

"You were so cute." He stares at a picture of me from fifth grade, with trees in the background, me in a turtleneck and an overall dress, and my hair pressed by my mom. "I mean... y-you still are," he stammers, "but you get what I mean."

I blush, which he thankfully doesn't catch since apparently he's unable to look away from the photo of me.

"Your hair," he says. "It's practically to your butt in that picture. I mean, I knew you had a lot of it, but what did I sign myself up for??"

I chuckle. "I'm not going to make you take down the whole thing. But you're wasting time right now the longer we avoid this."

"If you say so," he replies. "My hands are gonna be cramping hard after today."

We enter the basement alone and my nerves kick back up.

"You have a pillow you want to sit on?" Prince asks.

Damn, he *is* a pro at this.

I take one of the couch cushions and hand it over to him as he sits on the couch and places the cushion between his legs, which are long and muscular.

My pulse races. I can feel his body heat. The hair on my arms stands up. I think about what it's going to feel like with his hands in my hair. I've only ever had Mom's hands in it.

And Esi's. But never a boy's.

As if reading my mind, Prince puts both hands up. "I won't touch you without permission. And I'll walk you through every new thing I'm about to do, okay?"

I nod.

I ease myself onto the floor, right between his legs. I sit cross-legged, with both hands grabbing onto my ankles, motionless. So many feelings whiz through me.

"You comfy?" he asks.

I nod again.

"I see one comb and one pair of scissors…but I hope you know this is a team effort, right?"

I laugh and my body relaxes. "You're such a smart-ass. Pass me the scissors…and a Kit Kat out the bag." My heart is about to pump through my chest as I anticipate his touch, and I realize I'm practically not breathing. He starts by taking the scissors and cutting the ends on a few of the braids before he passes me the scissors. "Don't cut my hair!"

"You ain't got nothing to worry about, Danielle. I can see them ends poking out these old-ass braids."

I playfully snatch the scissors out of his hand. With his fingers, he unravels a braid with precision, detangling along the way and dropping the extension in the plastic bag before moving onto the next braid.

My body buzzes…almost hums, and I feel like he can probably hear it, feel it. The stir of his steady breathing makes me shudder as he draws near while the braid unravels at the root. The only touch I feel from him is his hand gently grazing my scalp while he slides the rest of the fake braiding hair off my natural mane. I let myself sink back a little. Getting closer.

He doesn't smell like cologne, like all the rest of the guys my age doing the most, but rather a fresh and crisp scent, like someone who's fresh out the shower, their body-wash scent seeping through their pores.

A silence stretches between us as we continue to work.

I open and close my mouth, questions bubbling up, but then I swallow them down again.

He handles every braid with care, is really efficient and just like he promised, and he's made almost zero effort to touch me. I turn the television on low for some ambient noise.

"I take it that vinyl player works?" Prince says. "Probably better company than the terrible-ass news."

"It does." I look up at him. "You want to play something for us, Mr DJ?"

That dimple flashes.

"Actually, I think I might. Watch my legs." I move out the way so that he's able to get up and check out my parents' collection. "Let me show you something, young lady." He imitates his best old-man voice and I smirk, shaking my head at his goofiness.

And just like that, I've lost him. He's already on the floor, pulling out each vinyl, admiring the artwork and scrolling down the tracklist. He's studying the music like my grandmother studies the Bible: deeply, enthusiastically, and dutifully. I continue to take out my braids and stare at his warm undertone popping out of his rich, espresso-coloured skin, his fade looking extra tight. Prince may have looked like he made very little effort with his outfit choice, but he absolutely went to the barbershop for our date.

He pulls out the *Love Jones* vinyl next. "Who's the romance fanatic in your house?"

I point to the ceiling, rolling my eyes. "My mom. She has like every Black rom-com ever created."

"She's got the good soundtracks. This one, *Waiting to Exhale, Brown Sugar*...like they all got some heat on those."

He does that thing that I only see in movies. He slowly takes out the vinyl record, lightly blows on it for dust, and carefully releases it on the turntable. He sets the stylus on the black vinyl and lets it play. He stands there for a few moments with his hands in his pockets, like he's testing the quality, before his head slowly starts to bob to the music.

"I just love good movie soundtracks," he says. "The way they curate the artists, the mood they want to evoke, it's the best."

"Have you ever had a vinyl player?" I ask.

"Oh yeah, I've had one since I was little...well, a turntable, at least. My uncle bought me one the minute I showed an interest in music, and he wanted to set me up to be his little protégé," he replies, still vibing. "It's like a requirement to be a good DJ. But I also just like looking at people's music collections. It's kind of hard to do, since everyone has music on their phones."

"Sorry, I assumed because you were so excited to listen

that this was a treat for you. But I guess that's how I feel when I'm checking out someone's bookshelves."

He focuses back on me. "Yeah, I could tell in the library." I look away, guilt-ridden. "Danielle, don't trip. You—"

"*Hello!*" My mom walks downstairs with a plate of food.

Did she really just fry up some wings real quick?

I flash her a look, and she shoots one back.

"I thought you two might be hungry, so I made these appetizers. Oh! You're listening to *Love Jones.*"

"Yes, ma'am," Prince replies. "You've got quite the collection here."

My mother beams. "Dani's father is the reader, but I'm definitely the music fiend in the family. I guess being born and raised in the Motor City, it's in my blood."

"Same," he replies. "My uncle is DJ Romes, so I knew lyrics before I knew how to walk."

My mom looks confused. "Waaaiit, are you DJ LoveJones?"

He smiles and shrugs, his hands still in his pockets. "Yeah. I mean, yes, ma'am."

"Oh my god! I've been following your uncle for years. I used to listen to him every evening on my drive home from work! I was so bummed when they moved him to late night and put a younger host in his spot." My mom is doing the *most* right now. "I knew your voice sounded familiar, but I didn't know you were so young! I mean…you give such good advice for someone who's in high school. And you have your own show?"

"Well, it's only an hour… DJ Mike is really the rush-hour host."

"Only! That's like prime time. All of Detroit knows you now."

Prince smirks. "Everyone but your daughter."

I'm over this, so I cut in. "We should eat these wings before they get cold."

"Oh, you're right! Make sure to wash your hands before you eat up."

"Absolutely," Prince says. He's practically salivating, even though he's already punished two candy bars and a bag of chips. Like, where does it even go? It's clear Prince is ready to dig in, so I point him in the direction of the bathroom and he bolts around the corner.

"Mom," I whisper, "where did those even come from?"

She moves closer to me and puts the platter down on the side table.

"I ran to the store to grab a bag of wings. I knew if I asked for him to stay for dinner you would have killed me," she replies in a hushed tone. "But I couldn't let this boy go hungry in my house. Plus, I wanted a reason to check in." *No* shame. "How's it going?"

"It's fine," I mumble, questioning whether this was a good idea after seeing my reflection in the TV and realizing half my hair is all over the place. I cringe and quickly attempt to braid the exposed hair and wrap it in a ponytail holder. "How crazy do I look?"

"You look beautiful, doll," she replies, coming over to

re-plait my hair. I know my mom is lying, but still, I'm thankful for the confidence booster and for making sure I'm looking right. She finishes up just as Prince walks out the bathroom.

I make my way to the bathroom and keep the door open, attempting to make sure my mom doesn't embarrass me, but I can't hear much but giggling from her, and when I come back into the common area, I find Prince extra animated with a wing in his hand, and my mom cosy on the couch like she's about to watch a movie, fully into whatever story he's telling. I clear my throat and she pops right up.

"Oh, I'm sorry, I got a little comfortable," Mom says.

"Thank you again, Mrs Ford," Prince says, wiping his bone clean.

"Of course," my mom replies, touching his shoulder as she walks upstairs. "Holla if you need anything." She gives me a wink and is finally out of our hair.

Prince wipes his hands with a napkin. "Your mom is adorable." He sits back down and holds out his hand to help me position myself on the floor. As I settle back in, I instinctively rest my arm on his leg and quickly remove it. "You – you can keep it there if you want. I need you to turn your head anyway."

I slowly lift my arm back up to his thigh, using it as an armrest. My insides are tingling all over.

"What's your favourite song on this soundtrack?" he asks.

I don't even hesitate. "That's easy. 'The Sweetest Thing.'"

"Aah, Lauryn Hill. She absolutely seems like your style."

"Yeah," I say wistfully. "I wish I was born around the time she was making music."

"From what I heard she never came out to her concerts on time—"

"Ow!" I yelp, wincing as I give him the death stare.

He smiles at me. "Is Danielle tender-headed?"

I pout as I turn back around. "Maybe a little, just up top." It's a cruel joke, really, for me to have all this hair and not be able to handle it getting combed.

"Should have told me. I would have been more careful. Here," he says, taking his time with each strand and delicately loosening up the knot.

"You were doing so well up until this point," I grumble, my head still throbbing.

"Well, my mom is also a little tender-headed, so I guess I'm naturally gentle. But every once in a while I mess it up." Duke Ellington's piano fills the air, with a tenor saxophone not far behind. "Now *this*. This is my favourite song on this soundtrack. It's so smooth."

I smirk. "I didn't take you for a jazz person."

He palms my head like a basketball and turns it toward him. "Why not?"

I slap his hand with my comb. "What happened to asking for permission?"

"You came for my music taste," he replies, shaking his hand in pain, "but you're right. I deserved that." He looks at me two seconds too long, and maybe it's the song, but suddenly I do feel like I'm in a sentimental mood.

"Well, Mr Jones. Why do you like this song so much?" I ask, not taking my eyes off him. He fidgets, then clears his throat.

"Well," he says, "it's the perfect collaboration. You have two iconic musicians who find a way to play into their strengths, without overpowering each other, and create a sound that's sultry, that's soothing…that takes you to a beautiful place and yet, so expertly crafted. It doesn't matter that this song came out before our lifetime. It's timeless." I nod, at a loss for words but fully understanding what he means. "Where does it take you, Ms Ford?"

"It takes me to a place in the near future, maybe right after I graduate from college and get my MFA."

"What's that?" he asks inquisitively.

"Oh, master of fine arts in creative writing."

His brain seems like it's processing for a second, and then it clicks. "So, an author, huh?" I nod. "That's why you were in the library, looking like you just won the lotto. Where do you wanna go to school?"

"New York City."

"Of course," he responds, cutting the ends of one of my braids. "It seems like that's where all the creatives go. What type of books do you want to write? Like rom-coms and shit?"

I laugh. "Nooo. No shade to those who do it. But it's just not me. I wanna write about stuff that matters."

"You think love doesn't matter?"

"I didn't say that. I just…" I'm stumped. "It's not that I don't think love is real. I mean, my parents are a good example of that. It's just…I don't know. I don't buy it right now. I don't see myself falling for any guy our age." Prince huffs while unravelling a braid. "No offence," I say.

"None taken," he responds. "Okay, Danielle the author, set a scene for me. What does your life in New York look like?"

I smile. "I'm walking down the streets of New York City. The city's alive with lights as I'm leaving my first book event, but I feel so…free. Like everything is falling into place. Like everything feels right."

"I feel that," he says, and bites his lip. I quickly realize I'm blushing and look away, suddenly feeling weird that I'm even allowing this attraction to pull me in.

Suddenly feeling regret.

"Why are you here, Prince?"

"What do you mean? I told you upstairs. To spend time with you."

"But like, what's the ultimate goal here?" I ask.

"To get to know you." He pauses. "And who knows? You might mess around and fall in love with me."

I whip my head around and a snicker comes out of my mouth. "You have got to be kidding me," I say with a snarl.

He throws another wad of the fake hair into the plastic bag. "Actually, I'm not."

Deadpan. No inflection or anything in his voice.

No laugh. Nothing.

This cocky boy just told me he thinks I'll fall for him, like he can just come in and sweep me off my feet with a few pieces of candy and some jokes. Who does this guy think he is? "What makes you think you can make that happen? Is this some type of stupid bet between you and your friends or something?"

"Dani…" he says.

"Danielle," I snap. "Dani is reserved for people close in my life."

He nods with a smirk, and that dimple that I thought was cute is now getting on my nerves. "You wanted me to be honest, right? What if I said my intentions were to have sex with you?"

"I would throw you out of my house without a second thought." I pause. "Wait, is that what you want? Are you just telling me what you think I want to hear?!"

"No," he says sternly. "I'm telling you the truth. I'm not trying to play games here. I like you. I've liked you for a while now. You just never seemed interested, so I assumed I didn't have a chance and moved on."

"You don't *know* me, Prince."

"I know that when you laugh, it comes straight from your belly. That your poems in our sixth-grade English class were some of the best I've ever heard. That you could be one of the most popular girls at Mass Tech if you wanted to be, but that's never been your thing. You've always carved your own path."

Thinking about that class, it makes sense. Middle school was the last time I read anything on the page aloud, before writing became a serious endeavour. Before I began comparing my writing to the work of authors who've had years of experience, writers who I knew had lived rich lives and had lots of worldly insight they could bring to the page. Before I began to analyze my work so critically that I felt it was never good enough to show anyone.

Prince sat in the back with his friends, and anytime I read a piece of my work, he always clapped and forced his friends to do the same. "You...you *were* in English comp," is all I reply.

"Yeah, I was. I know you're not into music like me or your mom. But your writing was always like music to me, Danielle."

I turn back around, a tiny quiver vibrating through me. I can't believe he still remembers my writing. But none of that really matters, because there is no way I'm doing this, falling for a guy like him, or any guy, period. I have so many other things to think about – college admissions, scholarships, freaking New York City – and I can't have anything, or anyone, stopping me from getting there. "I don't mean to hurt your feelings, Prince, but you and me, that's not happening."

"And why is that?" he asks, still taking out my braids, unfazed at my reaction.

"Because. I'm not ready to fall in love. I know men think they can get women to fall in love easily, but that's not how it works with me."

"Actually, all that is bullshit. Studies show men actually fall in love faster than women. We know sooner but are just afraid. It's why we'll ghost a girl as soon as we start catching feelings."

"Why do you even know that?"

"'Cause," he says, "being a relationship expert is kind of my thing. But love is tricky, so I like to do research to understand people better."

I don't say anything for a minute. "Okay, you're the expert. How long does it take a woman to fall in love?"

"One hundred thirty-four days," he declares.

I turn back to him, doing the math. "That's almost five months. Who says I'll let you stick around?"

"Fair point," he replies. "Let's try for less than five months."

I eye him suspiciously. "How much less?"

"Just give me three dates. I'm up for a challenge. I *am* the love expert, after all."

I laugh, mocking him. "You think you can get me to fall in love with you on two more dates?"

"Oh no, miss. You put me to work today...this ain't a date. I want three *real* dates. Let me woo you."

I swivel back around, facing the TV again. I almost want to believe him, which makes me feel like I must be crazy now, even entertaining this thought. But I just can't shake that something isn't adding up. Just like it didn't add up that summer night with Destiny. I can't keep that memory from invading my head.

Guy number five, who had been in and out of the apartment since we got there, walked back into the house, saw me sitting on the couch, and made his way over to me.

"I don't think I caught your name," he said, extending his hand for me to shake.

"Dani," I replied, shaking his hand, finally feeling a little more comfortable.

"Short for…Danielle?" he asked, and I nodded. "Everybody got a nickname. But I like learning people's government."

A smile crept out before I realized it.

"Nice to meet you, Danielle, I'm Drew. You want a drink?" I shook my head. "Well, I'm gonna get one."

He walked over to the kitchen and grabbed a beer out the fridge. His friend pulled him to the side and whispered a few things, and then headed toward the door. Drew walked over toward me and sat on the armchair next to the couch.

"Good luck," the other dude mumbled as he walked out.

I rolled my eyes and Drew laughed. "Don't trip. He just mad Destiny wants everyone but him."

I hesitated before I asked, "Does she come over here often?"

Drew took a swig of his beer. "I'm not sure, actually. Last time I saw her, she seemed pretty familiar with everyone, so I'm assuming she comes over often enough." He took another swig. "So, what year are you?"

"A junior," I replied.

"You ready for it?"

"Ready for it to be over," I whispered.

He laughed. "I was like you. Ready to get out and go to college. Now I'm not so sure."

I was surprised. "You don't like college?"

"Oh nah, I do. It's just, there's so much more pressure here. I play ball for the school, so it's tons of practice, lots of work. I tend to be low-key 'cause my time is so limited. I thought I'd have more free time, but I feel like with this full ride I'm a slave to the school."

"Hmm, I never thought of it that way." I thought about the scholarships I'd hope to get that seemed so unrealistic at the moment. My grades were great, but listening to Drew talk, I could only imagine how good he must be to get a scholarship at one of the top NCAA schools in the country. And here he was striking up a conversation with me.

"So, what about you? Where are you trying to go…wait, let me guess." He stood up and examined my look. I laughed. "You got the flowy sundress on with some flat sandals. It's got just enough edge but shows you classy. Natural hair. I bet you been natural your whole life, huh?"

"Oh, so you got a side gig on *Project Runway* now?" I smiled.

"You can tell you and your girl in there ain't cut from the same cloth." I gave him a look and laughed. "What can I say? I may be nineteen, but I'm an old soul. I bet you understood it, though." He gets up. "Hey, you want a beer? I'm getting another one," he said, already halfway through to the kitchen. This time I nodded. I watched as he popped open both bottles and plopped back down next to me. "I see you wasn't messing with that punch, huh?"

"Hell no!" I said.

He laughed.

I grabbed the beer from his hands and caught him staring, studying me. "What?"

"Why do you hang out with her?"

I shrugged, sipping my beer.

"Nah, not buying that," Drew replied. "You don't strike me as a girl who can't pull friends."

"Destiny is a sweetheart. She's funny. She's smart, too, when she really applies herself, and she's creative like me. She wants to move to NYC and pursue theatre. She knows how to captivate an audience, but she thinks the only way she can do that is through seduction. And it's so not true. She just doesn't see it yet."

"Damn," he said. "If I didn't know she was in there with three dudes, I'd be all into her."

I rolled my eyes at him. "So what," I said. "Let her do her! As long as she's not hurting no one."

"Ooh," Drew said. "I get it. So you sort of see her as a free spirit."

"Exactly." I guzzle down more beer.

"And what is it you want to do?" He leaned closer.

I could tell I was starting to feel the beer, because I felt warmer and more connected to this guy. And my dreams came bursting out. "I want to move to New York. Go to NYU or Columbia. Get my MFA. Become a writer. Like, be the next Maya or Audre. I mean, those are big shoes to fill. But I want to make it, you know? I want to win all the awards and acclaim and be on all the bestseller lists and maybe write a screenplay and attend all the literary parties and just...

be around dope-ass people who are changing how we view the world."

"That's cool." Drew nodded. He sipped his beer and then paused. "I like talking to you."

I blushed. "Me too."

"Hey, Danielle, you fall asleep on me?"

I'm snatched back to the moment. Prince is gawking at me. I jump so hard the bag of treats in my lap spills onto the ground.

"Sorry." I scramble to pick up the candy bars.

"It's fine, it's fine." Prince is studying me. "You aight?"

"Mm-hmm." I throw everything back into the *Frozen* bag.

"Danielle," he says, in a voice so calm it feels like silk. I see why he's in radio. Listening to him makes me feel like I've known him my entire life.

I face him, still crouched on the floor from gathering our snacks. I realize that more of my hair is out in that moment and start patting it down, attempting to look a little less wild.

"You've been sitting in silence for the last fifteen minutes, working on one braid. Something *is* up. You want to talk about it?"

I shake my head and realize I've given more of myself away by acknowledging something is bothering me, which immediately irks me. He has the upper hand. "Prince, I know you think you have the answers to everything, but some things you can't solve."

I start picking up any loose hair extensions on the floor that escaped the plastic bag. I feel so silly, my hair sticking out like Medusa, trying to convince a guy I barely know that I'm fine when we both know I'm not.

Prince looks confused. "Why do you think I know everything?" He pauses for a second. "Wait, have you listened to my show?"

I wince. I can't believe I just blurted that out, so I try to play it off. "I mean, I needed to know if you were normal."

He smiles, satisfied I've heard his show. But instead of pressing it more, Prince rises from the couch and begins helping me pick up hair stragglers. You can tell he's trying to be mindful of what comes out of his mouth next. "I didn't say I had all the answers. Part of getting to know you is all of you, right? The good, bad and indifferent."

"It doesn't mean I *want* to give you that access," I snap.

Prince raises his hand in surrender. "Okay, okay. I won't prod anymore."

"It's getting late." I look out the basement sliding door into the darkness. "I'm sure my dad is going to pop down soon, so I can take care of the rest." I lift the *Frozen* bag to hand him, laughing awkwardly to fill the silence.

"No sweat, Danielle. You keep it." He nudges the bag closer to me. "I brought it for you. Just don't go eating everything at once."

I nod, still crouched on the floor, looking up at this gorgeous boy in my basement who seems to be really trying. But I don't trust him, and I don't even trust myself anymore.

My judgement feels cloudy, and I've never before wanted a guy to stay and leave equally as much.

I finally hoist myself up and lead him upstairs. He steps into the family room, where my mom is once again excited, and my dad is relieved he didn't have to kick Prince out. Prince thanks them again for allowing him into their home, compliments us on being a wonderful family, and ends it by saying he hopes to see them again sometime soon. Mom squeezes him tight, and Dad's handshake seems firm, his expression adoring.

Prince steps out the front door, pauses, and turns back around. I attempt to pat my hair one last time, realizing this will be the last memory he has of me from the night.

"You don't believe me yet, but you will, Danielle Ford. Good night, beautiful."

"Good night," I say, slowly closing the door. I lean back against it, my pulse throbbing through my chest. My hair is a mess, I feel so raw, my emotions are a wreck. But somehow, I smile. Because the way he called me beautiful, I know he meant it.

Dear Toni,

How do you reckon with a friend like Sula? A friendship that starts so deep, so pure? A friendship that you love and trust even when others have their reservations, only to get hurt your damn self?

My female friendships have always been complicated. Women are powerful, and I wanted to learn from them –

their strength, their confidence – even if it looked different for different people. It rubbed some the wrong way, when I chose to hang out with girls who didn't fit cultural norms or weren't deemed appropriate or "good." But they were good for me. They showed me worlds I didn't know and would never have known without their friendship. They've taught me life lessons. A good friend will tell you their darkest secret. They'll ask you for advice and you'll give them your best. And somehow, you have felt what they've felt and have grown from their mistakes like they were your own.

But what happens when the company you keep doesn't make you feel safe? What happens when a friend refuses to acknowledge their destruction in your life? When your sister becomes dangerous? How does it make you feel, when the people who viewed her as an outsider, who warned you to stay away from her, are right? And the very thing that attracted you to this person is what rips the friendship apart? Maybe I should have known better. Or maybe I thought our love and friendship were so raw and genuine that she would.

Dani

Chapter Six

finger on the Pulse

PRINCE

Detroit has never had earthquakes, but I definitely woke up convinced we were having one. I spent half the night analyzing Dani's body language, which was so hot and cold she could be a brand ambassador for IcyHot.

Then I woke up to my bed shaking and almost rolled on the floor, until I realized Mook had decided to be my alarm clock and cannonball onto my futon.

"Wake up!" he whines. "You promised you'd twist me today!" My little brother is so self-absorbed. I mean really. This kid is only seven, and for someone who hates getting up early and has a hard time staying focused, he somehow remembers LIKE CLOCKWORK when it's hair day. I never picked an official day, but he knows it's usually one Sunday out of every month. Working at the station and going to school during the week means my weekends are dedicated to fam, so I should have known he'd come running downstairs at the crack of dawn asking me to do this. I just thought since I was out and unable to read his bedtime stories last night, he would sleep in pretty late like he usually does. I was counting on that for today. Joke's on me.

I think about last night with Danielle and her emotions, which were so damn chaotic. My goal was to make her laugh as much as possible and ask her about her writing, and for a moment I felt my jokes hittin' and even watched her eyes dance as she relished her dreams of moving to New York City. We *were* connecting, and then once she got in her own head about something, she switched it up on me completely. She retreated, got colder, and for the life of me I can't figure out what I might have said or did to cause such a drastic change.

And yet…the fact that she's listened to my show. The way she looked at me at the door. You can say I'm feelin' myself, but I knew. I knew she was into me. She's scared for whatever reason. I've already done my research around school, and Danielle has been on a couple dates here and there but nothing serious, so if she was ever serious with someone, it wasn't at Mass Tech. I mean, my ex didn't go there either… I shudder thinking about her. You know that saying, the best way to get over someone is to get under someone new? I don't recommend it, but in this case my little wager with Dani has definitely got me laser focused. If only she'd actually let me get under her…

Figuring this girl out is like figuring out quantum physics. But I am never one to shy away from a challenge. And last night might not have been a success, but it was a start.

"Okay, okay, chill, lil man," I groan, sitting up and rubbing my achy hands.

"Where were you yesterday?" he enquires, holding on to my neck in anticipation of a piggyback upstairs. He's a big ball of energy, but he also knows how to use it to his advantage. This is how he brings my energy level up fast in the morning. My poor mom never stood a chance with two boys in the house.

"Why you all in my business?" He gives me his cute little grin and I rub his head. With Mook hanging over me, I scoot off the edge of my bed and fumble around for my socks. Winter is coming, and this concrete floor is getting more and more frigid.

I break upstairs with him on my back to start our day. He's distracted all the time, but having him do daily rituals with me can somehow keep him focused. I almost have to treat everything like it's a game, so I'll have him do things like count while he's brushing or be my sous-chef in the kitchen while I'm making breakfast for the fam. I'll play tag with him while we're getting dressed for school, anything to give him balance. Each day is different, but it's one less thing my mom has to worry about.

As we approach the top of the steps, I smell the scent of bacon and hear crackles and pops in the kitchen. I turn the corner to find my mom, leaning on her cane, fixing breakfast. She likes to avoid using it when she's feeling better, but with this relapse, I think she's realizing it's safer for her to have it nearby.

"Ma, what are you doing?!" I ask as I come up beside her and kiss her cheek. Mook copies me and does the same. He grabs her neck while still on my back and nuzzles her face. She giggles.

"You always cook breakfast, so I figured I could do it since you slept in late from being out last night." She gives me the look.

"What's that?"

"Your uncle told me you had a date. Why didn't you tell me?"

"Ooh, was it that girl who came over? I like her. She gave me books!" *Come on, Mook!* He talks too much.

My mom stops mid-flip and looks at me. "What girl brought books over for him? When was this?"

"Both of y'all chill out. Ma, you were napping. Yes, Mook, it's the same girl. Also, you're choking me." I set him down and he darts down the hall to do who knows what.

"And go brush your teeth!" I yell. "Yo breath is funky!" I hear a faint giggle as he races off.

"Did you schedule a doctor's appointment?" I ask her.

"I'm feeling much better, baby, so I think I'm okay for now."

I sigh. "But Ma, you know when you have falls…"

My mom faces me. "Prinnnnnce." Anytime she says my name with that cadence, I know the conversation is over. So I'll drop it…for now. I make a mental note to schedule something in the next few days just in case. "So, who's this girl?"

She has that motherly look: inquisitive, but with a dash of concern. I'm still her cub and she's still my lioness. I know she wants me to find love, but I know she's also concerned about another heartbreak.

"Don't worry, Ma, I'm taking it slow." The bacon is starting to crisp, so I take the fork out her hand and flip it myself. You kinda get used to multitasking in this house. "She's a girl from school. I just went to chill at her place and got to know her a bit."

"And she brought books over? That's very thoughtful."

"Yeah, it was 'cause our first interaction wasn't exactly... pleasant." I explain the situation and my mom chuckles.

"That's extremely big of her to do something like that. Sounds like she comes from a good home."

"Yeah," I respond, thinking more about her house. The pictures that line her walls, the massively cosy fireplace in the family room, the finished basement with carpet and a plush sofa where Danielle and I sat, which wasn't nearly as drafty as my room and included a bathroom, a laundry room, and two separate bedrooms. She also had a sliding door that led to their backyard, filled with patio furniture, a grill, and a garden of flowers whose species I can assure you I don't know. Meanwhile, our basement is barely finished, and Mom and I have a rule: no laundry past midnight, so the buzzing from the dryer doesn't wake me out of my sleep. In some ways it feels like me and Danielle are from two different worlds.

As if reading my mind, my mom intrudes on my thoughts. "Hey," she says, "don't let this girl make you feel inferior for one second because things for her are a little different than they are here." She sighs. "I know I haven't been the best example when it comes to love…"

"Ma, don't do that." I begin to choke up. "Pops left you and that was fucked up…"

"Prince Jones. Watch your—"

"But you know it's true," I declare, seething. "He was the one who left us after you were diagnosed. What kinda coward does that? You shouldn't have to apologize 'cause he's a man that can't take care of his."

My mom grabs my shoulders, her eyes filled with sorrow. We don't talk much about my dad, but somehow my mom still blames herself for my dad's departure eight years ago. "PJ, I know you're mad at him. I am too. But your dad didn't sign up for this. When we met, I was perfectly healthy. Between him losing his job, the financial stress that took a toll on the marriage, the diagnosis and my health…and then when I got pregnant after the doctors told me I would never carry again and I told him I was keeping the baby…" Her voice is cracking. "I think it was all too much for him."

"Did you sign up for all that? And MS?" I wait for her to respond, but she just looks away. "And what about the vows you both made? In sickness and health. Shouldn't that have meant *something* to him?" She takes one hand off my shoulder to wipe her tears.

"Maybe, but life gives us free will. He wanted more from life, and he felt I was holding him back. But look what God gave me," she replies, holding my chin. "You. He left us and you stepped up and became a young man right before my very eyes. So that's what I mean, baby. You've been more of a man than your father *ever* was. And you show me daily the type of husband and father you'll be to someone. You're my greatest accomplishment. Don't you dare let this girl for one second believe you don't deserve her. If she can't realize how wonderful you are, then she doesn't deserve *you*. Understood?"

I nod and bite my lip, overwhelmed with emotion. My mom said so much there. She believes I deserve the world but doesn't think she does. I *am* her world. How can I pursue my dreams without breaking her heart?

Even when my dad was here, he was never fully present. He always managed to find a reason to get out the house; he'd start an argument with my mom and somehow that was his excuse for "needing some air." Air meant a reason to be out with his boys at all hours of the night, usually going to places a married man had no business going to.

Mook is two years shy of the age I was when Pops left us. He'll ask about him here and there, but not as much as you'd think. Once, when he asked me why he left and I told him the truth – that Pops wasn't happy here with Mom and me – I asked him if he wished his dad was around. His answer was simply, "No. I don't want him here if he wasn't happy. Plus, you make me happy enough."

I didn't want him to see me cry, but that night I pulled the covers over my head and cried like a baby. I never had much of a relationship with our dad, but the black hole I feel in my heart for not having him around is deep and ferocious.

It's different for Mook – he can't possibly miss something he didn't have. I wish I was as nonchalant as my brother and felt nothing, that I wasn't grieving for a relationship that never was. Sometimes I think it's better that way.

The cold air pinches at my skin the next morning as I slam the door of my Ford Taurus shut. My uncle Jerome gave this car to my mom years ago, and then she passed it down to me. Moms calls it Ole Faithful, and I'd have to agree with her – this car has been in our possession for what seems like an eternity and somehow manages to survive the brutal winters and still keep it pushing. It's one of the most reliable things I own.

I look up at the colossal construction of my school in downtown Detroit, forged from brick and glass, which holds almost three thousand students. Mass is one of the few magnet schools in Detroit and a beast to get into, but I love this place. It holds some of the brightest minds in the D, and we're in school grinding it out early. Some of the areas of specialization include science, engineering, and for people like me and Danielle, arts and communications.

Dani. I still can't shake this girl and have been contemplating my next move, trying to figure out a way I can impress her on our first official date. I gotta be real, the three dates idea came out my mouth because I've heard it used before and at the time, it sounded nice. But in all seriousness, how the hell am I gonna impress this girl with three dates…

on a budget? I probably should be focusing on applying to schools and all that other stuff, but home life is too stressful for all that. I need something fun, and Danielle is just that. The girl of my middle-school dreams is finally giving me a chance, and I wanna ride this out. See where it takes me.

I walk through the glass lobby, past Tech's Hall of Fame bulletin board and up the stairs to put my things away, and catch Malik in the hallway at his locker. He pulls his brush out his backpack and sweeps it through his hair, letting the bristles stroke his waves. I swear this man wakes up trying to figure out what girl he's gonna trap that day. People are lingering in the hallway, socializing until the last second when the school day officially begins.

I pull up beside him and bang on his locker door.

He shrieks and I laugh hysterically. "P, you play too goddamn much!" He's mad I messed up his cool in front of our peers, but that's my boy, it's what we do.

"Copped this the other day. Bro, check out my drip." He poses a few times in front of his locker to show me his new outfit, and I shake my head.

"Them gym shoes cold," I say. "The outfit? Eh." I give him one good look over and shake my hands as if to say it's all right.

"What!" he says, sucking his teeth. "You a hater, this whole fit is Gucci." I laugh, clearly annoying him again, and he changes the subject. "What's the move for the day?" he enquires, dapping me up. I lean against the locker next to him.

"Nothing, man, just gotta catch up on some work. I think I'm gonna go to the computer lab and work through lunch. I got too caught up yesterday helping around the house…"

"Excuse me," Makayla coos, "you're leaning on my locker. Unless you came to visit me."

"I came to visit this clown," I say, pointing to Malik and scooting over. "How you been?" Malik is grinning ear to ear, watching us interact. I can't fake, Makayla is a cutie, but in the obvious sense. Sandy-coloured skin, hazel eyes, she's got tons of guys fiending for her, including Malik, but there's something about her that's just…boring. I see her and I see a mannequin doll that wants to be doted on but offers nothing in return. But for some reason my lack of interest makes her obsessed with me.

"It's better seeing you." She hangs her brown leather jacket and backpack in her locker, grabs a notebook, and shuts the door. She edges closer, completely infringing on my personal space. "Did you not get my text messages?"

"My bad," I say, rubbing the back of my neck. "Things have been…busy. Between doing extra hours at the station and midterms, life has been kicking my ass."

"Well, if you wanna hang, let me know," she responds, biting her lip. "I know it must be tough for you with the break-up and all." She pauses. "My parents are out of town next weekend."

"Good to know," I say, my eyes darting across the hallway. I don't see Danielle often, since our classes are in different parts of the school, but it'd be just my luck to see her today of all days. I need to find a way to get rid of Makayla fast. "I'll see how my weekend's lookin'." That perfect smile spreads across Makayla's plump pink lips, and I'm reminded why almost everyone wants her. But me? I want more.

I can tell she thinks she got me, though, and I let her. It buys me some time before she blows up my phone again. I've told her I'm not ready to be serious, but it seems like "no" is not a word she hears often, 'cause she won't leave me alone. She sashays away, her black leggings hugging her small waist, and I swear if feels like she exaggerated her walk, hoping I'm looking.

I turn to face Malik, but he's still in Makayla's trance. "Now *she* cold. What are you doing?"

I shrug, grab his textbook for our first class, and close his locker door. "She's cute, but I've been there and done that with girls like Makayla. She don't impress me much." I give Malik his book to snap him out of la-la land.

"Cuffin' season is approaching and I'm tryna be booed up with someone like her. I got a few options, but I'll take her if you don't want her." We pick up the pace as the bell rings.

I shake my head. "M, you gotta stop talking like that. She's not mines to take." I unlock my phone to text Danielle.

PRINCE: We still on for Saturday? You not ready for what I have planned.

I'm not ready either.

DANI: Sure...just don't get too elaborate on me.

We keeping it casual, right?

PRINCE: I'll try my best 😌

"Okay, Captain Liberation," Malik replies, and my smile molds into a grimace as I make a mental note to school him *again* on misogyny later.

"But some advice, if you want to actually get her attention? Ignore the hell outta her, 'cause apparently that's her thing."

"Caller twenty-two, you on?"

"Heeeyyy, DJ LoveJones!"

"What up, doe?! What's your name, sweetheart?"

"Jessica," she chimes.

"So, what can I help you with today, Jessica?"

"Okay, so…I met this guy on a dating app, we started dating and everything seemed cool. I even paid for us to go on a cruise, and then when we got back, he ghosted me. Like, I got no texts, no DMs…no nothin'. Even after I texted him a few times to see if he okay."

"Hmm." I ponder, adjusting the microphone so that Jessica will hear me more clearly. "But he's still posting and stuff online?"

"Yessss! He even had the nerve to post something on his feed a day after I DMed him! But when I responded to it, tryna be cute, I got nothing." She sighs in defeat. "I felt like he was the one."

"I'm gonna go out on a limb and say that if he ghosted you after you paid for a cruise, he's definitely not the one for you. How long were you dating him?"

"About two months."

I cringe. It's amazing how people will use someone even though they know they aren't into them. It kinda reminds me of my ex, Morgan. And clearly Jessica is naive and willing to do anything to find her match. She's just going about it the wrong way. "I know two months might *feel* like enough time, but that's mistake number one. You can't get caught up that easy. There's no rushing love, and there's definitely no rushing your search for the one."

"But I am in a rush!" caller twenty-two says. "I don't have time to waste, LoveJones. I'm old. I need love like now."

"How old are you, Jessica?"

"I'm about to be twenty-five," she replies.

I laugh. "That is *not* old," I declare.

"Tuh. Tell that to my ovaries."

I chuckle. "Okay, hear me out. There was this study done by a group of scientists. They tested a few different things – how a person decides on buying a painting, how managers determine who they hire, and how people fall in love, right? And they realized people think they have more than enough information to come to a logical conclusion, but they're actually letting emotion cloud their judgement. That's not a good thing when it comes to choosing a potential spouse, right?"

Jessica is all in. "Okay, okay, so maybe I jumped in too fast. But how long should it take to find the one?"

"You'd know after the honeymoon phase, which lasts about three months. That's when the masks come off, and you start to see a person's flaws. And you decide even with all that if they're worth it."

"Damn, that's a long time…but I get it. So like, when will I know if a guy even likes me for real for real?"

"The theory is, in any heterosexual relationship it takes guys eighty-eight days to fall in love, and girls a hundred thirty-four. So if you keep it casual, you won't have to be extra with it. He'll fall right in your lap."

Jessica pauses. "My girls did tell me I was doing the most by paying for that trip so soon."

"Yeah, you went all in way too fast. Slow things down, let the guys come to you. Let them show you they are worthy of *your* time. If it's easy, it will come naturally." The door opens on the other side of the studio glass and Ant, Malik and Yaz pop into the green room. They all throw up the head nod, with Malik's extra-ass throwing his body against the glass, making the studio reverberate slightly. I swear this dude is gonna get me fired.

"When a guy starts to show you the real him, there might be some traits you don't like. You have to decide what traits you need to make you happy and fulfilled in the relationship. But don't invest anything else until you see the return, you feel me?"

"Thank you, DJ LoveJones, you da best."

"You got it, babe. Got a song just for you. And make sure to get your tickets for the annual Boo at the Zoo in a few weeks. I'll be spinning all the hits. This is your high-school love coach signing off." I fiddle with my audio console and play a song as DJ Mike walks into the booth. I turn up the sound, just as I slide my headphones off. Then I dap Mike up and clean up my workstation, setting him up for the shift switch so I can go chat with the boys for a bit.

Just as I walk out, my uncle opens the door to the studio.

"Damn, I just missed you," he says.

"Romes!" my friends yell as they rise up to greet him. They haven't seen him in a minute, and it's showing through their enthusiasm.

"How you young brothas doing?" my uncle responds, just as smooth as ever, embracing everyone.

Yaz shrugs. "I haven't seen you around the house much. Where the hell have you been?"

Uncle Jerome rubs his recently dyed goatee and sits down. "Been working overtime, man. These late-night hours are something vicious, but I'm not gonna let it mess with my coins. So I've still been doing birthday parties and cookouts and fundraising events and tryna find time to sleep in between. And I've been doing a few sets before some concerts at Chene Park."

"It's the Aretha Franklin Amphitheatre," Ant replies.

"No disrespect to the Queen of Soul, but it's always gonna be Chene Park to us," my uncle says.

I chuckle. "Hardest-working man in radio," I retort.

"Not anymore," he declares, giving me a good slap on the back. "You're doing your thing. I'm so proud of you, PJ. You carrying the family torch."

"Pretty soon Prince is gonna be taking over DJ Mike's shift," Ant whispers.

My uncle shakes his head. "Nah, if there's anything we learned, it's that you can't be loyal to these local stations. I had that spot for twenty years and they pushed me to the *Quiet Storm* spot just like that. Prince gotta think bigger."

I nod along, but in my head I feel so deflated. My uncle is absolutely right. I need to be using this as a résumé builder to do bigger things, but I just don't know how that's possible. My uncle barely has time to help around the house like he used to. I know he loves his sister, but he's doing all these gigs to stay relevant, and hopefully to land a better spot at another station. Who's gonna help my mom if he's too busy and I'm away at school?

"PJ, you okay?" my uncle enquires.

I shake myself out of it. "Yeah, yeah. I was just thinking about the first time I told you I wanted to be a DJ who gives relationship advice, and you threw me right in! I had barely started high school."

Uncle Jerome chuckles. "I mean, you were already helping me out at the station by then. And I knew they weren't gonna fire me if I tested it out, so why not? We threw you on for a few spots and the city couldn't get enough of your segments."

It was weird when people started to call in, requesting more of me. My uncle had pretty solid ratings already, but my spot made his ratings skyrocket. Instead of being bitter, my uncle used my new-found fame to hook me up. He was the one who pitched the concept of the high-school love expert segment my sophomore year, with the hope that the station would give him more of a producer role. But they just took his idea and ran with it. That's why my uncle wants bigger for me. He wants me to do my own thing, and he wants to be my right-hand man, to protect me. Whatever I do, I'm definitely putting him on. "A love expert your age? People really took to it. You were always wise beyond your years."

Malik cuts in. "Look, P, you know how to give some damn good advice. I'll give you that. But when it comes to taking your own..." He throws me the *eek* face and everyone laughs.

"Did you not hear the advice I just gave to my girl Jessica?"

"Prince, you and I both know that caller was basic as hell..."

My friends ain't wrong, though. My personal dating life hasn't lived up to my radio rep, so I'm trying something different. After Dani and I establish on Monday that we're seeing each other this weekend, I don't text her for a few days. Not because I don't want to, but she's been so caught up with college apps that she hasn't been super responsive with text messages, and I can take a hint. She needs some space. It seems like the right thing to do, according to my friends, anyway, who think the fastest way to get a girl to fall for you is to ignore them. And for as much as I go in on their love lives, I wouldn't say my last relationship ended happily ever after.

But now that I'm actually listening to them, they won't

stop "instilling" their "words of wisdom." It's like they finally got some power and don't know what to do with it. And the longer Dani and I don't talk, the more I'm doubting if this was even the right move.

"I'm still waiting to see if this no-texting thing even works," I respond, shuffling through my backpack to make sure I'm not leaving anything behind. I grab my phone and check my messages, I guess hoping there's some world in which she would text me first. But why would she? I had to chase her down and practically beg her to take out her hair just to spend time with her, and unlike Makayla, Dani doesn't seem like the type to pursue someone. What I see is a comment notification on my most recent post. From Morgan, of all people. I slide the phone into my back pocket.

"You literally just told that girl not to be pressed. What do you think texting someone every day makes you?" Malik says.

I laugh. "You can't even put me in that category, bruh. That girl out there buying trips around the world for a man she barely knows. I'm just tryna see how Danielle's day is going." I plop on the leather couch next to Yaz.

"I agree with Malik," Yaz responds.

"Et tu, Brute?" I respond.

"And stop saying that wack shit!" Malik says, throwing his hands up. "Where is that even from?"

"Shakespeare," my uncle responds, shaking his head. "You young boys need to read more."

I laugh at Unc's discontentment. "With yo uncultured ass."

"So, who is this Danielle?" Uncle Jerome asks.

"This girl I finally convinced to go out with me—"

"That Prince has been crushin' on since before we had facial hair!" Ant butts in.

"Man, whatever," I huff. "She's cute and smart. I wanna get to know her is all."

My uncle gets up and pats me on the back again. "Prince is a chip off the old block. He got this." Malik rolls his eyes and I throw him the middle finger behind my uncle's back because...I'm still respectful. "Aight, I gotta head out. Emceeing Saturday at the rink for Sweetest Day. It's old-school night, you guys should come through – it's the perfect date night."

"Nah, my mom and stepdad be going and they be all touchy-feely on the floor. I'ma pass." Ant shivers just thinking about it and we all giggle.

"Fair point," my uncle says, giving everyone the fist bump. "PJ, let my lil sis know I'll be over next Sunday. I know there are a few house projects I need to finish."

"Bet," I reply, and throw up the deuces while my uncle slips out the studio.

I turn to Yasin. "So I'm taking everyone's advice, but what about you? Any headway?"

Yasin's infatuation is with Jordan, a junior on our varsity track team. Jordan seems sweet, a quiet girl in the classroom but a monster on the track, which makes it even funnier when girls from other teams be talking mad shit before they race against her. Jordan keeps it humble, but they don't want that smoke on the pavement.

Yasin and Jordan had AP Chem together last year, and ever since they became lab partners, Yasin has been smitten. He spent a whole damn summer talking about her, and I've been determined to get him to ask her out. But Yaz is afraid she'll reject him because he ain't...Black. I guess stepping to a girl is intimidating no matter who you are, but I think it's just a cop-out because he's afraid of being turned down.

Now it's Yasin's turn to rub his facial hair – he's had stubble since he was twelve and would brag about having to shave while me and Ant were looking in the mirror every day, hoping for our peach fuzzes to grow in. "She posted something last week about getting ready for track season, and I told her I can't wait to see her on the field. We talked for a bit then."

I probe. "And what did she say?"

He pulls out his phone to read the message. "She said she really appreciates me coming to see her run and she wishes I could see her sooner. Track season is so far away."

Ant's eyes perk up and Malik rubs his hands together. "Okay, okay. We getting somewhere! How did you respond?"

Yasin sulks. "You think that was my cue to ask her out?"

"Yes!!" we all holler, and then I quickly shush everyone, realizing we're still in the studio.

"Hell, give me your phone, I'll set the date up myself." Malik attempts to snatch Yasin's phone out of his hand, but he's too slow. "Man, Yaz, track season's not till spring. You need to hit her up tonight on some 'you free?'"

I shook my head. "You gotta play off people's strengths. His sincerity is what Jordan is into. Yaz, ain't she a part of some indoor track club that lets her train in the fall? You should casually show up to one of those meets. Surprise her with flowers after the meet is over and ask her if you can take her out to eat and load her up on carbs to help her muscles recover." I pat Yasin on the back. "You got this. Trust the kid."

The bell chimes as we step into the shop, which is surprisingly packed for a Wednesday night. My shop is your typical barbershop, always loud, with either the music blasting, ESPN sport highlights cranked up to the loudest setting, or a disagreement happening that requires everyone in the shop to yell at the top of their lungs. Which means it's always a good time. But my boy Theo knows that I'm coming to get my sides and back touched up for my date this weekend. So he's already on his job.

"My man Prince!" he calls out. "Let me finish him up and then I got you."

"Bet." I throw him the head nod and turn to see my boys already getting harassed by Mr J, our neighbourhood hustler.

"Mr J, no one, and I repeat, *no one*, buys CDs or DVDs anymore! Like, I wouldn't even know how to use one."

"It's true," Ant responds, currently focused on an annoyed Kisha, who just got dropped off at the shop by Ant's baby mama and is flustered and ready to take off her coat like yesterday.

"Oh, 'cause y'all be using those iPods and such to play your music now," Mr J responds, irritated.

"iPods? You mean this?" Malik responds, holding up his phone. "My music? Is all in here. I don't have a Runman or whatever you called that thing."

"A Walkman!" Mr J answers back, shaking his head in discontent. "You kids don't know nothing."

Mr J is a fixture at the barbershop, which is sort of hilarious, 'cause I've never actually seen this man get a haircut. He's somehow either already there when I show up, or pops in when I'm in the chair. And every time I see him, he's got a new hustle. Last time he was selling vacation packages to Cuba, and the time before that, off-market kicks. His most popular one was probably a pyramid scheme, which the young folks could sniff through, but everyone over forty-five was really into. No matter how much the signs are there slapping you in your face, people wanna believe a hope and dream. Apparently I walk up just in time.

"My guy Prince!" Mr J responds, dapping me up. "People still use CDs, right?? He's on the radio, he'll know."

"It's kinda hard to believe, but I gotta side with Malik on this one." Malik flashes his huge, mischievous smile.

"Damn." Mr J holds his hand to his heart. "That one cuts deep."

"Let me see your packaging, though." Mr J pulls a few CDs out of his suitcase (I know, right?), hands one to me and one to Kisha, who has both arms out, grabbing the air. She immediately attempts to stick it in her mouth, but Ant's daddy superpowers kick in real fast and in one swift motion he distracts her with a toy from his backpack, while simultaneously sliding the CD over to Yasin. Parenthood is a true art.

I have to say, I'm impressed with Mr J's presentation. He's cut up little sheets of his own art, obviously created from Microsoft Paint, has his tracks on the back, and even created a fake barcode. If this was twenty years earlier, he might have had a real hustle here.

My phone buzzes and Dani's name pops up on my screen. I'm about to damn near hyperventilate, but instead I play it cool and put the phone back in my pocket. It's gonna eat me up not checking the text immediately, but I know if I open it I'm going to psychoanalyze every word she types and spend the rest of the time trying to come up with the perfect response. Let me not feed into my anxiety right now.

"Mr J, have you ever thought about selling vinyl?" I get a few people's attention in the barbershop with that question, including an older gentleman getting his receding hairline completely shaved off.

"Now this young man is onto something!" someone yells behind me.

Mr J huffs. "Nah, man, that's too much money!"

I sit down on the bench next to Ant and grab Kisha. "Not if you really break down your costs. How much you paying for those blank CDs?"

"I can get a hundred on Amazon for sixteen bucks."

"SIXTEEN DOLLARS?!?" Malik retorts from across the shop, attempting to flirt with the new shampoo girl. "Dawg, how are you even making a profit? 'Cause I know no one is buying them shits!"

Even I have to laugh. "Mr J, you could go to some vinyl shops around the city and buy at least three to four classics with that and sell them for double."

"Who gon buy that?"

"I would," I say, raising Kisha's hand. I kiss the heck outta her chubby cheeks and she giggles.

Ant raises her other hand. "I would too. I'm not a big listener, but my mom loves 'em. She stay in the record shops."

I decide it's time to check Dani's text and open the message app.

DANI: Hey Prince, I know we talked about linking up on Saturday, but can we hang some other time? I really need to focus on finishing my essays and submitting my college applications.

You know when babies are unaware of their strength and will sometimes just swat you in the face with their hard-ass baby toy for no reason? After Kisha did that to me the first time, I learned my lesson. But this? Feels ten times worse. I must have made a noise of defeat, because Anthony stares at my phone.

He smacks his lips and grabs Kisha, who's attempting to snatch my phone like a shiny new toy. "Damn, Prince."

I slouch over on the bench, rereading the text. "This

sounds like she's gonna keep blowing me off until I go away, right?" I whisper. Anthony nods. *Great.*

Malik looks over at us and can sense something is wrong, so he comes back over and pulls Yasin away from Mr J, who is now tryna sell Yaz some herbal shit.

"What happened?" Malik prods.

"She tryna flake on him," Anthony responds for me. "Something about having to work on her college essays."

Malik swats his hand dismissively. "Man, that was a dummy mission anyway."

I shake my head. "We already talked about this, dawg. I'm just tryna get to know her, that's *it*."

"I still can't believe Yaz co-signed your idea to take down her damn braids anyway. He was the only one that thought that shit was cute," Malik replies.

"You did what?" Mr J says. Some of the guys in the shop groan.

"That's what y'all doing nowadays? What you gonna do next, wash her clothes?" receding hairline guy says, looking around for support and trying a little too hard to impress everyone in the shop. A few of the guys chuckle.

I'm annoyed. "Maybe. But I guess when you have a mom with a debilitating disease, you don't mind doing shit like that." The shop goes silent, and you can tell Mr J feels horrible, since he grew up with my mom.

"What you know about that anyway, Yaz?" Mr J changes the subject, extra loud for everyone to hear. "Whose braids you been taking down?"

Yaz smirks. "Ya mama." The shop erupts in laughter and Malik daps Yasin for that one. Even Kisha is laughing and clapping her hands. We taught him well. "But seriously, my sister helps her friends all the time. They'll be in our living room for *hours*. I don't get how anyone can sit through that. My legs get numb just watching them."

"Yeah, that's like six hours! Like I said, a waste of time," Malik responds.

"Or a fast track to getting her to fall for me," I say, and Malik rolls his eyes. "Hear me out. I've dated enough girls that complain about taking their hair down and will bribe anyone. I mean *anyone*."

"That's true," Theo replies. "I've had girls I dated offer to buy their friends dinner, take them to see a movie afterward, fill up their gas tank…hell, anything to help them shave off some of the time!"

"Exactly," I respond. "It forces you to open up when you in a chair for hours. Women be telling their braid lady their whole life story."

"And how did that work out for you?" Malik shoots back. I suck my teeth, not sure what to say next, and Theo goes back to finishing up the guy's lineup in the chair.

Receding hairline tips his barber and walks toward me. "Look, son, I take back what I said about the braiding. That's a genius idea for winning over a lady. Shoot, I should have done more of that back in the day." He leans in closer. "I've been married to my wife for thirteen years, and you know what she likes? Surprises and thoughtful gifts. It doesn't have to be a grand gesture, just something to show you put some real thought into it. Sometimes that's enough to change a girl's mind. Doesn't hurt to try something different. It might work in your favour. Ya hear me?"

I nod, shaking the man's hand.

"My son makes me put on your show when I pick him up from school. He's only twelve but already trying to impress the ladies." He pauses. "You're doing good work, and you give good advice. Let your instincts guide you." He pats my back, and I turn to watch him step out the shop, the door chiming on his way out.

I look at my phone and begin tapping away.

PRINCE: I promise I will have you home at a reasonable hour. You deserve to enjoy life a little.

Her response is fast.

DANI: I'm just getting close to deadline. I don't know if this is the best use of my time, and I'm having serious writer's block.

I have to think. I quickly google how to overcome writer's block, and then I think about the night I went to her house, trying to remember if there was anything there that could give me a clue... I got it! I frantically text away.

PRINCE: I hear sometimes the best cure for writer's

block is to move your body…that when you get your body into flow, your mind follows. Maybe going out to do something fun and active will get you going, and I know just the thing.

Still no answer, so I give it one last attempt.

PRINCE: Don't give me a quick no, let me work to a slow yes.

The three dots appear, then disappear, and then reappear again. I got her stumped.

"What she say?!" Malik asks, attempting to look at my screen. I pull the phone close to me. For someone who thinks I'm wasting my time, he's all up in my space.

"She hasn't responded yet."

For four agonizing minutes I get nothing. Finally, the dots disappear and a text pops up.

DANI: Let's see if you can live up to your show's hype.

Chapter Seven
Got My Head Spinning

I open my locker to a pair of suede, retro-style Moxi roller skates staring back at me. Turquoise, with magenta shoelaces and a tan sole on top of black wheels. I would absolutely wear these if they weren't skates.

As if that wasn't enough, I lift a skate out of the locker and discover that the wheels light up. I have to laugh at the ridiculousness of all this. Where did he even find these? When I go to grab the other skate, a note falls out and I unfold it to find a message from Mr You-Know-Who.

Yes, I got you custom LED skates, because why not? You're coming to Northland with me Saturday night because the fact that you haven't been skating since like middle school is unacceptable…and this is exactly what you need to help you get over your writer's block. Let's see if you still got it.—P

I set the skates back in my locker and shut the door. Dang, he moves fast. I just told him yes yesterday and he managed to buy skates and have them in my locker by the time I got to school. Which makes me…slightly impressed. I'm going to make a complete ass of myself, but it's been a while since I've been this excited about anything. I've been so caught up in the past and focused on my future that I feel like I've forgotten how to enjoy the now. Which is probably why writing about myself for my college essay has become incredibly daunting to do. It feels good to focus on the present, even if it's just for a moment, and makes me glad he convinced me to go out with him when I tried to cancel…again.

I did have fun with Prince when he came over, but his cockiness turned me off. Love isn't a game, and his little bet made me feel like a trophy, which is one thing I'm not. He's such a typical dude. But somehow, I can't stop thinking about the end of the night and how he seemed to have a genuine concern for how I was feeling. And even when I snapped at him and attempted to cancel our next date, he found a way to tie getting out to my writing, as a way for me to loosen up. There is an interest in helping me with the things that are important to me. If it were just a game to him, he would have lost interest by now, right? Maybe underneath some of that arrogance is more depth? I'm thinking about this as I step into the girls' bathroom, almost colliding into Rashida.

"Oh!" I say, startled.

"Hey, Dani." Those soft eyes. Rashida always had a way of making you melt with her genuineness. I see longing in her eyes in this moment. The same longing I've seen for the past several months when she's attempted to approach me, and I always had "somewhere to be." Eventually she gave up and I didn't blame her. I just didn't know how to make myself available anymore, and blowing her off was easier than trying to engage. "How are you?"

"I'm good," I say, nodding my head and trying to convince myself that what I'm saying is true. "College applications have been taking over my life and I've just been busy…"

"Right. So busy you couldn't even answer a text or return a phone call for almost a year?"

She got right to it.

"I don't know what you're talking about," I say, feeling incredibly uncomfortable. This is the first time I've been alone with Rashida, and she's practically blocked the door. I can't just slip out.

"Don't play me, Dani," Rashida responds curtly. "I tried giving you space, hoping you'd come around when you were ready to talk. Clearly that didn't work, but guess what? We're going to talk right here and right now." I stand there frozen. I'm not really ready to confront anything, even this friendship. But being forced to hear the words coming out of the mouth of someone as sweet as Rashida makes me realize how selfish I've been. I can see her round jawline tighten up, her honey-coloured skin exuding a reddish hue. She's furious. "I know you don't hang out with Destiny, and now she's spreading rumours about you hating on her 'cause you liked a college guy that ended up giving her play."

"What!" All this because I don't want to hang out with her messy behind? I'm ready to slam Destiny against a locker and attempt to storm out the bathroom to find her when Rashida yanks me back.

"Danielle, stop!" She spins me around to face her. "This isn't like you. None of this. The detachment, the anger…" She slips my hand into hers. "I know something happened."

I hear the drip-drop of the sink faucet, and I try to force myself to mimic it. To hold in as much as possible, not to let Rashida's words cause my emotions to pour out. I want to leave, but her grip is too strong.

"Esi is mad at you, because she's hurt. She feels like you abandoned us. But I know better. I know something happened, Dani, and you've ignored us because of it." She squeezes my hand tighter and sighs deeply. "I know I can't force you to tell me, so all I can say is, I'm here. Whenever you want to talk, or if you need help getting help. Whatever it is, I'm still your best friend." She hugs me, her embrace firm and warm, and I am overwhelmed by her kindness, even though I don't deserve it. The tears stream down like a faucet running. I let her hold me until someone opens the bathroom door, and she turns us around so that whoever walked in can't see my face, only hers. She waits until the person goes into the stall before grabbing me a few paper towels. The bell rings. "Shoot," she says, looking at her phone. "I can't be late for Mr Brown. I have a date on Saturday, but can I stop by your house Sunday? I'll bring you Superman ice cream."

She knows that's my favourite. "It's too cold for ice cream," I say.

"Please, it's Detroit. It's always too cold for ice cream."

I snicker, then sigh. "I'd like that."

She smiles. "Good. Sunday then." She points her finger at me. "No backing out." She kisses my cheek and skips off. Rashida wouldn't be able to live with herself if she had a tardy mark for class, but she was still willing to risk it for me. It shows me how much she misses me...and I miss her, too.

She has a date on Saturday. It would be nice to have something positive to tell her about my life when she comes over. I think about how cute I'd be in those skates, pull my phone out, and text Prince to give my thanks.

DANI: You know you can get into serious trouble for breaking into my locker?

PRINCE: Was it worth it? Are you going to say yes?

DANI: Only if you tell me how you got them in there in the first place.

PRINCE: Well I ain't no snitch, but let's just say I got friends in high places. High places being hall monitors.

I laugh and put my phone away. One official date won't hurt.

Prince and I decide to meet at the skating rink, since he had a prior engagement at the radio station, but he promised he would drop me off at home after. My mom drives me to the rink, but as soon as I step into the building, I start to regret my decision. I haven't been to a social outing since my family reunion this summer, and let's face it, family reunions don't count as social events, they are cultural rituals. This, on the other hand…

I am hit with a blast of music and chatter as soon as I open the door. The mirrored reflections from the disco ball sparkle against the wall and ceilings, and waves of purples, greens and blues fill the air, playing up the red, orange and green streamers hung up from the ceilings and tables with scotch tape. There are HAPPY SWEETEST DAY balloons tied up along the skating-rink rails and tables, and a slight annoyance washes over me, thinking about how silly it is for me to be out tonight. I grab a locker to store my Adidas kicks and purse, and sit on the nearest bench, tying my skates and people-watching. The concession stand is filled with skaters grabbing a hot dog or nachos to snack on, and the rink is crowded with groups young and old, skating and gliding and moonwalking to Michael Jackson, currently blasting from the DJ booth, which is located at the side of the rink. I realize it's Prince's uncle spinning and for some reason that makes me gooey. He thought enough of me to show me off to family.

Too bad I'm about to make a fool of myself, I think, too afraid to move from the bench. I look down at my skates. Every move I make lights up the wheels, which looks baller on the pros in light-up skates drifting across the polished wood floor, but me? I'm going to fall so much my skates are going to be in the air longer than on the ground. I survey the gaudy carpet, filled with confetti and spaceships, and watch the items dance under my light-up wheels. A pair of Jordans enter my floor space and I look up to find Prince.

"You don't look awkward at all staring down at the floor," Prince says, smirking. Smart-ass.

"Whatever," I respond, embarrassed. I know I look out of place here because I am. This is a normal crowd and lately I've felt anything but normal. I don't know why I assumed being here with Prince would make me feel any different. If anything, I feel even sillier, knowing that Prince is in his element and everyone knows who he is.

I mean, this guy even has his Rollerblades hanging over his shoulder, tied together by their laces, like he's a pro. "You okay?" he asks, and it's clear he feels bad about the joke he just made.

"I'm fine," I snap a little, and realize I'm taking all my frustrations out on him. "I mean, I'm cool. Just a little nervous. I haven't skated in so long and I don't want to look stupid."

Prince sits down next to me and takes his shoes off. "I've been coming here for years. I used to help my uncle deejay, and when I wasn't in the booth, I was in the rink. I'll hold your hand the entire time."

"Yeah, but you're gonna outshine me on the floor," I rebut, with a pout.

"Are you competitive, Danielle?" he asks, lacing up his Rollerblades.

"Of course I am," I reply. "I'm a military brat."

He looks at me. "The way you look tonight, there is no way I can upstage you. I'm just going to look like a lucky-ass dude holding hands with the prettiest girl at the skating rink... who happens to be a klutz." I'm happy the lights are down so he can't see me blush. For the occasion I threw on some green, high-waisted utility pants with a cropped tie-dyed hoodie. I put my hair up in a curly, messy bun, rocked my biggest hoop earrings, and finished the look with my One Love lip gloss. I would have liked to wear my hair out today, but the last thing I need to be known for is as the girl constantly on her butt with her hair flying everywhere.

Tonight is Soul Skate Night, so Prince's uncle is serving all the old-school hits. The speakers blast Montell Jordan's "This Is How We Do It," and I give Prince the combination to my locker so that he can store his shoes. After he throws them in my locker, he glides around our bench, does a slick-ass spin like old-school bands used to move back in the day, and offers me his hand. I slap it.

"Is this gonna be a thing? Your slaps?"

"Why didn't you tell me you skate like the Temptations?" He laughs.

"What does that even mean?"

"It means you're way too smooth for me to skate next to you."

"You can't be that bad," he responds. Guess I gotta show him. I ignore his hand and hoist myself up, and as I attempt to skate, I stumble and trip over my front wheels. Prince swoops in and grips my forearm to keep me steady, and slowly leads me to the hardwood floor. He looks at me warily. "You ready?"

"What happened to confident Prince showing me how it's done?" I ask.

He chuckles. "You're right. You ready?!" He sounds like a hypeman, which makes me laugh, and I relax. A little.

But then I hold my breath and get ready for the rush. Once you're on the skating-rink floor, all bets are off. And there's two types of skaters: the ones holding on to the rails for dear life, and the ones in the middle of the floor, spinning and dipping like pros. The number of people in Detroit who could probably be professional ice skaters blows my mind. The lights flash as we manoeuvre around the rink, Prince still holding on tight while I watch my feet move, making sure I don't trip over myself.

The really good skaters move through the crowd, lapping us up as they soar to the music. They drift and glide, and one girl speeds right past us and turns around to wave at Prince. He acknowledges her with a nod and she spins back around, prancing in her neon-pink bodysuit and fanny pack. She slides down on the floor, one knee bent and the other leg out, cruising through the crowd like it's nothing. I almost trip watching her.

"Whoa," Prince utters. "Eyes back on your feet." I pinch him.

"Leave me alone," I mope.

"Actually, you're already getting better. I can tell it's coming back to you." I want to call BS, but maybe he's right. It might be hearing songs my mom played when I was a kid, or just being out and doing something fun for once. But it's feeling a little bit easier with each lap, and leaning on Prince helps. Plus, he smells good. Whatever he's wearing smells fresh, but with a light scent of citrus to it. Goodness, I can't believe I'm analyzing this man's cologne like this again. Anything to—

"Watch out!" someone yells. A child has gotten loose from his mother's grasp and is flailing out to the middle of the rink, right into my pathway. Prince tries to move me, but instead I do the only thing I know how: I try to make a hard stop and plop right on my ass, almost bringing him with me. After he composes himself, he leans over and grabs me by…my waist. My skin prickles at his touch, how easily he's able to stand me back upright.

He's holding back a smile. "You okay?"

"I see you wanna laugh, so go ahead," I respond, rubbing my backside.

"No, I don't," he replies, while *actually* laughing. I roll my eyes at him; my butt is throbbing by this point.

The mom tries to skate over to her little one as fast as she can, but it's clear the mom skates only slightly better than I do. "I am sooo sorry," she says, while grabbing him. "I told you *not* to let go of the rail! I can't take you nowhere!" The little boy just laughs in his mom's face. He doesn't look older than five, and absolutely seems like a handful. "Are you okay?" she asks me. "That was a pretty hard fall." *Thanks, lady.*

"I'm fine," I respond. "I couldn't risk hitting this cutie." The little boy hides behind his mom's leg. She laughs.

"Oh my god, he *never* gets this shy!" she taunts him. "Someone has a crush."

"Hey!" Prince exclaims. "I'm right here. Don't be tryna take my girl, homie." The boy laughs again, and Prince daps him up. He looks at me. "Let's take a little break. I'm sure your glutes could use it." The mom laughs as she skates away, and I limp-skate while Prince leads me over to the DJ booth.

"Wait, what are you doing?" I ask him.

"I want to introduce you to my uncle," he says.

"No! Not after that fall! The whole building saw me!" I try to push him to another area of the rink but fail miserably; balance and strength aren't my friends right now.

Prince touches my hand. "It's okay, there's so much going on, people barely saw." He smiles. Dammit. My first inclination is to follow him wherever he leads me. My next one is to run.

"Sounds so soulful, don't you agree?!" his uncle shouts to the crowd, while mixing the next sound. The crowd cheers and DJ Romes slides his headphones off to say hello, his Coogi sweater just as bright as the lights flickering across his face. We skate up to the booth and Prince introduces me.

"Nice to meet you," his uncle yells, extending his hand out to shake mine. "That was quite a fall, young lady." I grimace at Prince while he's cracking up.

"How was I supposed to know he saw?" Prince exclaims.

"I had to take one for the team. It was either me or the kid," I respond. His uncle laughs as he and Prince slap palms.

"I see you, nephew." They both nod in approval, and I clear my throat.

"I'm sorry," his uncle says. "You're right. I should give you the compliment directly. You're a fine young lady."

"Thank you," I say, smiling. "My mom is going to be so jealous when she finds out we met."

"Is she single?" he asks. Oh goodness.

"Unc!?" Prince shoots back, his hands up like, *What are you doing?* His uncle shrugs and I shake my head.

"No, sir," I respond. "Happily married for almost twenty years."

He nods in approval. "Your dad must be one lucky man then."

"Well, I'm going to get her something to eat," Prince intercedes. "Maybe that will help distract her from the pain she's feeling." I giggle.

"If you both get a snack at the concession stand, tell Trina to put it on my tab."

"Appreciate ya, Unc." I lean on Prince as he leads the way to the food concession.

In the background, we hear his uncle hyping up the crowd. "Aight, let's really get this party going with Chic's… 'Le Freak.'" A few people, who honestly look like they could be my grandparents' age, rush out of the concession area to the rink.

"I swear that song is a mating call for old folks," Prince

says, shaking his head, and we chuckle. As we arrive, pink-bodysuit girl approaches us, with a big smile on her face.

"You okay? That fall looked like it hurt."

If one more person mentions it...

"Luckily, I got enough padding in the back to break my fall," I respond, with a tight-lipped smile. "Danielle, by the way."

She clears her throat. "Trinity," she replies. Is that a smirk on her face? "Hey, Prince, haven't seen you here in a minute. Me and the girls were just asking your uncle where you been." The *girls*?

Prince looks mildly uncomfortable. "It's the last year of high school. Gotta make sure my grades are on point and I'm making time for what's important." He glances at me, and I look away.

"Well," Trinity interjects, "you've never brought a girl to the rink before. Didn't really seem like your thing."

I eye her. "What's his thing exactly?"

"Oh, I didn't mean anything by it. I thought you were his ex or something..."

"No shade," I say, turning my gaze Prince's way. "I just want to know what kind of guy I'm dealing with." Prince's eyes dart between me and Trinity, with a look of uneasiness.

She fiddles with her crochet braids. "I mean, I'm just surprised he's booed up is all. There have been a lot of girls who tried. And he was dating this girl from Southfield, so I was just surprised to see him here with you."

Prince tenses up. "That was over a while ago, Trinity."

"Well, look at you snatching him up before the news got around!" Trinity replies.

This girl is getting on my nerves. She's making assumptions about Prince and giving me Destiny energy right now. Just hatin' to be hatin'. "I didn't have to snatch anything," I respond with a shrug. "He just wouldn't leave me alone."

Prince is amused and lets out a hearty laugh. "You didn't have to call me out like that!" We look at each other, and his muscles relax again. I grin at him and then direct my attention back to Trinity.

"Well, I think we want to continue enjoying our date, if you don't mind. But it was nice meeting you."

"Oh," she huffs. "Well, good to see you, Prince." I roll my eyes as she skates off.

Prince skates out in front of me. "Danielle, I am so sorry. Whatever you think it is, it's not that. I used to come here and—"

"Pull all the girls?"

He gives me an uncomfortable laugh. "No, no. I just would come here and skate. And the girls would see me and see I was with my uncle and I was starting the radio thing and…"

I put a finger up to my lips to shush him. "We're in high school, Prince. I get it. It's cool. But if you're trying to get me to fall in love with you, this isn't the way to do it," I say half-jokingly, playing with my earring. "One thing I don't do is share. You got it?"

"I got it, Danielle." He smiles as we roll up to the counter. "Popcorn and pop on me!"

"I think it's on your uncle," I respond, laughing.

Prince tells the girl behind the counter our order, and as she's grabbing popcorn from the popcorn maker, he turns to me. "Just so you know, I don't like sharing either."

As me and Prince are talking, I notice the music shifts a bit, and DJ Romes puts on something smooth. Something more... romantic. Did he do that for us? Prince looks around.

"I know what this means."

"What?" I ask.

"The night's about to end. My uncle has a few songs that he plays toward the end of his set before roll call happens." It's been so long since I heard that term. Roll call is the part of the night where things get live, when the best skaters in the city all pile on the floor to one-up each other. And for me, it's the best time, because I will no longer have to die of embarrassment from my lack of skating skills.

But still, I have to stop myself from physically sulking. Roll call means we are close to curfew, which means closer to the end of the night, and I haven't had this much fun in such a long time. I didn't realize how long we were skating, and how long we sat in the concession area chatting. It seemed like I just got here and now we'll have to call it a night soon.

Prince throws our trash out, and then glides back over to me. He holds out his hand for me to latch onto and lifts me up.

"We can't let the night end without skating to a few slow songs. I bet this will be a breeze for you."

I smirk. "We'll see about that." He's still holding my hand and his eyes are locked on to mine, and I just can't take it. So, for the first time, I lead the way.

It snaps it right out of him. "Okay, Wayne Gretzky!!"

"Who is that?" I ask.

"He's like the G.O.A.T. of hockey, but it doesn't matter, since the joke went over your head."

I smirk. "Black people don't watch hockey!"

"I used to say that until I went to a game. Maybe I'll take you one day." We get back on the floor, and Prince spins around to skate in front of me, facing toward me.

"What are you doing? If you skate like that, you won't be able to see."

"Then I'll have you to guide me," he responds. I have to force myself to concentrate, because looking at him is an absolute distraction. Those long eyelashes that make him look *almost* innocent, his baby-smooth skin, and the little peach fuzz that's growing around his pink, round lips.

As the melody of Aaliyah's "Miss You" fills the air, I feel like Prince and I are practically floating on the rink floor. Our bodies are in rhythm as we bob and weave through everyone, and you can feel the energy in the room. Groups skate in unison and couples on the floor are snuggled up together. One couple is ballroom dancing on skates – the guy gracefully spinning the girl behind him and then back in front as he pulls her close to him again, casually taking his towel out of his back pocket to wipe his girl's face. It's the most hilarious yet sweetest thing I've ever seen. It's an energy of Black people of all ages filled with…love. It's hard to describe, but it's a beautiful feeling. I had so many reservations about going on a date with Prince on Sweetest Day, a holiday that's so overrated and commodified. But now that I'm here, I don't want the night to end. Prince's uncle tips his hat to me as we ride past the DJ booth, and I give him a wink.

"What did my uncle just do?" Prince says.

"Oh, nothing," I respond. "But my mom is going to be quite jealous when I tell her I made the voice of Detroit blush." He laughs.

The music fades out, and DJ Romes fades in. "Aight, ladies, fellas, playas and hustlers! I see you guys on the dance floor showing out. But now it's time for everyone to get ya ass off. I want my flyest groups to get ready…'cause it's ROLL CALLLLL!!!"

Just like he asked, everyone heads out, except for the groups who've been waiting all night for this. You see certain people begin to hype themselves up, trying to wake up from the R & B song DJ Romes just played not too long ago. Prince escorts me off the floor and takes me to the best seat in the house, the DJ booth.

"I've never been in one of these before," I sort of shriek as we step in.

"That's the benefit of having the voice of the D as an uncle," he says, smiling. The booth isn't that big, so he places me right next to his uncle, who is in the zone, and attempts to position me in front of him. But just as soon as we get comfortable, his uncle interjects.

"We got a special person in the house. Everyone welcome DJ LoveJones!!!" The crowd cheers and I am astonished. These people really love Prince. I turn back to look at him as his uncle hands him his headphones, and Prince looks almost...mortified?

"Unc, what are you doing?" Prince yells into his uncle's ear so that Jerome can hear him.

"Go ahead and show this little lady what you can do." His uncle smiles at me, and I can tell I like this guy. He's so proud of Prince – you can see it in how he passes the headphones to him, like he's passing the crown. Prince places them on top of his head like the prince he is. He knows he's got to prove himself to me, and he knows he can't let the people down.

I watch in awe as he quickly goes to work. "Aight, how is everyone doing tonight!" The crowd screams. "Hell nah! You all can do better than that!" And somehow the room fills with more noise, more stomping and more cheering. To see someone who has that much command of himself, to be able to read a room, and to get a whole community of people pumped, I'm impressed. The energy in the rink is electrifying.

"You know the drill," he says, while multitasking something serious. He quickly scans through his uncle's vinyl collection until he finds the perfect song, all while still giving instructions. "First group step up, everyone else on the wall. I wanna see ya go off – I need to see ya hair sweated out, T-shirts untucked, faces all grimy – show me you the best crew on the floor. Let's see what you got." He licks his fingers before placing them on the record, scratching it a bit before

Drake's voice blasts through the speakers. There are so many groups post up on the wall waiting for their turn, all rocking completely different gear. There's track pants and durags, Detroit Lions jerseys and crop tops. Some groups are skating in their custom-designed shirts to show what crew they're a part of. And this is the time when you see all the personalities, when the skating-rink floor comes alive. One guy does the running man on his skates. Another attempts to Jit and fails miserably. The crowd laughs, some boo, and Prince attempts to cover up his amusement with, "Aight, y'all, he tried. Show the man some love anyway." The crowd is obedient and claps it up for him, with some even patting his back while he walks off, defeated. Poor guy. A guy with a 'fro and a vintage green-and-red Afro pick starts popping and locking and has the whole crowd on their feet, cheering. There are crews skating sideways across the rink, and one guy is skating only on the balls of his feet. And under the dance lights, Prince is incandescent, keeping up with the mood of the skaters, eyeing their moves and switching up the music based on their taste, going from R & B to funk to trap in no time flat.

As for me? I'm having the time of my life.

I'm so lost in the moment that I hardly notice when Prince hands the headphones back to his uncle and taps my arm. He leans in closer and whispers in my ear, which causes me to tense up. "We should head out. Your curfew is coming up and I have one more surprise for you." Who *is* this boy? I was so caught up in the moment, I totally forgot to check my phone. Yet somehow he remembered?

"How did you even think to check your phone at a time like this?" I ask back.

"I didn't. I set an alarm before our date. Your parents are just starting to like me. The last thing I need to do is mess this up." His uncle squeezes my arm while taking over, and he and Prince pound their fists as we exit the DJ booth.

I rub my ankles down while Prince is driving. He looks at me and snickers.

"It will get easier the more you do it, I promise," he says.

"I hope so. I don't remember my ankles being sore when I skated before." I watch the street signs, trying to determine where he's taking me next, but we just keep driving down 8 Mile, the route to get to my house.

"So, do you feel loose? Like maybe you can finally write that amazing essay?" I look at him, surprised he still remembered my writing funk. *I* barely remember it after the time we just had.

"I mean, if not thinking about it means loosening up, then yes," I say.

"Sometimes not thinking about something helps you get out of your own head."

He's probably right. I haven't felt this light in a minute. "I can see that. I think the pressure of wanting to go to NYC is getting to me. It's so competitive, ya know?"

He nods in agreement. "Yeah, I can see that. Before your application, though, what was your writing style? Like you know how some rappers go into the booth and freestyle, and others write their flows in their notebooks first. What do you do?"

"I like writing in a journal too. But for me, it's more writing letters to writers I love. Writers who inspire me. I just keep the letters to myself."

I look over at him while he's driving. The brake lights from the cars surrounding us cast a slight red hue to the silhouette of his face. His perfect face. We brake at a stoplight and I think he senses my gaze, because he turns to me.

"I think it's pretty dope that you write to people you admire. Maybe one day you'll mail one of those letters off. Are they sort of your confessions?"

I nod, and suddenly a car honks at us. The light is green and he's back to looking at the road. "It makes sense," he continues. "It's the same with what I do. People overshare and I talk them through it. I think it's something about pouring your soul out to someone who will never see you. It's not like family and friends, where you're afraid they'll judge you." This hits closer to home than he could ever realize. Thinking about the friends I shut out and my parents, who have no idea what to do with me, I sympathize far too well.

"Why do you think people are so willing to open up to a radio host like that? Especially one that can't legally drink? No offence."

"None taken," he says. "It's kind of like a therapist. When you admit you need therapy, the very act of starting it is a big step. So you go in knowing that the therapist's job is to listen.

Not to judge you. They don't know you like that, and their job is to maintain a level of space. They're not gonna try to be your friend afterward. And you know if they put your business out there, they can lose their licence. I think the stigma of therapy is still real for Black people, so they feel more comfortable talking to someone like me. Plus, music itself is healing. You put those two things together, and you can cause a lot of people to open themselves up. And when it comes to being under eighteen, well, one thing I realized early on is that adults are just big kids themselves. It doesn't matter how old you are, good advice is just good advice. You give enough of it and you gain people's trust."

Wow. This boy really is into this. "So you always knew you wanted to be a relationship expert?"

"I always knew I wanted to be a DJ, just being around Uncle Jerome. And then the older I got, the more I knew I wanted to help people. I saw radio shows would bring in experts to give advice, but why couldn't the host be both? Why couldn't a deejay be the expert too...on things outside of just music?"

He's right. Why not? "Have you thought about double-majoring in psychology?" I ask him.

"Hmmm," he responds, a bit astounded. I think he never considered this as an option, and to me it makes so much sense. He is so invested in...people. He believes in them, in their ability to change. I wish I was as optimistic as he is. I also never realized that writing in my journal is my own little form of therapy. "That's not a bad idea." His face scrunches up like he's deep in thought for a second.

"I'm sure there are a ton of books on love psychology or love therapy you could probably read up on. Even books on music therapy. There's so much you could do…wait. I thought you were taking me somewhere?" I ask, a bit disappointed. Prince turns on Woodward Avenue, which is absolutely home.

"I am," he says, cheesing hard. And before I can process, he makes a Michigan left and begins to parallel park in front of one of my favourite spots, Dutch Girl Donuts. I squeal, and then quickly cover my mouth. He laughs. "I could tell you didn't love the idea of going on a date with me for Sweetest Day, but I couldn't let the night go by without getting you some type of sweet. It's tradition."

I try to hold back a smile. "Who told you I love Dutch Girl?"

"Your mom. I actually ran into her at Meijers this week and swore her to secrecy. I hope you don't mind."

"I am impressed you managed to convince her to hold a secret," I respond, laughing. "This is actually really sweet, Prince." I giggle, pun intended. He shakes his head, smirking. "Thank you."

He nods, gets out the car, and opens the door for me to do the same. We walk up to Dutch Girl and are greeted with a long line. Apparently, everyone else had the right idea, so we stand outside in the cold for a few minutes too long. But it's worth it. Once we go inside, the building has a warm feel and smell. The aroma of fresh donuts being made.

The shop itself is pretty small, with most of it used for the actual donut-making itself. As soon as you walk in, you're practically at the counter, but you can watch the batter being made and the staff cutting donuts by hand directly in front of the customers behind a clear acrylic wall. When it's our turn, I walk right up, ready to place my order. Prince is still browsing the donut display underneath, which is filled with every type of donut you can imagine – red velvet, custard-filled, powdered, maple cake, cinnamon, plus a few cookies sprinkled throughout and, of course, their signature glazed raisin donuts.

"Hey, baby, how are you doing tonight?" the woman behind the counter greets me.

"I'm fine, Ms Waters," I say.

Prince looks up with a smile. "You clearly do this often – you want to order for me?"

I get some glazed raisin, red velvet, and glazed donuts, and I get Prince a few donut holes and glazed blueberries for him and his brother. Prince hands the money over to Ms Waters, and I proudly grab the hot box of fresh donuts and a small white bag.

Since there are no seats in Dutch Girl, we head back to the car, shivering. Before Prince can even pull off, I'm practically closing my eyes as I bite into the doughy goodness, my sweet tooth completely satisfied. I look over, realizing we haven't moved, and catch Prince staring at me, fascinated.

"What?" I say, my mouth full of dough, suddenly embarrassed.

"Nothing. I'm just…happy to see you look so content. I hope one day you look at me the way you looked at that donut." I almost choke from laughing. For a minute I did almost forget he was here.

"Aren't you gonna try yours?" I ask.

"Not till I get home. Me and dairy don't mix well, and I forgot my Lactaid pills," Prince says.

I nod. "Well, if you took me anywhere else for this fabricated holiday, I would have been offended. But this was worth it."

"Do you know the real meaning behind Sweetest Day?" I shake my head, taking another bite. "Apparently it was started by this White man in Cleveland, who worked at a candy company and wanted to spread love. So he passed out candy and gifts to orphans and people confined in their houses, to show there was someone in the world who cared about them."

How does he do this? How does he find a way to make me melt a little more each time he opens his mouth? Everything about him feels so pure.

"Can I ask you a question?" I say, swallowing the last bit of my donut. "Do you talk to your friends about your random love facts?"

"I try, but they don't usually listen," he responds. "But they *do* listen to my segment every day. My boy Ant even confessed they have a group chat so someone will record the segment if someone else can't watch it. So even if I ain't giving them advice directly, they still receiving." He smirks. "Which, I don't know, makes me feel a little special." I catch myself smiling. "Oh!" He grabs a napkin from the bag. "You got something on your mouth." He steadies my chin and tenderly wipes away some frosting, looking intently at my lips. My breathing gets more faint, my insides quiver. He looks into my eyes, and I know he can tell that if he kissed me right in this moment, I wouldn't pull away. I'm wishing he does it. That he sees the desire in my eyes, that he goes for it. He doesn't disappoint and leans in closer and closer until...

...his phone's ringer goes off.

We both jump, and the donut in my hand falls on the floor. "I'm so sorry!" I exclaim.

"No, no, it's okay, I'm sorry. I gotta take this," he says, looking frazzled.

"Go ahead," I tell him, trying not to let him see my disappointment.

"Mook, Mook. Calm down. Wassup, man?" He's quiet for a moment, and I realize things are way more serious than I thought. "Put Ma on the phone." His face changes from jumbled to defeated as he listens to his mom. "No, no. We were just wrapping up. We're right around the corner from her house, and she has a curfew. So it's okay." I feel so bad for him as I watch him hang up and stare at his phone for a moment. He doesn't look at me when he says, "Danielle, I'm sorry."

I rush to say anything to make him feel better. "No! It's okay!"

"My mom went to put leftovers in the fridge, and she had a fall, and Mook called me in a panic. I usually keep my phone on silent mode when I'm on a date, but I always allow calls from my mom, just in case…" He doesn't look at me.

"Hey," I reply. He still doesn't look up, so I touch his shoulder, and that causes him to slowly turn to me. "I get it. Family comes first, so really, it's fine. Okay?" He nods, dispirited. "Besides, I don't want you to get a big head or anything, but this is the most fun I've had all year." He smiles, and I breathe a sigh of relief.

"Well, you know, this is what I do best." I try to shove him, but he quickly dodges my hand and leans against the driver's door, laughing.

My house is only five minutes away, so we drive in silence until he pulls into my driveway. Not knowing what else to do, I take two extra donuts out my box and add them to his bag of donuts.

"Give these to the people you care about. Happy Sweetest Day." I grin. "Thank you for making this night special, Prince."

He nods. "You got it." He goes to open his door, but I stop him.

"I'm a big girl. I appreciate you wanting to walk me to the door, but go home. Take care of your family. I promise I'll be all right." He nods again, and I open and shut the door, a box of my favourite donuts in tow. I reach the steps and unlock the door, but turn to find his car still idling and Prince waiting to make sure I get in safely. A smile escapes onto my lips. *He's a stubborn one*, I think, waving with my free hand as I close the door.

Chapter Eight
fine Tune
PRINCE

"You're back!" Mook yells, jumping off the couch and grabbing my hand like I can't see Ma right in front of me. When I walked in, Mook was seated on the couch, talking to her and holding her hand. I know he's anxious beyond repair at this point, and I'm so proud of him for handling things well. I crouch down next to my mom, who's disoriented.

"What happened?" I ask her softly.

"One minute I was holding all the Tupperware, putting the food away. Then I just felt…weak. I couldn't hold anything anymore. And then I felt dizzy…" Her voice is so faint.

I turn to my brother. "Did she fall on the floor?"

"No. She stumbled, though, and I helped her sit at the kitchen table," he replies, his little chest sticking out all noble like. I pound him up for that.

"I'm so proud of you. You did a good job, lil man."

He smiles. "Thank you. I was so scared." He pauses. "I know

you went on a date with that pretty girl, but please don't leave me here alone. What if she falls and I can't help her next time?"

I am distraught, so to clear my head I put everyone to bed and inspect the kitchen, which is…sort of clean? I mean, not really. Remnants of leftover mashed potatoes, green beans and oven-baked BBQ chicken are on the floor. Mook attempted to clean it but instead created a rainbow of colours on the kitchen tile like a painting. I let out a long sigh, exasperated. I go on *one* date in like three months, and the whole household collapses. Of course Mook is afraid. He's only seven. I remember how I felt the first time she fell. That's a lot to put on a kid.

But it's also a lot to put on me. I'm finally getting this girl to feel me, and I can't even enjoy that. I do so much for my family, and I'm already sacrificing a lot. This is why I told my mom to schedule a doctor's appointment. It's clear her health isn't in a good place right now, and her pride isn't doing anyone any favours. Something needs to change.

I call my uncle that night, and the next morning my mom is awoken by me and Jerome hovering around her bedroom, waiting for the right moment to chat with her.

"What is this?" she asks.

"It's what you think it is, Lori. It's an intervention," Uncle Jerome says.

My mom scrunches her nose. "Can I at least go to the bathroom and brush my teeth before you both go ganging up on me?" I nod, and my uncle and I help her out the bed and lead her to the bathroom with her walker. When the door is closed, we stand on opposite sides of it, waiting and hoping we won't have to go in and save her. The only person who is probably more pained than me by my mom's new normal is Uncle Jerome. Jerome said that back in the day my mom used to accompany him to all the industry parties and album releases in between her shifts at Lee Beauty Supply. After seeing her spend her teenage life and much of her young adult life so carefree, the grief for him to be present at times like this goes even deeper than mines. I sneeze.

"Are you guys really waiting outside the bathroom door? I'm fine. I'll call you if I need anything."

"This chick," my uncle whispers as we go to the living room. He settles on the couch as I look out the blinds, watching the first flurries of the season trickle down from the sky. The snow is light, which means it probably won't stick.

"Damn, it's coming early this year," I huff, worrying this will be one of those winters where I question whether I want to move somewhere warm.

"Yeah, and it's cold den a mug outside too. I definitely should have worn my coat." My uncle takes inventory of the house. "How you guys doing over here? I know it's been a while."

"Well, I could use your help with a few things that need to be fixed. Our landlord won't answer Mom's calls…"

"I got ya. My schedule is cleared up till later, so we can work on getting stuff done all day, after we work on your mom." I sigh, shaking my head.

"I'm frustrated," I say finally, letting the words I've been holding on to come out. I plop down on our matching love seat, resting my head in my hands.

"I know you are. You got a lot on your shoulders, but once you get into school and start really working on your radio career, things will change for—"

"How?" I look up in disbelief. "How am I supposed to go anywhere? She's way too private and too proud to ask for help!"

My mom clears her throat and we both jump. I look in her eyes and can see the immediate hurt. Pacing herself, she walks over to the couch, using her walker today instead of her cane, and slowly sits down next to Uncle Jerome. I watch him hold her arm to steady her into her seat. Once she settles in, she finally speaks.

"I don't ask for help because it's none of anyone's business. I'm not a charity case," she says, her voice cracking a little, but still carrying power. "Last thing I need is people in my home, judging me and telling my business to everyone who wants to listen."

I go to open my mouth, but my uncle steps in. "I can't begin to understand what you're going through, Lori, and I won't even try. But I do know what this boy is going through," he says, pointing to me. "Have you thought about that? How much he's taken on? He can't even go on a date without having to rush back home." My uncle pauses. "Don't you want him to succeed? Don't you want him to have it better than we did?"

"Of course I do!" my mom croaks. "I want the very best for

you and Mook." Her voice lowers to sort of a murmur. "That's all I want."

I move over to her, sitting on the armrest and wrapping my arms around her. She hugs my ribcage like a little kid. "You trust me, Ma?"

"I do," she declares. "There's no one I trust more."

My uncle huffs and we all laugh. I continue. "Then let us find a solution that works for all of us. I'm not gonna abandon you. But I can't work and do school and attempt to have a social life and take care of everything here." I think about what she just said, what I cannot ignore. "You are *no one's* charity case. It's just that MS isn't really something we can plan around. It just happens. You were doing so good, Ma, but you're relapsing. That probably means more trips to Henry Ford for immunotherapy. We just need help taking the pressure off both of us. So you can live your life and I can do the same."

I think about all the reasons my mom might be so prideful, so distrusting of others. When my dad dipped, that must have hurt for many reasons. Loving someone and having them reject you – maybe secretly wondering if your disability is the reason – would be enough to drive anyone to feel the way my mom feels. Maybe Danielle is right about this psychology idea. This whole relationship-expert thing definitely started the moment my parents' relationship fizzled. Me trying to figure out what went wrong with my dad, when my mom was doing all she could to hold their relationship together. It sorta feels like everything can be traced back to love in some way. And in my mom's case, the love was one-sided.

"Yeah, Lori," my uncle chimes in. "Let us tap into the community."

She looks up and nods in agreement, and I kiss the top of her head.

"Something's gotta give," I tell Yasin as we're in my room, attempting to study for our calc class (which I'm grossly behind in), the Pistons game playing in the background. If we compared grades a year ago, my grades had Yasin beat, but senioritis is really kickin' in for me. Everyone is focusing on keeping their grades up for college, and I'm just…trying to get by, honestly. College applications are probably due pretty soon, but I haven't applied anywhere because it doesn't make sense to. Mr Smith has been on my ass about it too and has even taken to commenting on my posts, telling me to come visit his office soon. Of course, I delete them every time. He's a passionate man who cares so much about the students at Mass Tech it's scary. But I don't have the heart to tell him I'm too afraid to apply. What happens if I get in? Then what? I break the news to my mom and tell her that her eldest son is leaving her to fend for herself? And me getting into my dream school only to have her beg me to stay. Being so close to my dream but not being able to go for it would break my heart. I haven't had the time or energy to put into anything really, outside of work, family, and now Danielle.

Yasin stopped by after me and my uncle chatted with my mom and scheduled a doctor's appointment for this week to run some tests and look at treatment options. Uncle Romes even offered to take her. Every little thing helps at this point. Yasin focuses in on me, the creases in his forehead showing legitimate concern. "You think she's open to what you and Romes are proposing?"

I shrug. "Who knows. I just hope...FOR REAL!?" I yell at a flagrant foul called. "That's BS."

Yasin laughs. "The Pistons not winning this game, Prince, no matter how much you try to will it."

I throw my pencil at him. "Get this blasphemy out my house," I utter, and change the subject. "How are things going with Jordan?"

He grins wide. "It's going great! Me and her have our second date on Friday."

"Second date! When was the first one? I see you, fam!" I say, dapping him up. "Look at you, learning from the love coach." He runs his fingers through his dark tresses, trying to keep it casual. "Thank you. I've been trying to tell you, but you've been preoccupied. Because unlike you, I can make time for both a girl and friends."

Damn. That stung.

"M was right, it *is* the quiet ones you gotta watch out for." We both laugh, but the notification on my phone causes my smile to wane.

"What's going on?" Yasin asks.

I shake my head, frustrated. "Morgan is what. Lately she's been liking and commenting on my posts, and she just DMed me."

Yasin chuckles, closing his textbook. "Let me channel my inner DJ LoveJones." He clears his throat and deepens his voice a little bit. He clasps his hands together in front of his chest, looking like a straight-up therapist. "And how does it make you feel, hearing from your ex?"

"Why is it every time y'all imitate me your voices go extra low?"

"That's the only way to do it." I heave a deep sigh. "Sooo?" he says.

"I figure she must have found out I took Danielle to Northland and was in her feelings about it."

Yasin looks a bit more serious. "But what if it was enough to make her realize her mistake? Would you take her back?"

I look at Yasin, a bit perplexed. "Do you *want* me to take her back? You never seemed to like her much."

"I don't," he responds, and I chuckle. "I just want you to analyze yourself like you analyze everyone else. If Morgan were to offer to take you back today, would you say yes?"

I give it some thought. I was pretty hurt when she dumped me, but I guess now, looking back, it was clear she'd been bored with me for a long time. At some point me and her just weren't connecting. We both wanted different things and had different obligations, and once college life became more clear to her, it seemed like everything I did started annoying her – my family responsibilities, my emcee gigs – but I could tell it was really me just being in high school. She wanted bigger and better. Which, I can't really be surprised that she was seen with Michigan's star football player.

"She's in college now and wants a guy who's big and flashy. I kinda feel like that's the whole reason she started dating me in the first place. But I'm still the same guy, so she's going to get bored with me just like she did before. I've moved on, maybe Tyrone's moved on too, and she don't like being left out in the cold, as my uncle would say."

"Okay, but what if she's changed?" Yasin enquires.

Damn, he's really coming for me today. I pause again before I respond, 'cause surprisingly, whatever lingering baggage I thought I would feel just…isn't there as much anymore. It's strange, but talking this out with Yaz is helping me put those pieces together. "Do I wanna risk it to find out? Nah. I like where I'm at right here." Yasin smiles, nodding his head. "You done with the interrogation?"

"For now." Yasin smirks. "I just wanted to make sure you were pursuing Danielle for the right reasons."

I nod in agreement. It's crazy how a relationship can be over long before you both call it quits. I started to feel it after prom and her graduation – it was like once she walked across that stage, she decided to step into her new life, and my presence just didn't fit anymore. The good times were good, but I had to be realistic and look at it for what it was: a time in my life that was fun while it lasted. The relationship for Morgan was transactional, but with Danielle it's different. Who knows, maybe she'll do the same, maybe she'll go to New York and forget all about me. But the difference is, I know that each time Dani opens up to me, it's 'cause she likes me *for me*. She's barely ever heard me on the airwaves, which is in some ways refreshing.

Maybe if I win Danielle Ford's heart, it really could be mines to hold. And even if it doesn't work out, if she goes her own way and I go mines, I'll be proud that I finally did something I had been wanting to do for ever, step to a girl who's had me for a long time. There's no way I'd ever regret that.

[LOVE RADIO TRANSCRIPT]

[CROSSFADE OF SONG HERE]

PRINCE JONES: What up, Detroit? I'm DJ LoveJones, the prince of love, back today for another segment of LOVE RADIO! I'll keep the hits spinning and give you my best love advice. Caller twelve, you on?

CALLER 12: Yes, hi. DJ LoveJones?

PRINCE JONES: What up, doe? What's your name, sweetheart?

CALLER 12: [sniffles] Misha.

PRINCE JONES: Misha, talk to me. What's on your mind?

CALLER 12: How do you let go of an ex? Like really let go?

PRINCE JONES: [pauses] I gotta be honest with you. The shit is hard. It just is. No matter if you've been with your partner for a few months or a few years, if you had a deep emotional connection with them, you can't turn on a light switch and make things better. It takes time.

The best way to get over someone is one, recognize the connection and its pull. So many people try to move on quickly or push it to the back of their mind without really *dealing with it.* You have to get it out. A...friend of mines told me part of dealing with her emotions is writing them down in a journal. Do that. Or even if you don't want to write about all the ways you're lovesick, get a pen and paper and write down the pros and cons of your ex. Seeing the reasons you loved them versus the reasons they were toxic or no good for you is a good first step to healing.

Next, it's time to practise that self-love. You might be in bed right now, wanting to do nothing but sulk, and that's okay for a few days, but eventually you gotta pick yourself up and keep moving. Start small – invest in something you enjoyed doing on your own, before your relationship. Or if you didn't, start. Choose up a hobby or something you've always wanted to do, something to pick your confidence back up. Hang out with other people in your life who genuinely make you happy, and don't spend your entire time with them talking about your ex. You're going to have to learn how to do things without your ex, but just like any habit, you can start one and break one. It just takes time.

And lastly, whatever happened between you two – whether it was something they did or something you did – you have to forgive it and let go. Whether it's forgiving them, or forgiving yourself, know that everyone is human and we all make mistakes, sometimes at the cost of losing someone. It all sucks now, but hanging on to hurt and pain will only negatively affect you and your life. And this thing we got is a gift, right? We need to appreciate it for what it is. Maybe in the meantime, imagine what your next relationship will look like. What were things about your ex you liked, and what were things you wish they did differently, things that you'd like to see in your new person?

We all deserve the partner we want, and sometimes doing an exercise like this helps you realize how much you've been settling.

I promise if you do these things you'll come around on the other side stronger and happier.

CALLER 12: You're right. I should write down the pros and cons, 'cause I put up with *so* much. I think once I see it, it will be easier to move on like you said. Thank you, LoveJones.

PRINCE JONES: You got it. Here's a song to help you cure that heart of yours.

[PRINCE PLAYS A SONG]

Chapter Nine

Mixtape of Love

Danielle

I wake up to a notification from my phone.

PRINCE: Morning, Danielle. Thanks for being so understanding about last night. I wish we could have hung out longer, but to make up for it, here's some music to keep you motivated while writing your essay.

I smile, looking at my phone in bed. Below is a link to an Apple playlist, entitled *Love Notes Mixtape: Volume 1*, which includes songs his uncle played at the rink. I respond back.

DANI: Love Notes, huh? That's a strong title. Also, what happened to Tidal?

PRINCE: Listen to the playlist first before you go judging the name.

I smile as I get a second ping.

PRINCE: I'll convert you eventually. But the biggest
priority rn is for you to vibe out.

I plug in my AirPods and do exactly that as I make my bed,
brush my teeth, and wash my face, thinking of all the moments
from last night and the songs attached to them. And for some
reason, it does clear my mind and my thoughts begin to come
together. I remove my earbuds and sit at my desk, feeling that
spark I feel when an idea is trying to force itself out, banging in
my head to be released. Somehow last night's events have
already made me feel so much more relaxed, and the words to
my essay begin to flow out like a melody.

An hour passes and by the time I go downstairs, I have so
much pep in my step, it's practically impossible to hide my
happiness. I'm humming along and bobbing my head to
Montell Jordan as I float into the kitchen, and my dad
immediately takes notice.

"What are you singing?" my dad says, laughing.

"Oh! Good morning," I announce, sitting at our kitchen
table, watching my dad pull freshly baked biscuits out of the
oven. I'm so used to chatting with him over the phone that
watching him in action is a real treat. He's mostly through
cooking breakfast and listening to NPR.

"Morning, baby. You're up later than usual."

I roll my eyes. "Don't worry, Daddy, I got home by curfew."

"Oh, I know. I checked," he responds, laughing. I'm not.

"I told your mom to wake me up if you were a second late, and she woke me up and told me you were thirty minutes early."

It would have been nice to have that time back, before we were interrupted. He brings over a plate, sets it in front of me, and kisses my forehead, squeezing me tight while still wearing floral oven mitts. I squeeze him back.

"This looks sooo good. It's been a minute since I had food like this in the morning."

"Don't start, Dani!" my mom says, walking into the kitchen, tightening her robe. My father and I laugh.

"She said it, not me," my dad chuckles, welcoming my mom with a kiss. I smile. Last night I almost had my first kiss with Prince and I was surprised at how comfortable I was becoming with him. He made me feel so at ease in his arms while we were skating, and I wasn't ready to pull away.

My mom heads to the coffee maker, sneaking glances at me while she grabs a mug and pours herself some.

I smirk. "Whaaat?" I finally respond.

"I didn't say anything," she says, smirking back.

My dad carries two more plates to the kitchen table and sits down. "You know what," he chimes in. "Your mom wants to know how your date went."

My mom walks over and parks herself next to me. "Well, he said it. Not me." These two. "But since he asked…"

I giggle. My mom probably watched me and Prince outside and would have asked me last night if she felt ballsy enough to do it. I have a strong inclination my dad told her to give me my space.

"It was…nice." I smile again.

"That's it?" my dad responds, a bit disappointed.

"Oh, she's being coy, James. But if you don't want to tell us, you don't have to."

"It's not much to tell," I say, chewing on a sausage. "We went to Northland and skated."

"Is he any good?" my dad asks.

"Yeah, he is, actually. But me, on the other hand…" They both laugh.

"I think the last time you skated was before you even had a car. When I would drive you, Esi and Rashida and pick you up. It sort of felt like old times dropping you off last night…" Mom says. The room goes silent. My parents never know how to broach that subject.

"I'm actually seeing Rashida today," I say nonchalantly, adding jelly to my biscuit.

My parents eye each other quickly, thinking I didn't catch it. "Well…that's great," my dad chimes.

"Yeah," I say, stuffing my face. My dad's biscuits are always so flaky and delicious. "We ran into each other in the bathroom at school and I told her about my date, so she just wanted to come over for a bit and catch up…if that's okay."

"That's totally fine!" my mom says, a little too eager. "I was going to run to Meijers to grab some food for tonight – I can make a little extra for her if you'd like and she can stay for dinner."

"Oh, no, we're just gonna kick it for a bit. I told her my applications and stuff have been keeping me busy, so she knows we can't hang for too long."

"Okay, well, your dad is coming with me, so you'll have the house all to yourself." My dad gives her a look like *I am?* and I want to laugh so bad. But that's one of the many reasons I love my mama. She'll try to get as much out of you as she can, but she knows when to back away. Truth be told, she's not buying anything I'm selling. She still knows whatever I'm dealing with is more than just college applications, but it's kinda nice to see her smile. To see her genuinely happy for me. A date *and* a friend over in one weekend? She's on cloud nine at this sudden change in me, so I appreciate her giving me the space I need to figure it out.

"Thank you, Mom," I respond. She nods and gives me her proud smile.

"Of course, sweetie. But you gotta clean before she comes over. You and I both know your dad can't keep a clean kitchen to save his life." I laugh.

"I'm sitting *right here*," my dad huffs, biting into the makeshift breakfast sandwich he created.

"I still can't believe you put jelly on your sandwich. Makes no sense," I say.

"You missing out, Dani baby, the best thing in the world," he responds, scarfing down another bite.

We enjoy breakfast and each other's company, me and Mom both basking in my dad's presence, which we've sorely missed. Once everyone is full, I rise from the table and start putting away ingredients and filling up the dishwasher. I watch my parents interact – how easily they're able to go from being playful one moment to having a serious conversation about the latest news cycle the next. Their body language, so in sync with each other, so natural. That's what love looks like. It's not always about the flowers and grand gestures, but this right here. Being completely yourself with another person in the moment, and them accepting no less of you. I smile to myself as I pull my phone and earbuds out my pocket, push play on *Love Notes*, and focus my attention on scrubbing these pots.

"Dani, this man bought you skates and took you out for Sweetest Day on date one? He sounds like he's into you for real," Rashida gushes. She's sitting on the couch with me, letting the TV watch us as we catch up. Her body is facing mine, with her arm resting on the top cushion of the couch.

"It seems that way," I respond nervously. "It's just, I don't know, Shida. I don't get him thinking he can get me to fall for him so fast."

"Why not?" she asks.

"Because that means it's basically some love-at-first-sight-type stuff. Which I don't think I buy into," I admit, taking another bite of my ice cream. "Also, you didn't have to drive practically to Novi to get me some ice cream."

"You know I didn't go for you. Guernsey Farms is halal friendly. You just gave me a reason to. This is a celebration, girl!" She chuckles, taking a bite herself. "Also, don't change the subject! You're looking at someone who definitely has."

"Has what…?" She nods, and I stop eating. "Are you in love with this guy?"

"Basically," she says, blushing.

"Okay, okay. I remember when you first met him, but tell me more about him," I probe.

"Malik's our age. He started Mass Tech second semester of junior year, so that's probably why you don't really know him. His dad moved the family from DC, but he's first gen…his parents are from Jamaica." I chuckle to myself. "What?" Rashida enquires.

"Nothing. I'm just realizing how many people I don't know. The guy I'm dating went to our middle school…" Did I just say *dating*?

Rashida smiles. "I know you don't want to tell me who he is, but I will find out."

"Is that a threat?" I smile back, licking my spoon.

"It's a promise." She giggles, and we look at each other. "I've missed you," she says.

"I've missed you, too," I respond.

I mean it.

There's an awkward silence and I know what's coming. "So…have you talked to Destiny since I last saw you?" Rashida enquires.

I shake my head. "I've been trying to avoid her, to be honest. Because I'm afraid if I see her, I'll likely get expelled."

"Wow, Dani. You get so angry every time I mention her name."

"You and Esi were right about not wanting to hang out

with her," I reply. "I wanted to believe that the girl I met in dance class was still in there, but she can't be trusted."

She places her hand on my leg, which is shaking. "Tell me *something*. I just want to know what's going on."

I pause for a beat. There's so much I want to tell Rashida. Stuff that I've wanted to tell her and Esi for months. But anytime I'd complain about Destiny, they'd make comments about the friendship not being worth it, even when I tried to defend her. It got so bad that I stopped talking to them about Destiny altogether. I didn't want to be judged then and I don't want to be judged now. Or worse, I don't want to see that sweet face of hers turn sour if she feels like I was the one that put myself in that situation in the first place. The writings were on the wall, but I refused to take notice. "Let's just say we went to a party and she put me in a...compromising situation."

"Did something happen?"

"I mean...yes and no." A tear slides down my cheek. Dammit. I quickly wipe it away, trying to laugh my emotions off. "It's silly, really. Nothing actually...happened. But it felt like—" Words are escaping me, and Rashida knows just what to do. She wraps her arms around me in a big bear hug.

"When my cousin was fourteen, a distant relative tried something unimaginable. She was able to fight him off, but no one believed her. They felt like she must have done something to provoke him. Can you believe that?" she says with disgust in her voice. "They didn't go after the sick uncle who tried to force himself on an underage girl, they went after my sweet cousin."

"But Rashida...I was drinking."

"Danielle, I don't give a damn if you were the drunkest girl at the party. That doesn't give anybody a right to force themselves on you. That's attempted rape. Period. *You* were the victim here." Rashida rarely ever uses a curse word.

I pull away and look at her. "It's so cute when you curse."

"Only reserved for you," she answers, "but don't tell my mom." Attempted rape. It's the first time I've heard from someone else what it actually was. The first phrase that makes me feel validated in my feelings, the first time I've poured my thoughts out outside of my journal. I wipe more tears from my eyes.

"You didn't finish your story about Malik," I say, changing the subject.

Rashida recognizes that I need to process everything, so she falls right in line. "Well," she says, slumping her shoulders a bit. "We've been on and off ever since he moved here. He's sweet. Like really. I know it's hard to tell with all the drama."

"You mean the no-sex thing?"

She sighs. "Yeah, I think it's too much for him. But he's trying."

"Do you...want to?" I ask.

"I know he thinks it's dumb, but this is something I want to hold for me. He's special, but there's still a part of me that doesn't know how serious he really is. Tomorrow I might tell you something different, but right now I don't think I'm ready to risk it if he's not serious. Plus, the anxiety of facing such a big decision like this is...a lot."

I smile. Same ole Rashida. Able to love hard, but I'm glad to see she's being rational. "That makes so much sense."

"Yeah," she sighs. "But his boys at Mass seem to be good for him. Like his one friend Prince…" I gasp. "What?" Rashida asks. I don't say anything immediately, but Rashida quickly figures it out. "Wait, wait, WHAT?" she responds, shaking her head in disbelief, her plastic spoon dangling in the air. "You're dating Prince JONES?"

I blush. "Maybe. Why, is that bad?" I get defensive. "What did you hear?"

Rashida laughs. "Nothing! I know he got out of a serious relationship not too long ago. But outside of that, absolutely nothing, D. It's just…funny."

"Why?" I ask. This is the second time I've heard about this ex, so I want to make sure to pry more about his past relationship later.

"Because, for you to be so low-key this year, you sure did pick one of the most visible guys at school. He's practically a local celebrity, Danielle!"

I suddenly become uncomfortable. What am I doing? I mean, I've cut ties with all my friends, and I expect things to work with a guy who seems to know everyone in the D? It doesn't even make sense. We don't even make sense.

"You're right. Maybe it's not a good idea…"

"Oh no, no, no. You will not use me as an excuse to get rid of him."

I put my hands up. "I…I wasn't even…"

"Yes, you were! Danielle Ford, you need to have a little fun.

He took you skating, which I can't remember the last time I've seen you do that. And somehow I feel like he's the reason I'm here now."

"No, *you're* the reason you're here now," I reply.

"Well, really it's the ice cream." We chuckle. "But I do think opening yourself up to him is allowing you to just… open up in general. Esi's gonna be proud."

Esi. She is not one to be ignored. And while Rashida has been persistent in rekindling our friendship, I am almost certain Esi isn't pressed to do the same.

"Don't worry, she knows I'm here," Rashida says, cutting into my thoughts.

"Did she tell you not to come?" I mumble.

"She didn't say much, except that I should let her know how you're doing. Even if she's cold, she still cares." I think more about Esi and Rashida and all the things we used to do together. Maybe I should enjoy my senior year and finally do things normal teens do, like date and hang out with my girls.

"Maybe…I can see Esi sometime? I don't want to force it if she's not ready. But I'd like to try," I say.

Rashida beams. "Yes! Let me warm her up to the idea, but I think she'd be down. And…if things go well with you and Prince, a double date in our future?"

"You're pushing it," I tell Rashida, and she laughs.

From the moment I step into those school doors on Monday, it seems like all eyes are on me. I so badly want to fight the feeling, to think I'm being paranoid, but after second period, it becomes all the more clear that me and Prince *are* the talk of the school. I catch stares from girls in between classes, and whispers and sharp glances while sitting at my desk. During lunch I do my usual, grab a sandwich from the cafeteria and scarf it down before heading to the computer lab. And while I made progress this past weekend, when I go to open my Google Docs to write my essay, all I can do for the first thirty minutes is stare at the screen, trying to distract myself from feeling like I'm part of the latest hallway tea. Soon enough, when words finally start to flow, in walks the last person I want to see. And she has the nerve to sit right next to me. I attempt to avoid her for as long as I can, but my fingers go numb and I'm unable to focus on my essay.

"Hey, Dani," she coos. I don't even look at her, nor do I acknowledge her greeting. She clears her throat. "So I was uh…just wanted to check in and see how you're doing. We haven't talked in a while."

"For good reason," I say.

She lowers her voice. "I was just thinking maybe we could hang out like old times…"

I whip my head her way. "Why do you keep doing this?" I ask.

"Doing what?" she asks.

"It's obvious you want something from me, Destiny. You always have. Whether it's a ride or a hypeman or to borrow whatever, it's always been about you. We were friends for so long, but I was too young and naive to see that."

"That's not true," she snaps back, leaning in closer. "Your friendship was always important to me."

I switch up my approach and soften a bit. "How have you been?' I ask.

"I've been good, trying to get the last bit of fun in before we graduate. I just miss having all this fun with my girl," she utters, and I smile.

So," I say, with fake enthusiasm. "What did you have in mind this weekend?"

She grins. "Well, there's this party on Saturday, and seeing as your new boyfriend is deejaying there..."

I laugh, shaking my head. "You don't even see what you're doing, do you?"

"What are you talking about?"

"This!" I scowl. "You only want to patch things up 'cause of who I'm dating. Get out of my face, Destiny."

Destiny stands up over me. "Excuse me?!" I've completely pissed her off, and we're starting to get an audience.

"What's going on here?" the lab assistant questions us from across the room.

I stand up, meeting her eye to eye. "I'm trying to work and this girl won't leave me alone," I respond. Everyone in the computer lab is glued to me and Destiny, ready to witness a fight. And in walks...Prince. *Crapppp.*

"Don't try me, Dani. You don't want this."

The assistant quickly rushes over to us, with Prince trailing closely behind. "If you both can't calm down, I'm going to have to ask you to leave."

I just want Destiny to take a hint. Our friendship isn't the same. She isn't the same. And now I'm realizing it's okay to let toxicity go, even if it used to be good at one point. What matters is how does it make you feel *now*, and right now nothing about Destiny makes me believe she cares about me or this friendship. Only her.

"Destiny, I have nothing else to say. And I don't want to fight you. But I *do* want you to leave." Some people mumble to each other, eyes all big as I stand tall. Destiny is fuming. Prince gently pulls on my arm.

"I see you haven't logged in," the lab assistant chimes to Destiny, "so unless you have work to do, I need to ask you to leave."

"Fine!" Destiny hisses. "You just mad Drew wanted me and not you!" She snatches her bag and storms off, with everyone in the computer lab oohing and aahing. Prince looks confused, and I'm shaking with anger. The only reason she let that come out of her mouth was because Prince walked in.

Prince grabs my backpack. "Come on," he whispers. "Let's get you some air."

"How are we supposed to do that?" I mumble.

"You trust me?" he asks. I give him a look of concern but slowly nod my head and follow him down the hall. Dave, our school salesman, gives me and Prince a look as we walk the semi-empty hallways, but that doesn't stop him from trying to sell us some candy and pop out his fully stocked locker. We politely decline as Prince takes me to the back of the school and daps up the hall monitor, who nods at me and cautiously walks the other way. So, this must be the guy who put those skates in my locker. Prince leads me directly to an emergency exit door where the alarm *should* go off, but doesn't, and we walk down some stairs to the back of the school. He drapes his leather jacket over my shoulders before he opens the door to the outside, the wind smacking us in the face as soon as the door is ajar.

"How did you manage to get that type of clout?" I ask.

"Let's just say I gave Bryce some relationship advice and he's a fan. It's impossible sometimes to get this school to let me run to the station or…run my mom to a doctor's appointment or something like that. And she can have so many at any given time – speech therapy, physical therapy, occupational therapy, emotional therapy – that I made a deal with him. He knows if I'm asking him to do this, it's 'cause I need it."

Wow.

"Prince, your mom…"

He puts his hands up. "I've been helping her eight years. To be real, I don't know anything else. It's fine."

I attempt to lighten the subject. "And he…didn't suspect anything when he saw you walking off with a girl?"

Prince pauses. "Well, you still look a bit worn out, so anyone could see something is wrong."

So much for lightening the conversation. "I know you're cold, walking out here without a coat on."

"I am," Prince says, blowing air between his knuckles. "So, pick up the pace!" I smile as we walk through the gated turnstile to our school's parking lot and rush to his car.

We jump in, attempting to shake off the cold while he immediately turns on the ignition.

"Where are we going?" I ask.

"Nowhere," he says. "We got about twenty minutes before classes start, but I thought you could use a moment away from everyone."

"You want your coat back?" I ask, hoping he says no. He shakes his head and I'm thankful, shivering a bit while Prince puts the heat on blast, a gust of cold air hitting us before the car settles into its warmth. "So. What was that about?"

I let an exasperated sound escape my lips. "Destiny…was a good friend of mine. I met her in dance class when we were little. We got along so well and I convinced her to come to Mass, but then she got here and…changed. All she wanted to do was party and be around popular guys."

Prince just looks at me. "Yeah, I heard a few things about her and seen her at a few parties I've deejayed at. But I used to see y'all hangin' from time to time, so I figured if you liked her, there must have been something good there. From what I've witnessed, though? She's…a lot."

"That's a nice way of putting it. But yeah, I'm starting to realize that." I look up at Prince. "How could I have been so naive?"

He softens his voice. "Danielle, we've all had friends like that. I have friends I had to cut ties with. And I'll always love them, but we want different things. I chose the radio, and some of them chose the streets. Some of them were smarter than me and had way more talent. But they still made that choice. It's why I hang so tight with the crew I hang with. We keep each other out of trouble." He pauses. "You feel like a sellout, don't you?"

I nod. "Very much so. I don't want anyone to think that I think I'm too good for her. Especially her. But I just don't trust hanging out with her anymore. The situation she put me in could have turned out much worse."

"Since when do you care about what people think?" he says.

I smirk. "I guess I do sometimes...when it's about my character." I look down at my fingers, and suddenly they're engulfed by Prince's hands.

"But that still doesn't explain what happened in there." I look out the window at the row of cars in the lot, attempting once again not to get emotional. Prince really showed me a side of him I didn't expect at the end of our first date. But it was still our first date. Having to explain *this* to him is another story.

"She used my naivete against me. And now she's spreading rumours about me because I refuse to be used anymore."

Prince sits back in his seat, pondering. We both sit in silence. Finally, he utters, "I wish I had more to offer you."

"It's okay. You took me out of an uncomfortable situation. This is more than enough."

I squeeze his hand tighter, both of us staring out the car window into the overcast sky, waiting for winter to show its presence.

Chapter Ten

One for the Record Books

PRINCE

Date two. This one has been tricky to schedule. I thought Dani was playing when she said she needed to focus on early decision applications, but more than a month went by before we were able to schedule our next official date. So I cheated a little and traded a romantic evening for a few meet-ups in places she was going to write. Those pop-ups were mostly the computer lab, the library, or a bookstore like John K. King, where she'd rummage the shelves for cheap rare books, or "collector's editions" as she called them, to add to her library. I found a few psychology books on love and some used picture books for Mook, and we'd sit there in silence, me watching her finish her applications with such a fire, like getting in *was* life or death for her.

College seemed like an escape for her. So the question was, what was she running from? I told her early admission wasn't as important for me, since I was gearing up for a few holiday gigs and toy drives, but I'd use the winter break to tighten up my shit. It was really a way to delay the inevitable conversation I needed to have with her, which was that I wasn't sure if going out of state was really even an option for me. While she was thinking about her life in the future, all I wanted to do was enjoy these precious moments, without all the fuss and uncertainty. Where I could make her laugh and loosen her up. Where the true Danielle was opening up to me bit by bit and causing me to fall a little harder each time I was around her.

I shake off my nerves, thoughts, and probably this weather as I step to her front door and ring the doorbell. Her mom answers almost instantly, gleeful as hell.

"Hi, Prince!" she exclaims, giving me the biggest embrace.

"Hi, Mrs Ford. How are you?"

"I'm doing great. Please, come in!" I step inside, and suddenly my stomach starts to turn. *Noooo, not tonight,* I think, freaking out in my head. This date needs to go perfect, and I don't need an upset stomach ruining it for me. But my gut doesn't give a damn about my plans.

Mr Ford turns the corner, with a smile on his face at that. Okay, things are shaping up with me and the big man.

"Prince," he greets me, giving me a firm handshake.

"Mr Ford," I say, returning the shake and meeting his cadence.

He lowers his voice and gets closer. "I have to say, you made a wise decision reaching out to me on Facebook for some recommendations. My Dani baby is going to flip."

"Thank you," I respond back in a hushed tone. "I can tell Danielle's a daddy's girl, and I wanted this date to be extra special now that her college applications are in. So I figured if anyone knew where to take her to make her really happy, it would be you."

Dani's mom clasps her hands in approval. "I'm so excited! Everything about it sounds so cute." *Grrrrr:* my stomach makes a noise and both her parents look at me with concern. Why is this happening to me?

"I haven't eaten all day. Nerves got the best of me," I explain.

"Oh, you poor thing. We're about to heat up some leftover Thanksgiving dinner if you want some..."

"No!" I proclaim. The last thing I need is something else in my stomach to set this off even more. "I'm sort of a... messy eater. And I know Dani will be down any minute. I'm sure y'all put your foot in the dinner and I don't want her seeing me pig out."

"Speaking of food, I should go check on it," Mr Ford says. "I'll be right back." Good, he's out of my hair. Now on to getting Mrs Ford something to do so I can make a quick bathroom run. I look at my phone and scrunch my face a little, showing concern.

"Something wrong?" Mrs Ford asks.

"I just want to make sure we make good time, and you know how traffic can be on a Friday evening."

"Oh! I can tell Dani to hurry up."

"Oh, no. I don't want her to feel rushed. I think if we leave in ten minutes, we should be fine."

"Okay," she says. "I can go check on her. You want to hang out in the family room?"

"Actually, can I use your restroom? I want to freshen up and could use the privacy to check in on our date location."

Her eyes brighten up. "Sure! Down this hall to your right." Thank god she took the bait. Mrs Ford scurries upstairs while I race to the bathroom, praying they have air freshener or *something* in there. What are the odds something like this would happen to me *right now*? Sometimes, the world is really cruel.

After a few quick courtesy flushes, and some matches I find under the sink, I walk out feeling...somewhat better. I hope it's enough to keep me going tonight. I rush back to the family room to find Danielle talking to Mrs Ford, with her back to me.

"Sorry, I had to make a call..." She turns around, smiling, and that's it.

She got me.

Dani's wearing a form-fitting blue dress that lands right at her calves, and she dressed it up with tan suede booties. She has a matching trench draped across her arms, and her beautiful, long, curly mane nestles right on her shoulders. I'm at a loss for words, and Dani looks at me with concern.

"Ummm, hi, Prince," she says shyly.

Hi, Dani.

Be my girlfriend.

Have my babies.

"Hey." I snap out of it. "You, umm…" I clear my extra-parched throat and think quick. "Your skin is so clear. You use Korean skincare products or something?"

The damn library all over again.

She laughs. "What do you know about K-beauty products? But thank you. I put on a mask this morning, so that might be it." She's never looked at me for such an extended period of time, and I don't think I can physically handle it. Thankfully, her father steps in.

"Dani baby, you look beautiful," his voice bellows. *Thanks, Pops, that's what I should have said. Plain and simple.*

Why is my tongue always betraying me at critical moments?

"Thank you, Daddy," she replies, walking over to him.

"Prince has a nice date planned for you. He's told me all about it." He looks at me and nods, and Dani suddenly eyes me with suspicion.

I swallow the frog in my throat. "We should get going." Dani kisses her dad on the cheek and walks over to her mom next. Mr Ford's brows furrow.

"Dani, do you wanna change…?" Dani and her mom both give him a look. I guess he didn't realize how much her dress highlighted her curves. Maybe he now understands why I'm unable to form coherent sentences.

"Oh, hush, James!" her mom fusses. "It's a long-sleeved turtleneck dress. She's not even showing anything." Her mom helps Danielle put her coat on and rushes us out the door before Mr Ford can object. "You kids have fun."

The front door closes on us, and Dani and I walk to my car, silent. I rush to open the passenger's side and hop into the driver's seat. When I go to start the engine, Dani's hand touches my arm and every ounce of my being tingles.

"You okay, Prince? You've seemed…uneasy this entire time."

Tell that to my nerves…and my stomach.

Just be real. It's got you this far.

"Honestly? You look divine tonight. I know I can come across cocky at times, but…" I gaze at her. "I don't know how for the life of me I convinced you to go out with me."

Dani suppresses a smile, and I bet she's hoping it masks her blushing.

But I peep it.

"Well, let's see what you got. Date three has officially begun." She sits back in her seat, staring at the driveway. Is she taunting me?

"Two," I gently remind her, and she chuckles. I put the gear in reverse and we're off to prove my theory right.

Her bright eyes shine like the freshly fallen snow as we both watch the skyline deepen to a blue-purple hue. We drive in silence, and even though it's almost December, we've lucked out. The sun is out and giving us a colourful sunset. We take it all in as we drive past trees stripped of the last bit of fall, before the horizon turns into months of dull greyness.

We drive to Midtown area and I find parking a few blocks away, so I won't give up our first location. But Dani begins fidgeting in her seat. Finally, she's out with it. "Where are you taking me?" she asks as I open the passenger-side door to let her out.

"Danielle, you're about to find out in like two minutes or less. Can you just relax and enjoy?" She huffs at me, letting me lead the way as we walk down the strip of Black-owned businesses in the area – the loft windows that hold a new hair salon, a vegan spot and a few more businesses housed along the old railway tracks technically called Milwaukee Junction.

We keep walking, and Danielle looks even more confused, which makes me happy. She seriously has no clue. Finally, we get directly in front of the building and she squeals.

"I knew it!" she shrieks. "I knew you were taking me here."

"Knew what? It's not even open," I say, looking directly at the building with the sign that says PEARL BOOKSTORE AND CAFÉ, OPENING SOON.

She looks at me, dumbfounded, and I can't contain my amusement anymore. I open the glass door for her. "You look so hurt, but you're right," I say. "We're going exactly where you think we're going."

Dani claps her hands in excitement, then stops herself. "I look like such a dork right now, don't I?"

I nod and grab her hand. "But it's cute as hell. Come on, let me show your dorky ass what I got planned."

We walk inside Pearl Bookstore and Café, and the owner is there to greet us.

"Hey, y'all," Ms Esaw says, coming up to me and giving me a big embrace.

"How are you doing, Ms Esaw?" I ask her. She shakes her head.

"You know, tired but grindin'. Don't get old, ya hear me?" Danielle laughs at her, since Ms Esaw can't be over forty.

"Ms Esaw, this is Danielle." They shake hands and Danielle is fangirling so hard.

"I've heard so much about this place and I've been following you everywhere, waiting for it to open."

Ms Esaw beams. "Aww, thank you, babygirl. It's still wild I raised that much through GoFundMe, but I'm happy the community looked out. My dad started this business as a record store, and the name has such a legacy, I wanted to preserve it. I'm so thankful the city named it a landmark." She pauses. "Well, you'll have to come back and visit for the grand opening, yeah?" Danielle nods repeatedly. "Tonight the bookstore is yours, and I want you both to take advantage. PJ, make sure you lock up, okay? This my pride and joy."

"On everything I will."

She nods, satisfied, and moves in closer. "And tell your uncle he could learn a thing or two from you." I crack up laughing and Danielle looks at me, amused.

"I will, he'll love it." She smiles and walks out.

"What was that about?" Dani enquires.

"That was in reference to a time where they dated, and my uncle sort of messed things up." Dani nods and looks around again.

"Prince, how did you manage to get us into Pearl before it's even open?"

"I hit Ms Esaw up and told her about you, and what you like. She's a good friend of the family and let me have the store for a few hours, right before it opens. She just told me not to steal anything or she coming for me." I laugh again.

Danielle looks me over. "So, what *do* you have planned for the night?"

"I thought you'd never ask." I clear my throat and settle into a baritone voice. Maybe Yasin is right about my voice going deep. "Danielle Ford, tonight we're gonna help you get out of your writer's funk." She laughs nervously, not sure what to do next. It's awkward and cute. "Your job, should you accept it, is to go through these bookshelves to your favourite authors and see if there's a surprise waiting for you."

She squeals again. "Oh my god, where do I even start?"

"Danielle, are you hyperventilating? Calm yoself, girl."

She chuckles. "Whatever. It's like you just asked me who my favourite child was. It's overwhelming."

"Okay, okay," I say, palms down as I attempt to settle her. "How about we start with some of the authors on your typewriter?"

She smirks. "My parents and their mouth."

"Care to lead the way then?" She grabs my hand as we make our way through the stacks.

"It's funny my mom gave me a typewriter, 'cause my dad's the reader. He used to take me to bookstores all around the city, but it's been a while since we've done that. He's been travelling a lot more recently."

"I told him my date idea, and he couldn't stop talking

about the typewriter and how important it is to you. Speaking of favourites, is your dad your favourite parent?" I ask.

Danielle laughs. "No! I kinda like both my parents for different reasons." She finds the classics section and we turn a corner. "I take it Mook is your mom's favourite?"

This time it's my turn to laugh. "I got you a date at this nice-ass bookstore that isn't even open to the public yet and you assume my younger brother is the charmer?"

"I mean, have you seen him?" she retorts.

"Fair point," I say, nodding. She stops in front of Hurston and gasps. Right on top of her collection of books is a black fedora. "Turn it around," I tell her.

She picks it up and reads the note attached. "'Wear this to channel your best ideas.'" Her attention is on me. "And it's even silk-lined!"

"Can't have that hair of yours breaking off."

"Aww, P." Dang, she's never called me P before. She goes for it and gives me the biggest embrace, and my stomach makes a noise. I try to play it off, and she seems in such a state of euphoria that I don't think she noticed.

She won't stop looking at me, and I feel so nervous, which is *not* helping my stomach. I'm finally getting her where I want her and my body wants to act like this. I try to push it out of my mind. "You want me to put it on you?" She nods. I place the hat on top of her head, and it fits perfectly. "So why is she one of your favourite authors?"

"She was one of the few Black women at that time writing in a lane that was male-dominated. Which is funny, since my dad was the one that put me on to her. She's from Florida, like him. He lived not too far away from Eatonville, where she's from, and my dad sort of idolized it. Have you heard of the town?"

"Vaguely," I admit.

"It was one of the first all-Black towns incorporated in the US," she says, pulling a book off the shelf and looking it over. "She bases a lot of her settings on the town. I think it's one of the reasons my dad moved to Detroit. To raise a family in one of the Blackest cities in America, so that I can be safe in my own skin to just…be."

"Your dad travels a lot for the army?"

"Oh yeah," she says. "He's been based everywhere, but my mom wanted me to have more stability, so we stay in the D while he was away. What about yours? You don't talk about him much."

I put my hands in my pockets and clear my throat. "It's not much to say. He's not around. Hasn't been for almost eight years now."

Danielle's shoulders droop. "I'm sorry, I didn't know…"

"It's all right. It is what it is. Do you have this book at home?" I grab the book from her hands and try to read the back nonchalantly, but my stomach rumbles.

"Yeah, I do, but this is a repackage. Are you…okay?" she asks with concern.

I feel myself sweating and I know she must see it, but I nod to reassure her. "Just give me a sec, I'm going to run to the bathroom. You want to look around a bit more?" Cute little worry lines frame her forehead as she nods, and I rush off.

I try to make things quick and hurry back. I find her at another spot in the store, and I can tell she's trying to distract herself from peeking inside a bag she just found on the floor, with the next clue inside.

I give Danielle an awkward smile and try to continue our conversation as if nothing happened. "Now we're in *L*."

"Yes, for our Lorde and saviour." Danielle laughs, amusing herself. She's such a dork and I love it.

"Well, I picked her 'cause she loved writing poetry and loved music. And I found out something special about her." I nod at the bag. "Open it up." She opens the bag to find a framed poem that I ripped out of a page of a magazine.

"What is thi—" She stops dead in her tracks. "*Seventeen* magazine?"

I smile. "I read that Audre was writing poetry in seventh grade, kinda like you in our English class. She wrote a love sonnet for her high-school magazine but they wouldn't publish it, so she submitted it to *Seventeen* and they took it."

She brushes her hand over the frame. "What year was this?" she asks.

"1951," I clarify.

She doesn't stop looking at the poem. "Thank you," she says, and reads the second note attached. "'You're never too young to get that poem published.'" She smiles. "Audre means the world to me, so having this is extra special. Do you mind if I make a copy and give it to a friend?"

"Do what you want. Can I ask who this friend is?" I ask, my eyebrows raised.

She laughs and gives me a light push. "It's not like that. It's for Esi. We started an Audre book club freshman year when Esi read about her on a message board. When she was struggling with coming out…"

"Oh," I say.

"Yeah, she's actually the one who told me about Audre's writing. But Esi was afraid that her parents would find Audre's books, so she'd only read them at my house. When she finally came out sophomore year, I gifted her our entire collection. I feel like this would make it complete."

She's even more beautiful right now.

"It would," is all I say. "You…still hang out with her?"

She sighs. "No, and it's on me. But I'm trying this new thing where I don't push people out my life. I want to make things right between us." She smiles at me and we stand there, taking in one another, until I'm the first to come out of the trance.

"So, this is taking longer than I thought."

"I'm sorry," Dani says. "I'm just having so much fun…"

"No, no, no, don't apologize. I just want to make sure we eat. The food is getting cold." Danielle gives me a puzzled look. "Follow me."

I lead her to the café portion of the bookstore, where a blanket is set on the floor with lit candles all around. I mean, there are candles all over. Yasin and Ant really committed when I asked them to do this and bought every damn candle they could find. Last thing I need is Ms Esaw being pissed at me for burning her new bookstore down. But the roses I asked them to get, sprinkled around the blanket and the food containers, were a nice touch. I can just imagine them in here fighting about where things should go, determined to show me they can outdo me in the romance department.

"Prince," she says with extreme gratitude, her hands crossed over her chest and her gold hoops sparkling against the backdrop of the string lights hanging on the wall.

Okay, maybe the candles aren't too much.

I take her hand to help her sit on the ground and settle down beside her. "I'm sorry I didn't have time to plate this, but my timing was pretty limited today." And my stomach wasn't helping. She opens her to-go container and is bursting with happiness.

"It's perfect, really," she says, looking around, and this time it's my turn to smile. "But to be honest, I was expecting matching *Frozen* plates."

I scrunch up my nose. "And what's wrong with that, bougie Danielle? This whole date is sponsored by Dollar General."

She laughs, taking a bite of the bread. "Nothing is wrong with it, nothing at all. In fact, I'm a little bummed we don't have them."

"Your dad suggested Andiamo and said it's your favourite. Tell me about it."

"It's sooo good! They make their pasta from scratch. The first time we ate there I was in middle school and loved it. I've never been to Italy, but my dad says the food there is like the closest thing to it in the area."

"How does it feel to have your applications finished?" I ask her, taking a sip of ginger ale.

"I have a confession, and don't tell my parents. I haven't technically finished."

"What?!" I say. I'm shocked she even let me take her out. "You've been working so hard at it. What about your essay?"

"Well, that's what's holding me back. I'm still getting tripped up on how to end my essay. I wanted to submit early so I could find out if I got in sooner for NYU, but I just can't get it right. So I'm going to use the Christmas break to enjoy my time with family and tighten up my essay. At least the rest of it is done, and most schools' applications are due by January. What about you?"

I take a bite of the bread with hopes that putting *something* in my system will settle my stomach. "I don't know. I'm thinking about maybe keeping it local for now."

"Maybe? Why maybe?"

"I mean, just trying to figure out what the best next steps are. I'll probably go to Wayne County my first year and then transfer."

Danielle's eyes light up. "You should definitely transfer! You gotta get the full college experience."

I wish. I want to tell her everything, but my burdens are mine to deal with. Not hers. "Maybe. It just depends. I have a lot on my plate and the station is treating me good…"

"But that's not what you want, Prince," she says matter-of-factly. "You want to revolutionize radio. Sometimes that takes learning from the best to figure out how you can do it your way."

"I know, it's just…" My stomach takes a major turn for the worse, and I can't even play it off. "I'll be right back!" I say, jumping off the blanket and walking very quickly to the bathroom.

Shit. I'm in the bathroom for like ten minutes and there's no way of hiding what's going on. It must have been that leftover mac and cheese I ate last night for dinner, knowing my ass is lactose intolerant. I shouldn't have risked it, but I just can't say no to Sister Beatrice's mac and cheese. I try to text Dani, but I'm at a loss for what to say to make me sound like I'm not sitting in this dope bookstore with the poops, spending more time staring at this bathroom wallpaper than the most beautiful and interesting girl at Mass.

I finally come back to the blanket, trying to act cool, and chuckle when I look down. On the blanket where I sat are four pink chewable tablets.

"You also could use some ginger tea or something. You seem like you're going through it."

I have never been so thankful to be called out in my entire life. I scoop the tablets and scarf them down immediately.

"Danielle, you're a lifesaver."

"I know." She beams. "You were about to ruin our date being secretive about whatever is going on with your stomach. I look too cute for that." She giggles when she says that, and blushes. I like it when she's in her bag.

"Yes, you do," I say.

* * *

We sit there slowly eating our meal, and she's right. This restaurant is bomb. I had to act like I wasn't impressed but damn, Dani's dad gave me the best spot, and my stomach is starting to calm down so I can actually enjoy the meal. He's definitely starting to like me. I'm going to have to take my mom there for Mother's Day or her birthday. Finally, I tell Dani it's time to finish the scavenger hunt.

"You still got a few more things to find in this store. Who is an author you've missed that is super common?"

Danielle stares into nothingness, figuring out what area she needs to go to next. She jumps up and I scramble to follow her, blowing out as many candles as I can before I do.

"No heads-up or nothing, huh?"

She laughs. "I told you I'm competitive, Prince." She goes to the *A* section and I nod. She got it.

She stops in front of the Maya Angelou titles and chuckles. Standing upright next to her books is a Maya Barbie doll.

"Aww," she says, holding it in her hands. "I debated whether to ask my parents for one, but it was sold out. So, thank you."

And it wasn't cheap on Etsy, either. I had to bargain like a street hustler to get the price down to something reasonable.

"Now it can be an endpiece you add to your bookshelf. What you call them things?"

"Bookends," she laughs. And this time she doesn't roll her eyes at me like at the library. It looks like she's searching for something, somewhat disappointed.

"What's wrong?" I ask.

"Where's my love note?"

Now it's my turn to blush. I look at the shelf until I find the note, which somehow fell off Maya's arm. This one wasn't tied as tight, I guess. I hand it to her, and she beams, reading the note out loud. "'You'll inspire millions of Black girls, just like her.'" She adjusts the headwrap on the doll's head, which somehow got crooked. "I hope so."

We walk the stacks some more and Danielle pulls out books that she's read, telling me what they're about as I watch her face light up like a sunbeam. She actually has me wanting to read a few of them, but there's also something in knowing she's read enough for the both of us and has no problem narrating the story herself to me. I almost don't want this part of the date to end, watching her enjoy herself so much. But I look at my watch, knowing we gotta go.

"Okay, the last two things I need you to find are for a future date."

"Date three?" she asks.

"Nah, four, five or six." I chuckle and she rolls her eyes. "Go to G and M."

Danielle ponders what I tell her, until it seems like a light bulb goes off in her head. "Gay," she says as she scurries away.

Next to Roxane Gay's books is a game of Scrabble. She giggles with amusement. "Why Scrabble?"

"You didn't know? Roxane is a Scrabble champ. Like hits up the tournaments and everything. She even wears her own portable board." Danielle is holding her belly from laughing so hard.

"What?" she manages to get out. "That is amazing!" She

tears off the note attached to the game. "'When you're feeling stuck, use your competitive streak to play a game of Scrabble.'" She nods. "This is a really good idea."

"I know. That's why I suggested it."

She looks back at me, her eyes filled with mischief. "You know I'll beat your ass, though, right?"

"Doubt it," is all I say, secretly eating this side of her up. "You got one more clue," I tell her.

She walks right over to the Morrison section with confidence and finds a container tube leaning against the shelves. She unravels the paper to find Toni's *Pieces I Am* movie poster staring back at her. "This will be a good one to hang up in your dorm room," I say.

She reads the note aloud. "'So that you always have someone to look up to.'" I feel like Danielle's face is going to hurt tomorrow from smiling so hard, the corners of her mouth turned upward for what feels like hours. I don't think I've ever seen this much joy radiate from her face. And it's intoxicating. "I have seen this documentary too many times to admit out loud, but I'd love to watch it with you," she says.

So she *is* planning for life after date three with us. I'm into it.

We drive down Woodward, past the blue, yellow and red neon Fox Theatre marquee and right into the heart of downtown to park. "Mook always says it looks like someone just threw up lights here," I tell Danielle, and she laughs as we walk through the thousands of lights surrounding us, taking in the tree-lighting with more lights than I can count on display. Dani's parents said she's a Christmas fanatic, so I wanted to do something that would put her right in the Christmas spirit. But I purposely chose to come after the actual tree-lighting ceremony, with the hopes that most of the crowd would be gone, and we'd be able to walk around and talk some more.

"You take him every year?" she asks.

"Last three, I think. It's a way to get him out the house and exert some energy. That boy has way too much of it." Danielle immediately looks guilty. "Don't worry, I'm bringing him tomorrow." Dani continues to admire the gleaming lights around us but takes a moment to look at me.

"That makes me feel better." She pauses. "You know, I've never met someone our age who looks after their siblings the way you look after your brother."

"It's all I know," I say. "If I don't, then who will? He's too young right now, but eventually he will have abandonment issues. I feel like it's inevitable, so I'm trying to do what I can to make him feel as complete as possible before those questions start coming up."

Danielle sips on the hot chocolate I bought her as we slowly make our way through the crowd. "Does he ask?"

I shake my head. "Not much. But I think between me, my mom and Uncle Romes, we give him so much love he doesn't have much time to think about it."

"It shows. Your family is solid, Prince. More solid than so

many other people's I've seen," she responds. And I blush. I'm always on go-mode and never have a chance to stop and look at how my family is a unit, how we hold each other up. I know so many families like this, but we somehow found a way to make what we have work. I feel proud.

"Yeah, my mom is one of the strongest people out here. But her not being able to trust others and let them help her makes our relationship feel smothering at times. Especially after my dad walked out."

"I honestly can't believe how much you're juggling. But I do get what you're going through in *some* ways. My mom and I are really close, with my dad being away for work. So, I feel like so much of her expectations fall on me." We pause at the ice-skating rink and watch for a few moments before she continues. "But it's nice to have moms who love us so much, right?"

I smile, thinking about what she just said. "I wouldn't trade it for anything in this world." I pry a little more about her family. "So, you told my uncle your parents have been together for like twenty years or something?"

"Yeah, it's crazy. It will be twenty years in February."

"Damn, ain't your mom twenty now?"

She laughs and points to some of the vendor stations. We walk in that direction. "If you tell her that, she'll love you forever. She'll be forty next year. I couldn't see myself being married so young. But I'm thankful my parents made it work."

I stare at Danielle's profile – her bronzed skin, those full pink lips – and see our future, our life, so much more. And I have to snap out of it. Why the hell did I just think that? Her and her mama must put some magic on men.

"Prince?"

"Yeah, huh?" I say, snapping out of whatever that was.

"What…were you doing?"

I look beyond her and point at something out in the distance. "Just eyeing that crazy-ass man over there." Dani turns to her right to find a slightly inebriated man in the distance dressed as Santa Claus, yelling, "Merry Christmas" to everyone he walks past.

She shakes her head. "We usually go to Wild Lights at the zoo, but I can't believe we haven't been here before. I guess my parents told you I like Christmas too, huh?" I nod. "Thank you for the hot chocolate."

"No problem," I say, smiling.

"I've been so greedy. You want some? I got it with soy milk, so you won't be running to the bathroom again."

I thought she'd never ask. The temperature has dropped a solid ten degrees since we got to Campus Martius Park. I grab the cup and take a gulp, but the shit is still *hot*. Before I know it, some has spilled on my coat, and my lower lip feels numb. Great. I'm so damn angry and almost throw the cup on the ground, until I feel Danielle's hands around mines, taking the cup out of my hand.

"Prince! Why did you try to drink it so fast?"

"Why didn't you tell me it's so hot?"

"Because it's *hot chocolate*," Dani says, trying to hold in a chuckle. "Have you not had it before?"

"You got jokes, Danielle," I mumble. "We've been walking around for a while now. I thought it would have cooled down."

"It's the Styrofoam, and I've been cuffing it with my mittens to keep it warm. A trick my dad taught me." She eases closer to me. "Let me see." She takes off her glove and examines my lip, lightly touching it with her finger. Suddenly the crowd around us sounds muffled and the only sensation I feel is her touch.

"I feel like I just got a third-degree burn," I whine.

"It doesn't look too bad. But let's go to the bathroom and run your lip under some cold water."

"I'm all right," I say.

"Prince," she exclaims. "Just trust me. Plus, you can use the time to clean off your jacket." I look down at my grey North Face to find a dark stain smack dead in the centre of my chest. My uncle got this for me as an early Christmas present. I knew I should've asked for it in black instead. *Great.* I find a bathroom and run some water on my lip and attempt to wipe the stain off my coat, but instead it just creates an even bigger one. I shake my head in the mirror. This is how Ant be looking after Kisha spits up all over his shirt.

I come out and find that Dani has wandered under a row of trees with about a hundred string lights wrapped around them, which transition from blue to green to pink to yellow. Her fedora is still on her head, and she's looking like she should be on someone's Christmas card. She couldn't have picked a more romantic spot, and I feel defeated. I wish the night was as magical as she looked. "This date is going horribly," I mumble. Dani is still laughing.

"I think it's perfect," she says. "For the first time I see the human version of the love coach. Today is one of the first times you've seemed like you didn't have the perfect words to say, or the exact right things to do." She leans in closer. "And I feel much closer to you."

"You tellin' me I'm not the only dork on this date?" She pushes me jokingly, but of course my ass is near some black ice and I slip and almost fall. Danielle grabs my arm with a strength I didn't even know she possessed.

"Oh my god, are you okay?" she asks, eyes wide.

My heart is actually racing. "You tried to kill me!" I declare, loud enough for other people to stop and look at us, which they do.

"Prince!" she whisper-yells, unable to stop laughing. "I can't help it if you're a klutz." Tears are coming down her cheeks. "I was trying to kiss you and it got ruined again."

Oh.

I can see her breath – visibly white from the cold air – getting more intense in the darkness, and I can't tell if it's from her lifting me up, or a result of being nervous that she even admitted that to me. I lean in closer to her.

"You want to kiss me? Even with this puddle on my coat?" She smirks and pokes at my coat puddle, nodding.

She parts her lips and they taste like chocolate goodness mixed with lip gloss. I already know when I pull away it's going to look like I just ate some fried chicken, and I could care less. Dani wants to kiss me. And in *public*. I've never been more turned on by her boldness. This is the shit you see in the movies, and it's just as rapturous in this moment as it is onscreen.

I forget that we're outside, that it's cold, that the coffee shop served us lava hot chocolate. All I care is that Dani's fingers are around my neck and her tender lips are taking over mine, causing every muscle in my body to buckle under her touch.

When we pull away, I lick my lips, wanting to relive the sensory overload I just experienced all over again. Wanting to taste her one more time. You know when you just finish a workout and you feel light-headed and get this adrenaline rush and start seeing them white, floaty specks in your eye? Yeah, those. Floaters. That's what I just experienced.

"Is the date still going horribly?" she asks coyly.

"Not at all," is all I can muster to say.

"Good." She slips her hand into mine. "'Cause you owe me another hot chocolate."

Luther Vandross's "Have Yourself a Merry Little Christmas" suddenly blares through the coffee-shop speakers. In this chaos of a night, with almost all of Detroit out for the tree-lighting, we were somehow able to snag a seat by the window. "Did someone turn the volume up?"

Danielle smiles. "They sure did, and if there's anyone to turn the volume up for, it's Luther."

"Oh, so you *do* like music?" I ask, secretly sniffing the aroma of coffee beans filling the air.

"I never said I didn't. I just said I didn't listen to your show."

I place my hand over my soggy chest. "Damn. I thought we were having a good time." She laughs. "You're so over the top. Everyone rides for Mariah, but they forget this song."

"Only reason I know Luther is because my dad attempts to sing this song every year around this time. He sang it a few days ago when we had family over."

Danielle eats her chocolate croissant, and I watch the goo of the chocolate attempt to escape her lips. She catches it with her finger and I just want to lean in and lick it off. I know, not my best moment. It's just that her lips are so luscious…

"Prince, have you ever considered that you might just be a music curator?" That comment throws me right back into the discussion.

"Those are heavy words," I say, contemplating what she just uttered. "Trust me, Danielle. I don't know enough about music."

"You know a lot more than I know or anyone else does. You know the music our generation listens to, the music of my parents' generation, and even my parents' parents. And you're only seventeen. Imagine what you'll know ten or twenty years from now."

She's not wrong. I want nothing more than to go to college and nerd out on music like Dani nerds out on writing. Meet professors and mentors who know so much more about music, people who would change my life. Just being in those spaces might help me dream bigger, as my unc would say.

"It really started when I was young, 'cause I would play a song, and it would give me déjà vu. But then I'd go look it up and realize it was sampled from another song. And then I'd go look that song up. And before you know it, I spent hours listening to five versions of a song that came out this year. I just like finding out the history of a song. But also figuring out what inspired a producer to take elements from that song to incorporate it into music today. How they make it new. It just shows how we're all inspired by artists before us."

Danielle stares at me with admiration. "See? I don't do that. I just Shazam it and keep it moving…" A light bulb goes off in her head. "Oh my god, you're a walking Shazam!" That causes me to chuckle.

I watch as a few people grab their orders, and my ringer goes off on my phone. Danielle glares at me.

"Is that for my curfew?" she asks. I nod, and she scrunches up her nose. "Who said I'm not breaking the rules tonight?"

I smirk. I like this version of her. "Not on my watch. Part of my charm is getting your parents to trust me. If they can expect nothing but the best from me, it makes my life easier."

"Easier for what? Dating me?" she asks, that gorgeous smile spreading across her lips.

Dating.

Has a nice ring to it.

"Yeah, dating you," I reply.

She a real one.

I strut into school on Monday like I just won the lottery. You can't tell me nothing. I got my first kiss from Dani; that soft, gentle kiss. I didn't think I could *possibly* like her more, and here we are. I'm reminiscing on Saturday night when I spot Ant, Malik and Yasin waiting for me at my locker. *Shit.* I'm in trouble.

"So that's what we're doing now? Blowing yo homies off?" Malik practically yells for half the hallway to hear.

"Chill, man, it's not like that," I declare, wiggling my coat off and hanging it up in my locker. "I just haven't had a chance to respond to messages."

"Messages? Bruh, we had a whole pick-up game on Sunday at the rec. You were supposed to come through," Ant responds. I feel bad. Anthony doesn't trip over most things, and maybe it's 'cause when you have a kid in high school you mature faster than most and realize most things ain't that serious. For him to not be into sports like that and still call me out? He's hurt.

I give him the most genuine apology I can. "Ant, for real. My bad. I am just finally making headway with" – I lower my voice – "Danielle. And I wanna ride this out."

Malik is once again looking at himself in his locker mirror. "Man, I don't know why you whispering like the whole school don't know."

I'm baffled. "How? Me and her barely see each other during school."

"Just 'cause you didn't tell us about that encounter in the computer lab with her friend doesn't mean it didn't get around," Yasin says.

"What has everyone been saying?"

Anthony sort of chuckles. "It's kind of ridiculous. They said Danielle almost ripped Destiny's earring out her ear and you had to carry Danielle out the lab."

My eyes widen. "What the fu—?"

Malik laughs. "I ain't know she threw blows like that." He puts his knuckles up like he's about to square up and gives me a quick jab to my side.

I cough from losing my breath. "You play too much," I proclaim, trying to compose myself and looking around.

"Don't worry, your precious little Danielle didn't see it." I roll my eyes at Malik. That's my dude, but sometimes he gets on my damn nerves. Like he ain't smitten over Rashida.

"You wanna link up to work out?" Anthony asks. "I have Kisha tomorrow for the next week, but then I'm free after finals, since her and her mama going to North Carolina for the holidays." Ant looks a little sad when he says it; he could use some company.

"I gotta work at the station for a toy drive next weekend, but you're welcome to come through."

"Bet," Anthony says. "I'll come after my shift." I knew he needed an escape.

"I'll be there too. I just can't hang too late 'cause I promised my mom I'd go to mass with her at St. Joseph that Sunday. Y'all know I hate getting up early," Yasin remarks. "You down, Malik?"

Malik's mind's gone to another place and we all look at him.

"Malik," Ant barks, snapping him out his trance.

"Yeah, what up?" Malik looks at us with a face that looks like…guilt?

I shake my head. "Tell me you not going to hang with Charte?"

Anthony and Yasin groan. Malik shrugs.

"What? That's the only time Charte is free before she goes out of town. And Rashida been busy lately with some show she doing with her friend Esi, and they tryna recruit Danielle…"

Danielle?

"Wait, wait, wait. Danielle is hanging with Rashida again and you didn't think to tell me?"

"I figured she told you, since for the past month every time she tells you she's free, you jump," Malik snaps back. "Now I got plans. The world don't revolve around your ass, P."

He's right. There's so much I don't know about Danielle, but I have been using any opportunity to meet her wherever she is. To do that requires my schedule to be a bit…flexible. Which means I haven't made time for anything else outside my family.

I throw my hands up in surrender. "You right. That's on me. I'm sorry, you guys. You forgive me?" I extend my hand out to dap Malik, and we clasp hands. Then I pull him in for a hug and pat his back and just to be funny, I massage his head.

"Get off me," Malik yells while half the hallway laughs.

"That's for earlier," I contend. "I promise I owe y'all a rematch next weekend. I just need to play catch-up on some things first."

I'm fidgeting in my seat after sixth hour later that day, watching Mr Smith glare intently over my file on the computer. His bald head is gleaming and I can't stop looking at it. Does he lotion it every morning? It's glistening like a bowling ball right now.

"Mr Jones!"

I jump. "Sorry, Mr Smith. Wassup?"

"I'm reviewing your grades, and it's not looking good." Tell me something I don't know.

"I'm not failing," I declare, chuckling a little. Mr Smith's face is stoic as fuck. I didn't even get a smirk out of him.

"You think this is a game?"

I throw my head back against the wall. "Come *on*, Mr Smith…"

"Prince. Don't play yourself." I roll my eyes. I hate when he tries to use slang. "With these grades, you can't apply to State, Eastern, or Western."

I finally spill. "I wasn't planning on going to any of those places. I think I'm keeping it local."

"State is local."

"I was thinking more like...community local."

Mr Smith sinks into his chair like I just knocked the wind out of him. Is he *that* disappointed in me?

I give him a lot of shit usually, but I really can't take it. Not from him. He always stayed on my ass, but I thought he'd throw me a bone with it being my senior year and all.

"It's fine, Mr Smith. Community college is a perfectly good plan. It's not like I'm not going anywhere. Plus, I got some offers lined up with the radio station. A few local frats and sororities have already been DMing me about emceeing at parties and stuff, which will put some extra money in my pocket. I figure between that and classes..."

He takes his bifocals off and rubs his eyes for a bit, which stops me in my tracks. I completely let him down.

"There's nothing wrong with community college. But Prince, you're so much smarter than this. You're not going to be challenged there," he contends, pointing to his computer screen. He sighs, and then leans closer to me. "Look, I get it. You think if you leave the station you won't get an opportunity better than this." I squirm in my seat some more, suddenly feeling a little light-headed. "I've had many kids walk through this door, and I promise you, it's not true. There's something greater out there for you. But you got to get over your own fear."

I bob in my chair and bite my cheek, trying to fight the urge to get emotional. "It's...it's not just that," I tell him, my voice cracking a little. "My mom..."

Mr Smith eyes me with concern. "What about your mom? You've never mentioned her before."

I look at the stark white wall and let a long exhale escape my mouth before I speak. "She needs me. Financially. Her disability cheque isn't enough…"

Before I know it, Mr Smith's hand is on my shoulder. "Why didn't you tell me that, son?"

I scale my teeth with my tongue, trying so damn hard not to cry. But my eyes are watering and before I know it, a tear falls down my cheek. I put my head down to avoid eye contact. "I thought I had it figured out."

Damn, I'm no different than my mom right now. This must have been what she felt when me and Uncle Romes were going in on her. I guess me and her are a lot alike. Trying to do it all on our own when there are people willing to help all around us.

"Prince, there are scholarships for students whose parents are disabled and struggling financially. Money that will help you. For this very reason." I'm floored. "You had no idea, huh?"

I shake my head. "When my grades were better, I was banking on scholarships. But once I started slacking, I just felt like there was no hope. I didn't think I'd be eligible for anything."

"And I know a few resources that will help your mom, too, as a single parent." He suddenly is back at his computer, typing away.

"But Mr Smith, this is all a lot and it's not your job—"

"The hell it ain't!" he proclaims, which startles me a little. "Let me worry about helping you finance your dreams. But in exchange, it might mean you have to retake some classes over the summer and bring your grades up your first semester of community college. Deal?"

"You'll help me even after I graduate? After I'm out of Mass?"

"Absolutely. Prince, I've been trying to help you for the last few years."

"I know, I know," I say. "And I've appreciated you getting on me, even when I ignore you."

He chuckles. "Yeah, that's one thing you know how to do well. But you're not the first student and you won't be the last. You keep coming back, which shows me you might be overwhelmed, but there is a part of you that still wants to try. My job is to figure out what's stopping you from doing the thing."

"Don't tell anyone I said this, but you're kinda good at your job." He laughs and leans back in his desk chair.

"I'll take it. Do we have a deal?"

I nod my head vigorously. Up until this moment, I didn't think any of those things were an option. And now, I've never wanted anything more.

Chapter Eleven
The Rest Is Noise

"Danielle," Esi says, her head turning abruptly when she notices me in her peripheral as I walk into the nail salon and ask for a mani.

"Esi," I respond, trying to measure how mad she still is with me. I sit at the station next to her and she turns her head, almost like she's over me that fast. The nail tech helps me remove my coat and then goes to town on a long-overdue fill-in.

"I thought you usually go to the nail salon by your house," she finally says, watching her tech bedazzle her nails. Esi is getting the works: her long, sculptured nails are decked out in a midnight-blue colour, with bursts of jewels and swirly designs. Just like with her hair, Esi is always one to pop up with the latest nail trends, leaving everyone in our school astonished.

"That's still my favourite spot." The nail tech rolls her eyes at me. Whoops. "But Shida told me you'd be here, so I came. Figured you wouldn't want me stopping by your house."

Esi shrugs. I don't press her any further. I just let my tech continue to buff and massage and pull back my cuticles. But I catch glances at her. She's got her hair in a high ponytail, her long fishtail braid cascading over her shoulder. I chuckle and Esi looks over at me.

"What are you over there giggling about?"

"I'm into this look. Remember when you tried to teach me how to braid?" She rolls her eyes, but her face warms up like she's trying to hold in a laugh.

"Oh god. You were such a lost cause. You complained about your fingers cramping within the first five minutes. Such a drama queen." I smile, and she returns the favour. "I hear a boy whose name shall not be mentioned took your braids out recently. I'm jealous. You used to let me play in your hair and now you found someone new."

I chuckle, relieved. Esi is much warmer to me than I thought she'd be. I was ready to do whatever it took, but even this is more forgiving than I expected. "You know there's no one who could take your place. My hair hasn't been right since you laid hands on it." I attempt to pat my hair, but my nail tech pulls my hand back. She really doesn't like me at this point.

"Yeah, it looks like a deep conditioning could do you some good. Have you been using that hair mask I made for you?"

I laugh. "I ran out and couldn't exactly buy it at the store."

"Well, if you didn't abandon your friends, maybe your hair would be healthier." She purses her lips and I nod my head.

"Dang, that cuts deep. But I deserve it."

Esi gets serious. "Danielle, I know I made it explicitly clear I didn't like that girl. But you choosing to still hang with her didn't change our friendship. Whatever you went through, whatever you're going through – that's an 'us' problem, okay? Not a 'you' problem. Me and Rashida, we always got your back. You hear me?"

I focus on the wall, the pictures of Black women posing in glamour-style shots, holding their hands to their faces and showing the intricate designs on their fingers. I really don't want to be the girl sobbing in the nail salon, but before I know it, a droplet falls, and somehow my nail tech is right there, wiping away my tears with a tissue.

"She's doing those sloppy nails *and* wiping your tears? Someone deserves a big tip," Esi says. A few people next to us laugh.

"Absolutely," I respond, and the tech smiles. She begins to handle my hands with a bit more care, rubbing them with a warm towel and lotion before styling.

"My mom asked about you the other day," Esi says. "Which, she's about a year too late. But you know for her that's a big deal."

I smile.

It is.

"She told me you should come over and she'll make you koko."

Esi's mom isn't much for affection, but she shows all her love through her meals. I'd come over on Saturday mornings and get my hair done, with a bowl of hausa koko waiting for me. And especially in the winter months, it always hit the spot for me. Her invitation is her olive branch, and I'm deeply moved.

"I will," I say. "Just say when."

Now that that's out the way, Esi changes the subject. "I don't know if you know this, but I'm putting together a hair show at the school."

I gasp. "Esi, what? That's amazing!"

"Yeah, I'm tired of everyone appropriating Black hair and nails. Making it seem like they are the inventors of it. When we do our hair up in certain styles it's ghetto, but when White people do it, it's fashionable."

A lady sitting next to us butts in. "You talkin' like Hair Wars?"

Esi smiles. "Yeah. I keep seeing beautiful hairstyles and long acrylic nails popping up on all my Instagram feed, and I'm like, it's time to let everyone know where this came from. Give us our credit."

"That's right!" the woman says, nodding her head with vigour.

"Esi, I am so proud of you!" I pause, my voice cowering a bit. "Can I come?"

She looks at me with that mischievous smile.

Uh-oh.

"On one condition."

"Whaaat?" I draw out, afraid of the answer that comes with it.

She sits up tall, knowing she has me. "You have to be my model."

Oh no. I knew that was coming. So, this is her initiation back to our friendship. I begin to let out a whiny noise and Esi stops me short.

"Danielle, you owe me."

I sit there, pouting. The lady next to us speaks up. "You betta put your behind in that show! You're cute and got all the hair. You'll be the star."

The star. That's the last thing I want to be. Extra visible for everyone to see. I'm trying to dip my toe back into social life and Esi wants to throw me into the deep end.

"I don't really have a choice, do I?" I ask. Esi shakes her head. I give in. "Fiiiine," I sigh, and Esi squeals with excitement.

"I already got your look down. You won't be disappointed."

I huff, my anxiety building just thinking about being on anyone's runway. "And when did you decide my look?" I ask.

"When Rashida called me after your talk to tell me how you're doing and asked on your behalf if you could reach out."

"You're such a scammer," I respond.

Her sinister grin returns. "The one and only."

I get the attention of Esi's nail tech. "Don't you dare let her pay. This is my Christmas gift to her."

"You got it, sugah," she says.

Esi smiles. "Well, if that's the case, put a few more rhinestones on my nails."

Before I head home, I text Prince. It's the weekend before finals and we'll both be busy, so a part of me just wants to see his face.

DANI: Hey, how busy are you rn?

PRINCE: My house is full of people, but it's a good thing, my mom is finally accepting help :-). Some of my mama's church friends came over to cook and help clean the house. And my uncle is over here just to eat lol.

DANI: How sweet! Okay, never mind. I was in the area and wanted to drop something off, but I can do it another time.

I feel like before I could push send he's already responded.

PRINCE: No, please come! I would love to see you. I feel bad. I still owe you a date and haven't had the time.

ME: KK

My third date. The one that would supposedly determine whether I'm in love with him. I'm sort of happy this is taking so long, if I'm being honest, 'cause I'm enjoying my time with him. But love? I'm not quite sure. That word carries so much weight, and it's something I'm not sure I feel just yet. Love is my mom and dad sitting out back in the summertime, my dad grilling, my mom bringing out Grandma's famous iced tea that she learned to make right before my dad's mom died as a way to remember her. Them watching the sunset together, not saying anything. Enjoying each other's company.

Love is the way my dad shows me he cares, the interest he takes in my boring life, even from hundreds of miles away. My mother's patience with my emo ass. The potential they see in me, to get it together, to become a better woman, even if I don't see it.

That type of love takes years of cultivating. Not three dates. But how do I tell Prince that? So, date three can wait. The pressure of this joke becoming a real thing worries me, because what if at the end of it all he starts falling for me and I don't return the feeling? Buying some time until the third date eliminates my fear of breaking his heart while I figure out what this is.

When I get to his crib, I have to park a few houses down. His driveway is full of cars, and so is street parking in front of his home. I text him to let him know I'm outside and walk up to a cracked door.

Prince is waiting on the other side of it, ready to greet me with that cute grin.

"Look who decided to pay me a visit," he leans down and says in my ear, trying to talk over the vacuum that's going.

He gives me an embrace, and I can't tell if it's the chill outside or what, but his body is so warm. I want to snuggle in his chest for eternity, but the church ladies are watching. One even turns off the vacuum, which snaps us back. Prince pulls away sort of abruptly. "Danielle, this is Sister Beatrice," he says, pointing to the burly lady with her hand on her hip, "and Sister Tammy," an older woman with curly salt-and-pepper hair who walks out of the kitchen to greet me, towel in hand.

"Nice to meet you both," I say, with my most innocent voice. Sister Beatrice is already looking at me like I'm a heathen.

"Very nice to meet you," says the sister with the towel in her hand. "You staying for dinner, right? I made more than enough for the family."

"Whoa, whoa, what you doing handing out our food like that?" Jerome's voice booms from the other room. I can tell it's him before he even hits the corner. "Ahh, Dani girl," he says, putting down a box of Christmas decorations. He hugs me affectionately.

"That's messed up, Jerome. I thought we were cool," I say.

"And since when did they make food for *you*?" Prince tells his uncle, chiming in on the fun.

Sister Tammy laughs at us all.

"Prince, don't be stingy," I hear another voice say, as a woman walks out of the kitchen with a cane. Prince's mom. Her skin is fair, her hair cut into a cute, short, finger-wave hairdo. Sometimes I wish I had the face to wear a style that short. Her gait is sort of a sway; her coordination is slightly off-centre when she walks, and she uses the cane to hold her steady. She gives me a look-over before she speaks, in true mom fashion. "It's very nice to meet you. I've heard so many things."

I meet her in the middle and shake her hand, using both my hands to engulf her free one. "It's a pleasure to meet you as well, Ms Jones. I hope you don't mind me coming over during family time. I promise I won't stay long. I just wanted to drop off a few things." I feel like I'm sweating, trying to impress the mother in front of me, who is every bit the woman of the house, demanding respect from anyone who steps foot in her door.

"Call me Lori, sweetheart. More books?" she enquires with an amused look.

I feel flushed. "How did you know?" Mook comes out of nowhere (seriously, lightning speed), and rushes right up to me, almost knocking me down.

"You have books for me!?!" he asks.

"Yes, I do," I say, holding up the small Spider-Man gift bag I brought, "but should you wait to open it until Christmas?"

"Just let him open it. He's gonna bug us every day if we don't," Lori says, already exhausted from the thought.

"*Sorry,*" I mouth to Lori. She nods with a smile. Prince eases up closer, trying to take a peek into the bag. I laugh. "You're worse than he is." He shrugs, owning his brashness.

I sit on the floor and Mook lies flat instead, belly down, feet dangling in the air, waiting for me to take each book out.

I give him the bag instead and he dumps the contents onto the floor. He grabs *Hair Love* first.

"This," I tell Mook, pointing to *Hair Love*, "is a book you should read to your brother."

"The dad has locs, like me!" he says, shaking his locs. We all giggle.

"That's right." I hope Prince doesn't mind that I brought this book, considering their home situation. But showing him a positive male role model could be a good discussion starter for them both. And maybe a way for them to bond and heal.

I pick up *Look Both Ways* next. "And this book is for someone a little older, but your brother can help read it to you," I say, talking to Mook but looking up at Prince. "One of the characters in it has locs, and he's closer to your age."

He gleams. "I can't wait!" he exclaims, and jumps up. "PJ, I want you to read this to me tonight," he declares, handing him the book.

"You got it, lil man," Prince says, looking down on us.

Mook passes me *Hair Love*. "And Danielle, I want you to read this to me now. Since it's a girly book."

"Oh, hecks nah!" his mom blurts out.

"Now why you showing out in front of company!" Prince proclaims, firm yet kind. "You know we taught you better than that."

"Whaaaat?" Mook whines.

"I'm going to do you one better," I say, taking my phone and earbuds out my bag and opening my audiobook app. I pull up

Hair Love and place my earbuds in Mook's ears. "You know who read this book?"

"Who?" he asks.

"A fierce girl who recorded this audiobook around your age. Blue Ivy. You know who that is?" His face scrunches up, similar to his brother's face when he was trying to figure out where he saw Kadir Nelson's art. I finally relent. "It's Beyoncé's daughter."

"Oh! She's cute!" he responds, cheesing hard. Which causes everyone to laugh. Prince folds his arms and rubs his head.

"Where does he get this from?" he says.

His mom clears her throat. "I wonder."

"Well, this boy is sitting in the middle of the floor and I am trying to vacuum," Sister Beatrice exclaims.

"Oh!" we both say. Prince yanks Mook up off the floor with ease, causing him to laugh, and sets him on the couch, placing the book in his lap.

"Can you hear it?" I ask. Mook nods quickly, but he's already into the story and we've lost him. Prince gives Sister Beatrice a squeeze on the shoulder and apologizes, and she smiles.

"Have you eaten lunch?" Prince asks, and I shake my head. "It's a bit loud in here. Let's go to the Coney Island around the corner and grab some." I nod. "We'll be back," he yells out. And before anyone can object, he throws his coat on and we close the front door.

* * *

"How much do I owe you?" I ask as Prince sits down with a tray full of food.

"I don't want to hear it today, Danielle. This meal is only like ten dollars, and most of the stuff on this tray is for me anyway." I inspect our order. Two hot dogs – one Coney Island dog and one regular with onions and mustard – a large order of chilli cheese fries and two Faygo pops. I prefer to take some of the chilli from the fries for my dog, but Prince is definitely a "more is more" kinda guy. He has it on *everything*.

"You get enough chilli?" I ask.

"I could get more, but I don't wanna turn you off." He takes a big bite out of his hot dog.

"Too late," I tease. His mouth bunches up as he attempts to keep from laughing with a mouth full of food.

"This is a thank-you. You brought over books, I treat you to lunch. Plus, you already tryna up my brother's reading level, bringing over chapter books."

"*Look Both Ways* is for ages nine and up!" I say. "Plus, I brought that one 'cause it talks about kids dealing with parents who have cancer. I thought it might be a helpful discussion for you both to have on parents with health problems."

Prince stops chewing. "That's…super thoughtful. Thank you."

He continues to stare at me, so I nod and change the subject. "I don't think Sister Beatrice liked me much."

"Don't sweat it. She mad 'cause she's been tryna set me up with her daughter for years. She ain't even close to my type."

I was curious. "Why isn't she your type?"

"She thinks this DJ thing is a silly dream."

"She told you that?" I ask in shock.

"Practically. Sister Beatrice *conveniently* left her phone at her house once and used my phone to call her daughter so that she could come and drop it off."

I'm cracking up. "So cunning."

"For real," Prince says. "So her daughter took it upon herself to text me later. We chatted on and off for a few weeks. But I just felt like she kept judging everything I said. And when she told me she thinks I should consider a more lucrative career…well…" He shrugs, taking another bite of his Coney dog.

Before I can respond, a few girls from Mass Tech walk in and immediately spot me and Prince. *Crap.*

"Hi, DJ LoveJonessss!" they all say in unison. With a mouth full of food, he gives them a closed-mouth smile and waves. Then he's tuned right back into our conversation. They sit in booths across from us and I can feel their stares from behind, like Cyclops from *X-Men* shooting red beams.

"So I've been meaning to ask you, DJ LoveJonessss," I tease, mimicking the girls. He shakes his head. "Why a DJ? Why music? I mean, I know you love it – but what do you love about it?"

Prince puts his Coney dog back on his Styrofoam.

"I just think of the influence music has. Whether it was watching my uncle spinning while I was growing up, or me and Uncle Romes listening to Questlove or D-Nice on

Instagram. Swizz Beatz and Timbaland brought all these artists together with Verzuz, and that was like culturally so important. I remember the ways music took my mom away from the moment while she was coming to terms with her diagnosis, how me and her were singing songs that I didn't even know I knew. Like, no lie, I could sing every verse to the song but at the time probably couldn't name the artist if my life depended on it. It all just shows the power of music. It's a testament that music saves. It's more than just a tune, a song – music takes you back to a time and place that's happier, that's somber, that's a relief…you listen to a song and it brings about a memory. And then you have emcees now like DJ Khaled, Va$htie and Amorphous, taking this deejaying thing into filmmaking, producing and all that. To me there's no other job more powerful than that."

I don't know what to say, so I stare at Prince, blinking. He laughs.

"Did I break you?"

"No," I manage. "I am just…blown away. By that answer. Your passion, it all makes sense now."

"I eat, sleep and breathe this shit, Danielle, just like you with writing. How is that going, BTW?" he asks, scarfing down the rest of his Coney dog.

"I have another confession," I admit. He raises his eyebrow, unable to say anything with a mouth full of food again. "I've been wearing the fedora before I start writing, and for some reason it's been helping and I'm almost finished." Prince almost chokes on his food.

"Anything to get those creative juices flowing," he responds, still laughing. "I'm glad."

"So…if you could have a dream job, what would it be? How would it look?"

"The radio station is giving me some pretty decent exposure right now, and it seems like if things continue to go well—"

"No," I cut him off. "I know big dreams, and yours are bigger than that. Stretch yourself, Prince. No limitations, what would it be?"

He sighs. "I mean, my dream job is to be someone like Sway, who has a show on XM radio and interviews hip-hop legends. Except I'd also offer up love advice, bring couples on my show, have them get real with viewers about their relationship ups and down. Make it honest and relatable. All these reality shows portray Black love full of drama and stuff, but I hate the way they flip it. Nothing about love is easy, but the drama is hyped up for ratings. What if guests could talk about overcoming infidelity or dealing with jealousy or the frustrations of losing their spark after kids in a way that makes them feel safe?"

"That's amazing, Prince," I respond, coming to a realization. "Wait…does that mean you want to move to New York?!"

Prince's dimple pops up as he blushes. You can see the sparkle in his eyes just thinking about it. "I've thought about it once or twice."

I huff. "Prince Jones. Don't do that."

"What?" he coos melodramatically with his palms in the air.

"Like we haven't just opened up to each other over the past

few weeks! Like we aren't acting like this is something more…"
I clasp my lips together as soon as I say it, surprised at myself.
Prince breaks out in a huge grin, leaning back in his chair.

"Like love…?" he asks, staring at me intently.

"No, I didn't say all that," I reply, picking at my chilli
cheese fries with my fork. I roll my eyes to try to break up the
tension, but I feel the nervous energy between us. Which
makes me want to open up a tad more. "But maybe a strong
like. You just…you just seem to have a lot of female admirers
and I don't know…how am I supposed to know when you're
serious, anyway?"

"Danielle, you already know the answer to that. Those
girls," he says, looking in the direction of his fandom, "the girl
at the rink, all of them don't matter. I know I made a joke of all
this, but getting to know you makes all this feel more…real.
I'm starting to think maybe I do want more." My heart is racing
and we're now in the dead of winter, yet my face has never felt
more flushed. For some strange reason, I believe him.

"Prince, I'm still not in love with you yet." I hesitate before
I let the words come out of my mouth. "I just…like what this
is so far."

He leans back, beaming way too hard. "Yet," is all he says,
grabbing a fry and placing it in his mouth.

We go back to an emptier house, his mother and uncle
sitting on the couch, playing Uno with Mook, who's leaning
against the coffee table, fixated on his hand.

"PJ, come help me! They won't let me win!" Mook whines.

"You gotta take what you want," Prince says, removing my coat. We both sit on the floor next to him.

"Un—!!!" Mook attempts to say, about to slam his card down with such force that you can tell he's watched his uncle and brother do this one too many times. I stifle a laugh.

"Nah, nah, not yet, Mook. What colour is that?" Prince says.

"Green."

"And what colour is this?"

"Blue," Mook replies. "But it's six! So I get to say it!"

Prince smiles sweetly. "No, it's a nine. See that little line at the bottom?"

"Ooh," Mook says, then huffs in defeat.

Prince points to a card. "It's okay, you can still get 'em. Put that one down."

Mook looks at Prince and his eyes glimmer with hope. He pulls the card out his hand with a sly look on his face. "DRAW TWO!" he yells at the top of his lungs.

"Oh *hell* nah!" Uncle Jerome proclaims. "I got something for you." He goes to drop down a draw four.

"Draw four! And Uno out!" he proclaims, throwing his card on the table and standing up, victorious.

"No, Jerome, you cheating!" Lori declares. "You can't stack draw two and draw four."

Jerome gives Lori a look of defiance. "Says who?" he utters.

"Uno, bruh!" Prince says, grinning.

"Damn all that! I don't care what Uno says. I been playing this game since before you all were even born," he broadcasts, pointing at us. "I win!"

We are all dying laughing, watching Jerome and Lori get into a yelling match, battling it out like true siblings.

The conversation evolves from Uno to other things, and eventually we all settle down, watching a holiday movie playing on the TV in the background. When Prince puts his arm around me, his mom glances over at us. "The sisters made enough for an extra mouth. Would you like to stay for dinner?"

"I gotta text my parents to make sure it's okay, but I'd love that," I respond, thinking about how thrilled my parents are going to be.

"Go ahead and do what you gotta do, baby. Jerome, bring yo crazy behind in this kitchen and help me set the table." Lori gets up and Jerome is trailing behind her, both of them making their way into the kitchen. I hear low voices on the other side of the wall.

While I'm helping Mook put the stack of cards back in the box, Prince's eyes are focused in the direction of the kitchen. He finally smiles. "She likes you," he whispers in my ear. "I just heard her tell my uncle."

"How?"

"I'm a DJ," he says. "We hear everything."

* * *

After dinner, I help clean up the kitchen with Prince. We're side by side at the sink, him soaping up the dishes with his sponge, while I rinse the dishes in warm water and wipe them off with a towel.

"I really need to remind Unc to help me fix this dishwasher," he notes, shaking his head.

I laugh. "You're such an adult," I say.

"Sometimes it feels like I have no choice but to be. My mom taught me how to do chores growing up, since there was so much she couldn't do. And I'm teaching Mook now how to do the same." His eyes are sincere, almost tired. But filled with compassion. That's why his mama is so protective. I would be too, if this sweet teenage boy was my son. Prince just steps in to do everything for his mom, without complaint. I already want to protect him and he's not even my boyfriend. *Don't change. Wait, what am I saying?* But speaking of relationships... I need to pry about something I've been avoiding.

"Can I ask you something?" I probe, taking another dish from his hand. He nods. "Why did you and your ex break up? What happened?"

He pauses. "Morgan was a year older than me. We initially talked about us both going to a local college and working things out. But before she moved into her dorm, I guess she had a change of heart and broke up with me."

"How long did you two date for?" I enquire, chewing on this information.

"Pretty much all of junior year. I took her to her senior prom and everything." I'm floored. And here I thought I was the special one. Is he a serial dater? And since Morgan was the one who broke up with him, are there still lingering feelings? Is she the one that got away?

"Aren't you worried you're jumping in too soon? With me?"

"I thought about that. This…us…being a distraction. I was reading up on this study in this psychology journal that said distractions make you feel good overall, but don't actually help you get over someone. But I *feel* over her. So I sorta conducted an experiment on myself."

Only Prince.

"And what did you find, love doctorrr?" I say, mocking him.

He chuckles. "One of the prompts was to negatively evaluate your ex. So I made a list, and the shit just would *never* end." I shake my head and flick a little bit of dishwater at him. He laughs. "But seriously, it said doing this would suck for the moment, but ultimately lessen the blow. And that's when I realized, I liked her when I first met her. But too much time had passed and too many things had happened. It just wasn't the same and the feelings are… gone."

I smile, setting a plate on the dish rack. "You're reading, huh?"

"Yeah," he responds. "You were right. There's something to this psychology thing."

I mull over his initial goal to go to school in-state, and while I feel like it's a cop-out to living out his dreams, spending time with him and his family today helps me understand why. It's just…the thought of him and Morgan being in the same state without me is enough to make me feel a jealous knot tightening in my chest, even after Prince explained why they're done. As we're washing, the music in the living room grows louder and louder, peppered with Mook's giggles and cheers. We finally finish up our chores and look out to see Mook controlling the volume on the Bluetooth speaker, watching his mom and uncle ballroom dancing. Prince creeps up behind me and whispers in my ear. Which causes a slight chill to tickle my insides.

"It's been a while since they've done this. They used to go ballroom dancing all the time back in the day."

I watch them take it easy, Lori's left hand on Jerome's side. Them stepping two up, then two back, getting the cadence right. Jerome is taking the lead and places his hand on her left shoulder, directing her movements so she knows where she wants to go next. But you can see her gripping his hand tight.

"Go, Mama!" Mook says, jumping up and down on the couch now. You can tell Lori is getting exhausted but pushing through. Her face lights up with each step, moving and flowing with the music. She's a natural. A few songs later, she finally gives in. A little out of breath.

"Jerome, you'll have me dancing all night, but I gotta sit down." She pauses. "I've missed this." Jerome sweetly pats his sister's hand and leads her to the couch. The music is still going.

He also looks a little sad it's over. But then Lori looks at me. "That's my physical therapy for the day, but you know how to do this, right, Danielle?"

"Of course!" I blurt out, shocked at my own confidence. Anything to impress Prince's mom, I guess.

"Well, come on, then!" Jerome exclaims. "Bring that nephew of mines over too so you can teach him." I look up at Prince and he looks…nervous?

"Do you not know how?"

"I…I'm just a little rusty."

I huff at him. "You're no fun." Then, feeling a bit more spirited, I walk over to Jerome and put my hand out. I then look back at Prince. "Let's show the prince of radio how it's done."

"I like her. She's feisty!" his mom says, laughing.

Prince's eyes go low, like he's trying to pierce right through me. He's annoyed, I think? Even that is cute. He pulls out his phone and changes the tune. Something more upbeat.

"Really? Beyoncé?" I look back at him. Don't get me wrong, I love the queen. But I was expecting something with a little less…pep.

"You're the one that brought up Blue Ivy earlier, so 'Love on Top' is fitting. See if you can keep up," Prince directs at me, a mischievous smile forming. So, there it is. Mr I'm So Good at Everything doesn't like to…not be good at everything. How childish.

I connect my right hand with Jerome, and we get right to it. We quickly get into the flow, the right foot being driven forward, me shifting my weight, us doing a half turn, then stepping right. "And finally you put me first!" Jerome is singing off-key while dancing. I laugh and lose my step. "Come on, babygirl!" he says.

"Leave the singing to Bey," I remark, stepping back into it. One, two, three…and our weight shifts. One, two, three… and then we step again. "Baby, you're the one that I need…" Beyoncé belts out, and we continue dancing to the pattern of the tune. Finally the song fades, and Jerome finishes with a side dip, me leaning on him, hip to hip. Everyone gives us a round of applause. Jerome bows and I curtsy.

"Wow, I haven't done that in a long time," I say, breathless. "My mom used to ballroom dance for fun and take me with her, and then we'd come home and she'd teach me the steps."

"Did your dad ever go?" Jerome asks.

"Nah, he was never a good dancer. It was something she did to entertain herself while he was away. I would just tag along and sit on the floor, watching her. It was just as much fun for me as it was for her."

Lori smiles. "You two are close?"

I nod my head. "Very," I say.

"Well, tell your mama if she wants a dance partner, I got her," Jerome responds, popping his jacket collar.

Everyone in the room but Mook shakes our heads in disapproval. "Unc, her dad is in the military. Try him if you want to…"

I lift one eyebrow, as a warning.

"Okay, I'm kidding, kidding. Damn, these babies so sensitive now," Jerome says.

Later on that night, while getting ready for bed, I come back to my room to find a text waiting from Prince. This time, it's nothing but a link. I open it.

Love Notes Mixtape: Volume 2. In it are the best songs to ballroom dance to. I text him back.

DANI: Are you gonna let me teach you one day?

PRINCE: After you tell me you love me.

I shake my head, this time not so put off by his statement, put my earbuds in, and let the music take me.

Dear bell,

I'm normally a fiction and memoir reader, letting an author's imaginary or real-life struggles consume me. There's imagery, there's symbolism, there's all the things that high-school students run away from in English class but are the very things I adore.

Maybe part of it is I haven't "lived long enough," as my great-aunt would say, and maybe there's some truth to that. Because here I am, taking the very advice I gave Prince and applying it to myself – reading a book about love.

Not just any book, though – yours. And it's changed me already.

I picked All About Love expecting to read a "self-help" book on how to be a feminist and fall in love, how to maintain my womanist ideas while committing to another person. What I got was a book that takes me on a journey of self-love. How self-love cannot flourish in isolation and how I must give myself the love I dream of receiving. That in healing from whatever hurt I experienced, whatever has caused me to retreat, nothing will change unless I commit to the change. It's becoming clear Prince is wanting me to like him more and more, but you've taught me there is no loving him without loving me. And there's no loving me without shutting down the negative voices in my head and replacing them with positive affirmation. So, beginning today, I affirm myself by saying I am love; and regardless of what happens with Prince, with any more of my friends, I know that I am deserving of it and that true love will find me, because I am finding it within myself.

Chapter Twelve

Right on Cue

Danielle

"I'm weeeeak," I utter, still trying to recover from laughing.

Rashida, Esi, and I agreed we'd hang after we turned in our applications, using the rest of Christmas break to finish them so that we could use our new-found freedom the beginning of second semester to brainstorm Esi's hair show in April. With my future looming, hanging with friends is a nice distraction.

I decided to write about my experience with Destiny and how much I've grown from it, even with me going back and forth about whether it was too personal to share with a college admissions committee. Did I want to admit to a group of strangers what happened to me? I've read enough about racism in college admissions to know they could very well judge me because I'm a Black girl. Did I want to face that type of bias?

But no matter how many essays I tried to write, how many

other iterations I came up with, I kept getting stuck. Until I devoured bell hooks and realized so much of this book was steeped in her being honest with herself, no matter how difficult it may have been for the reader to witness it on the page. She inspired me to allow whatever was in my heart to spill onto the screen, and once I bared my soul, I knew it was the incident that brought me the most growth, for better or for worse, and the life experience that needed to be told. I no longer cared if the committee looked down on my revelations. I was proud of me for finally starting to become the writer I always wanted to be. One who puts a little bit of herself in everything she does.

But I didn't show the essay to anyone. I kept it close.

"A silky hair sheet? They weren't even creative with coming up with a new name." I take another look at the screenshot on Esi's phone before passing it back to her. She's sitting on the bed with me, and Rashida is leaning back in my desk chair, her feet propped up on the bed.

Rashida is wiping tears from her eyes from cracking up. "I can't believe the new trend is durags disguised as a silky hair sheet. All this appropriation has got to stop."

"Right?" I say. "How is it even beneficial for them to wear? They not getting waves or laying their edges down using this."

"This is exactly why I'm doing this show," Esi declares. "Hair, nails, clothes…all these things that are staples for us are suddenly in style." She rolls her eyes. "But we've been doing this for years. They take the same thing we're doing, throw a new name on it, and call it a new 'trend,'" she says, using air quotes. "You know the other day I saw they're calling Bantu knots twisty knots? Like what the hell?"

Rashida gets up and combs through my bookshelf. "I love the industrial pipes for your bookshelf, Dani. Your parents really did their thing with your room." I look at the muted lavender walls filled with a few vintage photos I could find of my favourite literary heroes from scouring the internet.

"Thanks," I say proudly. "I love it in here…a little too much." I mumble the last part.

"What's that mean?" Rashida asks.

I sigh. "My mom helped me decorate this room right after everything. And I *do* think she did it to help get me out of my funk. But also…sometimes I feel like my mom gave me the perfect room so I wouldn't go away for school."

"Ahh," they both say in unison.

"Parents are weird," Esi says. "My parents could care less how far I go to school, but they don't understand my dreams to start a hair-care line and build the next Riri empire."

"I don't mind being local," Rashida chimes in. "I'll just come to NYC and visit you both when my family gets on my nerves." I look at Esi. Before I became a hermit, me and her decided we'd apply to the same schools and I stuck to the plan, secretly hoping we'd be in the same dorm or run into each other at a party and reconnect, my mind better after getting away from home for a bit. It was nice to know after we reconnected that she still had dreams to move to the city too.

"If I get in," Esi mumbles, which surprises me. She never gets frazzled.

"You'll get in, Esi," I declare. Then I shift the focus, knowing what she's feeling all too well, the applications too fresh. I snap us both out of it. "I wish I was like you, Shida. Are you going to live in a dorm?"

She shrugs. "Depends on where I go and what kinda scholarship I can get. If it's State, I'll probably stay home, but if Western gives me a minority scholarship...I'm out!"

We both laugh. "Oh, so you *are* trying to get away a little bit," Esi chimes in.

"Heck yeah! I just want to be able to get home quickly if I'm homesick. I love being around my little siblings, even if they can get annoying sometimes." We all sit in silence for a second, thinking about the gravity of the decisions we're forced to make and the anxiety of waiting for our dream colleges to determine the next four years of our lives. How we're trying to find our own happiness, even with our parents' expectations of what we should be doing.

To bring the mood back up, Rashida plugs her phone into my speakers and turns on the local station. "It's DJ LoveJones hour," she sings, and I laugh.

We listen to his love advice for the next hour and it's actually...good. This is the first time I've really listened to his show since he came to my house, and he's so in tune with each caller and their issues, and even when one male caller gets ignorant, he stays neutral, while still managing to check him. I hope he really considers this double-major thing. We bop to the music he's playing.

"He's not a bad DJ," Esi says. She hesitates before asking,

"You think he would emcee for the show?"

"I think he would *love* it," I say, remembering his set at the skating rink and his natural connection to the crowd. "I just got to make sure his schedule is free. He was pretty busy over the winter break."

I sulk a little, and Esi laughs. "Someone is in deep."

"I am *not*," I bark. "I don't know him yet."

Rashida and Esi look at each other and roll their eyes in unison.

"What?" I say, chuckling a little. "I worry he doesn't have enough drive. He's planning on staying local too, but it's different than Rashida. He *wants* to go to NYC and intern at a few stations and streaming companies, but his family obligations won't let him. I just don't want to date someone who is…settling. And the last thing I need is another person to convince me to stay here when I don't want to. I can't let anything or anyone get in the way of my dreams of going to NYC."

"That's tough." Rashida ponders. "Some people take a little longer, Dani…and some people need a push."

It's my turn to roll my eyes. "I am *not* trying to motivate anyone, especially a man."

"Maybe he's just scared to make the leap. Fear is a real thing. I don't think your job is to motivate him," Rashida clarifies. "But maybe your presence is enough to make him dream bigger."

"Speaking of presence, when's the next date?" Esi asks.

I huff. "He's been too busy to plan anything."

Esi and Rashida look at one another…again.

"What?" I ask.

"Our little diva," Esi says, chuckling.

I pull a pillow close to my chest. "Screw y'all."

"Dani, just plan the date," Rashida says.

"Yeah," Esi butts in without looking up from her iPad, sketching up ideas for the show.

"I just…I just don't know what to plan. I barely go out anymore, so trying to plan any sort of outing just gives me anxiety." Esi glances up at me from her iPad, the white screen illuminating her face.

"What about your godfather or whatever he is, the guy who does programming at the Motown Museum?"

I feel such a sense of gratitude for these girls. "E, you're a genius!" I yelp, giving her a big wet kiss on her cheek. She's so caught by surprise her iPad slips out of her hand.

"I need to start charging for my ideas," she says.

We hit the end of January, and it seems Prince is juggling more than I could ever envision having to do. He's helping his mom with her physical therapy in between his on-air time and making up for the lost time with his boys. As someone who's also been avoiding her own friends, I can sympathize with him wanting to do right by his close circle, something I can learn a thing or two about. So while we sneak times to see each other in between classes or at the computer lab, it's nearly impossible to get a time that works for us both.

I miss him. I'm feeling more creative than ever, and even got back into writing short stories. Once I began healing old wounds, it gave me space to be inspired again. But there's still one thing nagging me: whether my desire to get into NYU is a pipe dream. February is a reminder of how I botched my own application for early decision. If I had just gotten out of my head and turned the application in on time, I would have known in a few weeks instead of a few months. I'm still beating myself up for that.

If there's any good out of all this, though, it's that a decision like college feels so big that deciding if I love Prince after date three doesn't feel *as* scary.

I decide it's time to find out.

Prince is always one step ahead of me with the dates, so I have to think long and hard about how I'm going to top what he's done. And I do. I have my dad make a call to set up a tour after hours on a Saturday – on Valentine's Day, the weekend my parents will be out of town for their anniversary. A Valentine's Day wedding? Cheesy, I know. But it's what my mom wanted and it's what my dad acquiesced to.

Then there's the invitation. I can't just text him, so my mom and I search eBay to find the perfect gift: a vintage radio with a secret compartment. My mom reached out to the same person who restored my typewriter. As she's packing for her anniversary trip, she says what I've known was coming.

"I knew you'd find your love story someday. Enjoy it, baby." I don't argue with her. Love isn't perfect and Prince is far from it, but if this is what love is supposed to feel like, then *maybe* I am becoming more and more okay with the idea.

When I told Prince I'd be planning the date, his responses were extra, but clearly he was happy I was the one taking the initiative.

PRINCE: Oh, the wooer is getting wooed. Look like someone is starting to feel ya boy.

DANI: Okay, you're making me rethink this.

PRINCE: I joke ☺ I would love to have you plan something. I'm actually not used to this…not being in control. I'm pretty excited.

DANI: You should be because remember I'm competitive. I'm about to outdo you.

PRINCE: Ok calm down, Danielle. I'm the love expert here. That's not possible.

DANI: According to who?

PRINCE: Now you got jokes.

So yeah, he knows something is coming, but I won't tell him what until the night before our date, after he comes home from the station. I wait until he's home and leave the gift by his front door. I barely make it to my driveway when I get a FaceTime call from Prince, seeing nothing but teeth show up on my screen from his wide grin.

"So, you just come over, drop gifts off, and don't even say hello?"

It's my turn to smile. "I sent you a text to check your porch."

"Danielle, this is dope," he says, admiring the sophisticated detail of the wood and dial keys. I hear Mook in the background.

"Ooh, let me see!" he says, and Prince gives him the device. He holds it with a look of confusion. "What's this?"

"It's a radio," Prince says. Mook smacks his lips.

"No, it's not. A radio is the thing in the car and on your phone." Me and Prince burst out laughing.

"I think we're showing our age," I say. Prince huffs.

"Speak for yourself. You have the birthday coming up, not me."

I decide right then I'm going to have Mook help with the surprise. "Mook, do me a favour. There's a secret compartment, and I need you to be a detective and find it."

Mook's eyes get so big, they practically take over his entire head. "Okay!" he screeches, and sits on the floor, attempting to pull apart everything. Prince freaks out.

"Yo, Mook. Chiiiill, you're gonna break it!"

"Have him look at the side," I quickly chime in. "There should be something special there." On the side is a clasp, and when Mook clicks it, the back of the radio pops open, and a piece of paper falls out. Mook hands it to Prince, and he realizes it's not a note, but a pamphlet.

Those heart-melting dimples show up on his face. "The Motown Museum. That's where you're taking me?"

"Can I go?" Mook asks, and I feel so bad.

"Not this time. Me and Danielle are going on a special date. We might kiss."

Mook's face quickly grows disgusted. "Yuck! I'll see you later," he says, and walks out the room. I can't stop laughing.

"You scarred your brother for life," I say.

"I had to think fast, but he'll be all right," Prince replies, plopping down on his couch and looking at the programme. "I haven't been since I was little, which is actually pretty sad, right?"

"I'll do you one better," I say, finally getting out the car and walking to my front door. "I've never been."

"Ah, hell nah!" Prince chants. "Are you even from the D?"

I giggle. "Apparently not. Anyway, I'll pick you up at six thirty."

"But I thought the museum closes at six."

"It does."

Prince pulls his face back from the screen, surprised. "Let me find out Danielle Ford got the *plug*!" I shake my head. "Okay. Six thirty. Can't wait to see what you have planned in that brilliant head of yours."

Brilliant head of mines. The best compliment he's given me yet.

Chapter Thirteen

Love Is on the Air

PRINCE

"2648 West Grand Boulevard, where the magic happens," I say as we pull up to the museum.

"Okay, Berry Gordy," Danielle giggles, and I suck my teeth.

"You just wait. If you got us a private tour or something, I know this is about to be life-changing."

She smiles. "You're about to meet my dad's good friend Mr Harry, who is a beast in this space. Mr Harry's dad worked at Motown Records, and he's dedicated all his free time to learning about the history of Motown and the radio."

"Damn, how dope is that?" I say, looking over at the two-storey home standing upright.

"You ready?" Dani asks.

We walk up to the famous blue-and-white house covered in snow, with the HITSVILLE U.S.A. sign bold and flashy for everyone to take notice. It's crazy that so much of the music my parents and grandparents and great-grandparents listened to was created and produced behind this small, seemingly normal Detroit two-storey flat. I've always been inspired by the legacy of Motown and how you can make history out of humble beginnings. The building standing before us is living proof.

"Prince," Danielle calls. I look over at her. "Can you believe Berry bought seven houses on this block? It's all so fascinating, right? Just thinking about everything that happened here before we were even thought of."

I nod. "I feel like we're walking into a time machine. I've never been more excited to go to a museum in my life."

She grabs my hand. "Come on."

Danielle escorts us next door to the brick home attached to the Hitsville U.S.A. building, which is also part of the museum, and opens the entrance door as we step inside of history. The inside is pretty small, so as soon as we walk in, a somewhat short and stocky light-skinned gentleman greets us, anticipating our arrival.

"Danielle!" he exclaims, rushing to her. "It's been so long."

"I know. Things have just been so busy. Uncle Harry, this is Prince, the boy my dad told you about," she says, changing the subject. *She's really closed herself off from everyone.* "Prince, meet my godfather."

"Mr Harry, is it? It really is a pleasure," I say, shaking her godfather's hand zealously. I'm both nervous and excited and probably looking crazy right now.

"Prince, huh? If she named you after Mr Purple Rain himself, I like your mom's style."

I smirk. The number of times I've woken up to that album playing in my household. "She did. She's obsessed with the singer."

"Well, it's nice to meet you, Prince. Danielle's father has spoken well about you, even said he listened to a few of your shows and feels like you have some skills." *Oh no.* I give Danielle a look of horror. I know I don't say anything too crazy on the show, but it's one thing to know strangers or your homies are listening in. It's another to know the father of the girl you're trying to/maybe/one day make your boo is scrutinizing me, wondering if I'm taking my own advice and run game on his daughter. Mr Harry chuckles. "Don't worry, he's a no-nonsense man, so if he didn't think you had potential, he wouldn't have said it. I think he senses something in you. And please, call me Harry." He winks.

"Well, thanks again, Harry, and I'm…just happy Mr Ford trusts me," I reply, not really knowing what to say about that. I turn the attention back to why we're here. "I want to know everything there is to know about Motown. I'm a sponge."

"Be careful what you ask for. I'm known to be a bit…long-winded. But growing up here and watching my dad work in this very building has seriously been the best experience of my life."

He leads us right to the control room, which overlooks the infamous studio, the blue-and-white MOTOWN STUDIO A sign hung straight ahead a focal point of the adjoining room. The control room looks like it hasn't been changed one bit – the walls are top-to-bottom covered in wood panelling, and a green chalkboard is hung up on the other side, where I imagine they'd write down session schedules or some other cool shit like that, pre-internet. "When Berry Gordy bought this building in 1959, everything was done in-house. He even lived upstairs."

I look at the ground. "What happened here?" I ask.

"Oh, the recording engineers would tap their feet so much to the songs that they wore out the floor." I chuckle. Sick.

After observing the analogue recording tape strategically placed in back of where the soundman must have sat – the same master tapes that so many artists fight to have control of – I finally eye the second most beautiful thing in the room after Dani: the mixing desk. "I can't believe Berry Gordy and Smokey Robinson used to sit…right here." I don't move, taking in the gravity of what I just said out loud. "Absolute legends."

Harry smiles. "It's good to know it's not completely lost on your generation. So much of sound today was inspired by what was done in this studio. There were a lot of folks who tried, but few were able to recreate that iconic Motown sound."

"Why do you think that is?" Danielle asks.

"That's a good question, Danielle. What many didn't realize, even Berry himself until years later, was that the echo chamber was the bathroom upstairs. Berry hated it, but meanwhile all of these White producers were trying to imitate every instrument, every cadence, but couldn't figure out that 'thing' that set Motown records apart."

I smile. "The beauty in the flaws." I stare at the mixing console with my arms crossed, because I want to touch the keys so damn bad. Instead, I imagine what the audio engineer would be doing right now if they were in here: adjusting the sound, making sure the mics and levels were strategically placed and just right, starting and stopping the greatest singers of our time if something didn't sound just right. To be able to be in this little room and experience a live concert day after day and that's your entire life? Probably the closest thing to heaven on earth. I look through the control-room glass at the live room.

"You ready to go into the snake pit?" Harry asks.

Danielle and I laugh. "That's what it's called?" she asks.

He nods. "Follow me." We step through the glass door in the control room and down the steps to the space where legends were made.

The live room has the same wooden panelling around the walls as the control room but is also padded with acoustic dampers to soundproof it, to isolate the sound and keep outside noise from seeping in. The equipment includes the money piece in the middle of the floor – a classic grand piano, and an organ nestled in a corner behind it. Vintage microphones are lined up at the far end of the wall, and a grey-and-red-striped drum screen is tucked in the back of a drum set.

"The recording sessions back in the day would be the thing to do. People would come to Detroit, step off a plane or train, and come straight here because they knew at any given time someone was here, recording the next hit for the airwaves."

"I bet," I say, walking around the room and soaking in every accessory, every piece, every aspect of this iconic studio.

Danielle goes to the piano and admires the music sheet. She somehow always gravitates toward anything with words. "Have you ever read about some of the great songwriters, Danielle?" I ask, and she shakes her head.

"No, but these lyrics read so much like poetry."

Harry looks over Danielle's shoulder. "You know, someone once called Smokey Robinson 'America's greatest living poet.' I couldn't agree more."

"And he was taught by Berry," I chime in. "They used to have competitions, right?"

"Oh, all the time," Harry replies. "Berry Gordy sort of made that the record label's culture. Friendly competition. Writers were always trying to make a better version of the songs. Hell, even Smokey was competing against his *own* work. He wrote 'My Guy' by the Supremes, which was a smash hit, and then turned around and co-wrote 'My Girl' by the Temptations later on that year. And he said he wanted to write his own response to 'My Guy.'"

"Wow, it's like a sequel in song form," she says.

"Yeah," Harry continues, "and they'd also write a song, have artists sing it, and then go back into the studio to have another act perfect it."

Dani's all ears. "Like who?"

"So many, but what's a good one?" He rubs his chin, thinking. "Ahh, 'I Heard It Through the Grapevine.' It was recorded by three different artists."

"Three artists!" Danielle and I say in unison.

"Yeah, who do you know who sang it?" Harry asks. Danielle shrugs, but I know.

"Marvin Gaye," I reply, thinking about one of my TikTok mixing sessions where I showed the samples for this track.

"It was also sung by Gladys Knight and the Pips *and* the Miracles."

"Damn, Motown was the true inventor of the remix, huh?" I reply, and Harry and Dani chuckle.

"Apparently," he says.

"It makes deejaying easier for me. I could just mix the best parts of those songs together if I were emceeing for a cookout or something."

"So you like deejaying, huh? Why?"

"I just love music. I love where it takes me, and where it takes everyone. You can tell when you've touched someone just by the song you play. I like having the control of playing a certain artist and watching a person's emotional response to it."

"Yeah, Berry used to say you gotta get them in the first ten seconds."

"I agree," I reply. "Same with deejaying. You can't save all your heat for the end or you won't have people stick around long enough. So you have to *know* your music and hook people in the first few songs. You have to study music and always have a collection of songs in your head that you can pull out your back pocket at any given moment."

Harry nods. "You know, it's all connected. If it wasn't for radio, we wouldn't even be here – radio was one of the first things that showed Black folks' influence. It showed we were an audience that listened to the media and enjoyed it. At first, radio was mostly live music and theatre, then radio drama was created, and our folks loved it so much that by the 1940s, Black programming on the radio really began to thrive."

"Really?" I say.

"Yep. The late fifties were when we started to call radio talent 'announcers' and then 'disc jockeys.' And those became the local celebrities. Then from there, you started to see the need for DJs who played different tunes. So, for example, this cat by the name of Jack L. Cooper was one of the original personalities until Al Benson came along. Jack played more jazz, and Benson wanted to play more blues. Benson saw a need and filled it. Which I think is what makes a real DJ, finding out what niche needs to be served. 'Cause Black people are multifaceted. We want music that gives us different things.

"The real DJs at radio stations across the country would play a record they loved simply because they believed in it, and that's how Motown grew. If Berry was the chef, the DJs were serving the food on a gold-plated platter."

"Yeah, but that goes back to the geniuses who came up with this," I contend. "Motown had hit after hit after hit. And it was because they had a real pulse on what the people wanted and needed, they found raw talent, they kept true to the culture, and they mentored and trained talent that otherwise wouldn't have had an opportunity like this. People were skipping their high-school classes to come and learn under the songwriters here." I come out of my trance and catch Danielle and Harry just looking at me.

"Well, someone knows more than they let on," Danielle says. "I think he's trying to take your job, Uncle Harry."

I blush. "I'm sorry, I just…"

Harry waves his hands in the air. "Please. I love it. A *real* DJ. You honour the past, celebrate the present, and embrace the future, right? As Mr Gordy used to say, if you don't innovate, you stagnate."

"A true word," I respond, touching the studio walls. I feel that.

We walk up the steps back into the control room, and Harry stops before we walk out. "I know you want to touch the mixing console." He pulls the chair up to the desk. "Go ahead, but don't make me regret it."

I nod and sit in the chair, being careful not to let my nerves cause me to do something like hit the desk too hard or worse, for my clumsiness to cause *anything* to knock over. I study every knob and dial, ever so slightly playing around with a fader. I feel like the Hulk or some shit, gaining power with each thing I lightly graze, feeling like I can take over the world knowing a Black man before me did the same thing.

"And to think, he was able to build this empire when Black people didn't have nearly as many rights as we do today," I say.

"Oh, you're absolutely right. They'd travel for their Motown Revues and the tour bus would get shot up. They'd sleep on the bus for days on end because half the hotels wouldn't let Black folks sleep there, no matter how famous they were. But Berry Gordy just refused to accept no. Even with Motown, when an opportunity like this didn't exist for him and his people, he made his own."

I look at Harry. "When did he know?"

"To start Motown?" Harry asks, and I nod. "When he wrote a song and collected his first royalty check. Realized it was pennies. He knew he had a better shot going into business for himself."

I sigh. Motown was making hit records while the city was on fire from race riots. You start a business in the 1960s and it's guaranteed every Black person that worked there was going through something. Every single one. And far greater than anything I've ever experienced. If anything, they used the racism and trauma they experienced as fuel to help their family get into better, safer conditions. That's all I want, to use this talent of mine to hopefully put my family in a better situation. I keep asking my mom to trust the community, but I think I've been projecting. It's *me* that needs to learn to trust my community and trust that Mook will be okay and so will my mom, because there will still be people around them that love and support them. Because there are people who will be proud of me and know that everything I'm doing, I'm doing for my family. So Mook can truly have a brother he looks up to: the father figure he never had, a man who rolls his sleeves up and works hard to help those he loves.

Danielle touches my shoulder and I find myself back in the control room, my hands touching the edge of the desk, attempting to absorb some of the energy from the great songwriters, singers and producers that graced these rooms.

Harry pops out of the room for some reason or another, and it gives me and Danielle some alone time. I place my hand over hers and look up at her.

"Thank you."

She beams. "I wanted you to feel the same way I feel every time you take me somewhere. It feels like we're going on some grand adventure, and you never know what's going to happen next. I always come back feeling refreshed and creative. Even tonight. I knew you'd enjoy it, but it was fun seeing you get something else out of it entirely."

"Clarity," I respond. "In a way I've never gotten before." Her smile grows wider.

"I got something for you." Harry's voice booms back into the control room, and Dani and I jump. "Was I...interrupting something?"

"Oh, no! Prince was just thanking me for such a great time."

"Mmmh," Harry says, peeking through his glasses. "Well, just don't go thanking her in here." Dani looks mortified, and I can't stop laughing.

"I promise you, Harry, we're just talking."

"Mmmh," he says again, this time with a chuckle. "I wanted to hand you this." He passes me a pamphlet.

"What's this for?" I ask.

"Well, there's some summer programming coming up that requires you to register. You learn songwriting, music production, all that. I know it's not deejaying, but maybe learning the other side of the biz will help you be a better DJ."

"Like Questlove. Hell yeah!" I skim the programme so fast, looking at everything they have to offer. I definitely wouldn't mind spending my summer here between airtimes. I stand up and shake Harry's hand firmly.

"Harry, thank you. I truly feel like I got a masterclass tonight in music production and music history."

Harry waves his hand in the air again, which I'm assuming is his bashful response. "Anytime. Danielle asked if you two could be capped onto the end of a tour, but I felt like this was better, more intimate. I would give free tours all day and night if I could." He looks around once again, admiring everything this historic building has to offer, and smiles. "There's just no place like it."

We stroll outside and I ask Danielle where she wants to eat. "I figured since my parents aren't home, we could relax there."

"Ummm…" I say.

She grabs my arm. "It's okay. It's just ordering in and watching a movie. Plus, it's Valentine's Day weekend. Everything is gonna be packed and booked up. That sounds fun, right?"

I nod slowly. "That sounds like the perfect way to end a night like this." Even with the haziness of the streetlights, I can spot her blushing. But a pang of worry hits my chest. I don't want her to feel uncomfortable in any way. I'm fine with us eating and ending the night on the same high I feel right now. I don't want anything to screw this up.

I press my lips to her forehead, silently thanking her once more. And we get into her car and ride off into the moonlight.

Chapter Fourteen

Vibrations Heavy

I give Prince a tour of the house and open the door to the last room.

"And this is the office," I say.

Prince walks over to my dad's system and gasps.

"What?" I ask.

"I thought your mom said she was the music head in the house."

"She is," I respond. "She's the one who would drag my dad to concerts and everything. Even right now, she made my dad drive all the way to Chicago to see her favourite artist."

"Well, she definitely rubbed off on him," he responds, transfixed. "'Cause he got the Focal headphones. Serious drip." He carefully picks them up and flips them over, admiring every little detail of the headphones. Is he drooling?

I can't help myself and start laughing.

"What?" he says.

I shake my head, still in disbelief. "I can't believe how excited you are about these headphones. Like really. You're a kid in a candy store."

"You don't understand..." He pauses for a moment and then has an epiphany. "Have you even listened to these?"

"Sometimes when he's home, he'll come into the office with his beer, lean back into his chair, and just be gone for hours. My mom leaves him alone when he does it, but every once in a while, I'll come in to bug him and he'll let me listen."

"And??" Prince exclaims.

"I don't know." I shrug. "I just didn't get it."

"Well, let's see if I can convert you." That dimple appears, so I know he's up to no good. "You want to give it another go?"

"Why not?" I respond. I pull up my mom's office chair and we sit down next to each other. I log into my dad's computer and open his Apple Music app. Prince huffs and I chuckle again.

"Oh my god, we have a family plan!"

"Nah, we not doing this. I'm logging into my Tidal account." He opens the browser to access his account and downloads the app.

"Why can't you just use the browser?" I ask him, and he smacks his lips.

"If I can't get the highest quality of music for you to actually enjoy the headphones, what's the point?" I suck my teeth. "I'll delete this before I leave, promise."

I acquiesce 'cause that's the last thing I need – getting busted by my military father. He already warned me about having Prince over unsupervised and told me he has "eyes and ears everywhere." So I made Prince duck when we drove into my neighbourhood and parked my car straight in the garage.

"What makes a good DJ anyway?" I ask, watching him do his thing. "Help me understand with words."

He pauses for a minute. "A good DJ knows how to accentuate the best parts of a song, and also how to mix one song to another as smoothly as possible. One of my favourite DJs, Questlove, said a good DJ should know five songs that blend perfectly with each other. So, my ear should be able to spot that perfect part to transition to – do I need to turn up the vocals here, or does a certain instrument need more life for this part of the song, or whatever I need to do to mix in another song with a similar cadence or rhythm. Make sense?"

I nod, as I continue to watch Prince set up. It's literally just him, some headphones, and the computer, but he's already opened like three portions of the app and is doing too many things at once: fiddling with the app's audio sound, scrolling through his library of playlists that *never seem to end*, and placing the headphones up to one of his ears, testing the noise.

"The other part," he continues, "is highlighting the best parts of a song. The parts that are sort of an unspoken rule. Like when you out with your girls and your hands go up in the air when *that part* of the song comes on." I giggle. "You'd be surprised how music really connects people, because more people have that same feeling than you think. So like for instance, with some artists who can't sing, the music hits 'cause the bass is there, and the production is fire, but the artist's voice is aight. You essentially drown them out and accentuate the part that puts everyone in that space together. That gives everyone that connection, which almost feels… like a religious experience."

He explained it so clearly, with so much passion. I pry some more. "Why are these headphones such a big deal?"

"Because the good ones will try to recreate as close as possible what was created in the studio, so true music heads will spend thousands on equipment, just to hear those little things in the studio that make a song magical. Hold on." He puts the headphones on his ears and vibes out for a minute, adjusting with the audio a bit more. When he's satisfied, his head goes up and down and I can tell he's zoned out, like my dad. Finally, he looks at me and smiles, and hands me the headphones.

"You're an artist," Prince says. "I have faith in you." He pauses the music and puts the headphones on my ears, making sure they're perfectly aligned. "Your ears are completely covered, right?" I nod. "Cool. I want you to lean back, close your eyes, and just listen."

"What am I listening for?" I ask.

"Everything. Every note, every instrument. You are really going to appreciate everything that goes into a score, every hour that's spent perfecting *one song*. We truly don't give producers enough cred, man."

When Prince taps the play arrow, I wanted to clown him for playing an old song like Brian McKnight. For someone who plays mainstream music daily on the radio, it's striking to hear what he decides to listen to after on-air hours. Maybe going to the museum has put him in an old-school mood. I almost take the headphones off, and then I begin to hear what he's talking about, what my dad obsesses over.

Brian McKnight is an artist my mom said her mom listened to when she was younger, but when we talk about voices that are next level, I see why he's in this category. His voice warms your insides, like placing your hands in front of a crackling fire on a cold winter night, and it's surprisingly airy to have so much power. With all that beauty, though, in this song he isn't the star. It's the piano.

For someone who isn't into music as much as my parents, it didn't stop me from enjoying live concerts. My parents loved to take me to the Detroit Jazz Festival or even just Jazzy Nights at the amphitheatre, and I've enjoyed a solid piano performance or two before. But never like this. Maybe I was too young to appreciate it. But right now, it almost feels like Brian and the piano are one instrument, that the beauty in the song isn't just in his voice, but the fact that his voice and the piano hold the same weight. The keys are just as important as his vocals, and that is what makes it so brilliant. As we reach the bridge, I realize it's the first time his vocals overtake the piano, but it's also when you feel his aggression and his plea for a lost lover. I'm really astonished that headphones can do that – I feel like I'm actually in the studio, listening to him take his hurt out on the piano, begging for forgiveness through this ballad.

I open my eyes to Prince's sweet smile, watching me listen

to this song for the first time with a new-found appreciation. My legs are propped up on his lap while listening, and I've never felt more of an urge to be closer to him than I do now.

Before I know it, the words escape my mouth. "I'm crazy about you."

A boyish smile creeps onto his lips. "I've *been* crazy about you, Dani."

Adrenaline rushes over me as I take off the headphones and inch closer to him. We press our lips together and his feel so soft and supple, our kissing going deeper and deeper into one another. I can feel his tongue caressing mines, and everything about this feels so natural; it finally feels like I'm ready for whatever comes next. I stop kissing him and take Prince in. Everything that makes him, him. Everything that makes me madly attracted to him becomes clear. And I can't get enough of it.

"Let's go to my room," I say, panting.

Prince hesitates. "We don't have to go up there." And that's what I love about him. His eyes are telling on himself; he wants me so bad he can't stand it. His voice is shaky and breathless. Yet he still wants to make sure I feel safe with him. And I do.

"I know. I want to." I take his hand, but he quickly stops me to delete his Tidal app first. I'm glad someone is thinking. Once that's done, I lead him up the stairs to my room. It's the first time he's been in here. I see him quickly scan my bookshelves and the hung-up prints that line the wall of my favourite authors. He follows my lead cautiously, right to my bed.

* * *

He leaned over more and came in slowly for a kiss. I didn't object. Gently, he started nibbling on my neck. I felt so many things in the moment, but I was mostly trying to just take it in.

He whispered in my ear and started caressing my arm and moved his hand over to my chest. "Are you a free spirit like your girl?"

That statement disturbed me, and my body froze. Suddenly I wanted to be as far away from Drew, this apartment and this campus as possible. I stopped him.

"I don't feel comfortable doing this."

"Oh, come on. We were having a good time. Right?"

He moved his hand to my thigh and started to lift the bottom of my sundress up.

"No," I said, my muscles stiffening. "I don't want to do this."

"I'm not going to hurt you," Drew objected. "Just go with it, gorgeous." I tried to get up, but he aggressively started kissing me again, pressing me back against the couch.

I didn't want to cause a scene, but I felt frantic. Why wasn't he listening to me? I felt my stomach regurgitating and prayed I would throw up on him, just so he'd let me go. With his other hand, he made his way to my dress strap, pulling it down. Exposing me. I pushed him.

"No!" I objected, trying to cover up. But he held on to the strap until it ripped in his hand.

"Why are you acting like that? Like you weren't feeling me a few minutes ago!"

"I'm not, not in this way. Get OFF me!" I secured the top of my dress with as much strength as I could, trying desperately to wrangle myself from his grasp and finally breaking free once the rest of my strap ripped in his hand. But as soon as I escaped he grabbed my other wrist, hard. I was scared for my life, but if he was going to really try something with me, I was going to call him out on it.

"You're going to rape me in your friend's living room? Is it worth risking your full ride?"

"What?!" He was furious. "You wildin'! No one would ever believe you over me. You're just some high-school hoe putting out to an athlete."

"I don't care who you are. YOU'RE HURTING ME AND I DON'T WANT YOU. LET ME GO!"

"Crazy bitch," Drew said as he freed my wrist. I rushed out the door and to my car. I had no sense of where I was, but I cranked my engine on and drove off as fast as I could. To nowhere in particular. When it felt like I was a safe distance from the complex, I opened my door and hurled onto the parking-lot ground I found myself in. And kneeling over, with half my body out the driver's seat of my car, I bawled my eyes out.

Chapter Fifteen

Mixed Signals

PRINCE

She takes me upstairs to her room, and I look around. It's so Dani. Everything about it, from the bookshelves to her little writing desk...she even has the Audre Lorde poem I got for her hanging up next to some of her other pictures. *She must really like me,* I think.

"Come closer," she instructs. Damn, I want her so bad, but I'm so scared. I don't wanna fuck this up. She's sitting on her bed, her energy coy and ravenous all at once. Her breath deepens the closer I get.

"You sure?"

"You've asked me that already, Prince. I am."

I slowly take off my shirt and watch her, her eyes inspecting my newly formed pecs and abs. Moving to the foot of her bed, I get on my knees and pull her closer to me. She wraps her legs around my back as I grab her chin and kiss her passionately. I let my hands travel across her body, first touching her legs and then easing up to her hips. I let them graze across her back as we kiss and move my hands down to the end of her shirt, where I place my fingers underneath to touch her skin. She winces.

"Are you okay?" I ask.

She's breathing hard, and her demeanour has changed. A second ago seductive, and now…rigid. I'm ready to back away, but she stops me and begins rubbing her fingers on my chest. She explores my torso and shoulders with her fingertips in such a tantalizing way that I'm completely lost in her again, unaware of what happened just moments ago. My skin is on fire with each new area of my body she explores, and before I know it, she takes her shirt off and scoots back on her bed, inviting me to follow.

The whirring in my head intensifies as I draw near to her. Starting with her stomach, my lips touch her skin – which is every bit as soft as velvet. A sound of pleasure escapes her mouth, so I continue to travel my lips up her chest, kissing around her violet lace bra as she braces my back, causing my hormones to go crazy.

She begins to gnaw at my ear and tremors move through my body. The sensation is so intense I am almost unable to breathe. I grab onto her bra strap and she freezes again.

"Stop," she says. I look into her eyes, and it's clear this time. Fear. I climb out of her bed and grab my shirt from the floor. Danielle sits up against her headboard, her knees to her chin.

"Let me find your shirt," I say, scouring the room.

"You don't have to," she snaps, putting a pillow in front of her.

I don't know what to say. "Did I do something wrong, Dani? If I did, please tell me." She just shakes her head aggressively, and I know there's something more. Someone hurt her. "I knew this wasn't a good idea, Danielle. I could tell something was wrong…"

"I don't need a lecture from you, Prince!" she scoffs, her face hardening. "This was a mistake."

Fuck.

"I…I didn't mean to say that. Let me make this right. What can I do to make this right?" I plead with her.

"Just go," she responds, her lips tight. I sigh, beaten.

"All right," I finally say. "I'll go."

Chapter Sixteen

Scratch Beneath the Surface

Danielle

"Danielle Ford, get up!" The covers are suddenly ripped off my body, and I moan and turn the other way, curling up like a roly-poly. Rashida plugs her iPhone into my speakers and puts on Meg Thee Stallion, and Esi does something totally out of character: she gets up close to my face and starts shaking her booty.

A bit of joy creeps up inside me. "You never twerk for meee." I grin, slapping her behind. We all start giggling.

"I know, Esi be holding out," Rashida voices, vibing out and adding more songs to the queue.

"I reserve that for my lovers only, but I'll do what I must, if it gets you out of this funk." She sits down next to me and I hug her waist. "Why the hell have you been avoiding us?"

"What are you talking about?" I say with a sense of guilt. They've been calling and texting for over a week, and I haven't responded. I told my parents when they returned that I think

I caught the stomach bug and took a few days off school. My mom knew something was up, though, and that's probably why she let Rashida and Esi in the house without even warning me.

"You smell like him," I whine.

"And what smell is that, soap?" Esi responds, rubbing the top of my head. I nod.

"Aww, she's lovesick!" Rashida remarks.

"Don't let her change the subject," Esi advises. "She owes us an explanation."

Rashida walks over to my bed, crouching down so we're eye level. "Why would you ignore us *again*, Dani?" she asks, those eyes of hers showing the forgiveness I don't deserve.

"'Cause...I'm a bad friend," I reply.

"That's a cop-out, D," Esi counters, still rubbing my head with such tenderness. I don't deserve these two. "What happened, babe?"

I bury my face more in her lap, the sadness engulfing me. "I brought Prince here and...we almost went there."

Rashida and Esi eye each other. "Almost?" they say in unison.

"Yeah. I brought him up to the room...but then I just..." I sniffle. "I freaked out and asked him to leave. It was all too much, too soon for me. I was so sure it was what I wanted until we got up here." I break down.

"He didn't hurt you, did he?" Rashida asks.

I shake my head vigorously. "No, he was the perfect gentleman, even at the very last minute when I told him I couldn't and asked him to go. He didn't object once. It was all me."

"Aww, D!" Esi says in a soothing tone. Rashida grabs my hand, squeezing it tight. We sit like that for what feels like hours, Esi rocking me back and forth, Rashida massaging my hand. Both girls letting me release all my emotions. When my eyes are finally clear of tears, I look up to find them both wiping their own.

Finally Esi breaks the silence. "Shida, pass me that box of Kleenex. D got me over here looking like a raccoon with my mascara running." We all snicker in between sniffles. Instead of wiping her tears, though, Esi gently wipes my face.

"Don't be hard on yourself. When you're ready, you'll know," Rashida says.

"I thought I was, though. I feel so bad for leading him on."

Esi lets out a loud sigh. "We're in high school. We can barely decide what outfit we want to wear without changing our minds a million times daily. Why would this be any different?"

I nod. She's right. "As much as I like him, I just don't know if I'm ready for any of it right now. Love, a relationship, sex... he's been so determined to win me over, but I just don't know if I want the responsibilities of love right now."

"Well, we can't be sitting in this room crying with you all day. You need to get *out.*"

"Can't we just stay in and watch a movie? We can watch one of my mom's old romance movies," I say. And just when I can tell I got Rashida's vote, Esi snaps us both out of it.

"No!" she proclaims. "Shida, don't be fooled here. Danielle knows exactly what to say to appease the romantic in the group. Almost got me too." I roll my eyes.

"You're right!" Rashida jumps up. "Dani, the longer you isolate yourself, the worse off you'll be. We're not letting you dump us just 'cause you dumped Prince."

"Ouch," I respond, rolling over and placing my hand to my chest like I'm in pain.

"The truth hurts, kiddo," Esi says, slapping the hell out my thigh. They both laugh.

"Fine," I groan, slipping my feet into my furry white house-shoes. "But let me at least take a shower."

My friends get me out of the house to shop for pieces for the hair show I promised to be in, and I see what being a recluse does to me. Instead of facing my fears head-on, I let as much time pass as I can, putting space to what I'm going through instead of dealing with my feelings, whatever they may be. It's almost the first week of March, which makes it one more month till the hair show, and one more month until I find out if I got into my dream school.

While Esi is putting hair packets and temporary dye and who knows what else up to my face in the beauty supply store, getting feedback from Rashida, who is helping her by taking notes on her phone, I'm in and out of my head, trying to make one of the hardest decisions of my life.

I'm stringing him along. I am letting someone invest all this time and energy into making me his girl, and I still don't know if it's what I want. And all I can do is think of his ex and how she seemed to have some of the same feelings. Difference is, I don't want to keep leading him on and suddenly withdraw. Or worse, make things official when I'm unsure and end up breaking his heart. I know he'll be upset with me now, but at least things haven't gotten more serious, at least he didn't utter those words to me yet. Maybe pulling away now is the best idea.

I figured I put everything behind me when I wrote my college essay, but it's silly to think one essay or journal entry will help me face my pain. I felt like I had closure, but I never thought about how it could negatively impact my love life. It hit me after I told Prince to stop, when I saw my sundress balled up in the same corner as my shirt he offered to look for. I didn't want him to pick it up, to see the strap ripped and hound me with questions. He would try anything to save me, but it isn't enough. I need something more than a book, a distraction, or a prayer; I need a real counsellor or therapist. And whether or not I get into a New York school, I've got to let him go, or it will follow me right to the Big Apple.

It's what I have to do, I tell myself as I sit at my desk later that night, letting all the words pour out. Words about him, about us, about me. Things that have become so clear to me, now that I forced myself to revisit that night, to think how my friendship with Destiny had to end, and what I need to do to make myself feel good about me again.

I *am* crazy about Prince, but I got to deal with my own complications first. He doesn't deserve to be intertwined in all this.

Chapter Seventeen

Singing a Different Tune

PRINCE

I stare at my phone for the millionth time, willing her to push accept but instead listening to her voice as the phone goes to voicemail. Looking at my phone ain't changing anything. That shit is dead. I can't stop thinking about what Danielle told me before our date turned: *I'm crazy about you.* Danielle had been so stoic up until that point, so to hear those words come out her mouth means she even surprised herself. It means that when she let her guard fully down, she was able to finally be honest with me and herself. She cares about me.

So why the hell would she treat me like this? Why would she ignore my calls and texts? Why would she be so honest with me just to turn me away? I thought I was special enough for her not to shut me out, but joke's on me.

For all the things I've planned to impress her, last week's date was something I couldn't have planned even if I tried. She planned a date to help me tap into my passions, which is next level. There are people who believe in me, but she gave me a taste of what it's like to think bigger, to get involved with something outside myself and my normal environment. She made me appreciate the need to go away and do your own thing, to learn your way. To take that knowledge and bring it back. And then...she just flipped. Said she made a mistake inviting me over. Inviting me up. Truth be told, knowing her parents were out of town, I didn't expect her to even let me come over. 'Cause I knew she wasn't ready. And I should have found a way to convince her not to. But her sudden desire to have me made it hard to say no...

One thing Dani is consistent with is how she'll switch it on you. How she'll go from being into me to going cold. I thought I had a handle on it, but I don't know if I can solve this.

After my Uber dropped me off, I tried calling her and she didn't answer, and again the day after that. On Tuesday I asked Malik to talk to Rashida, and she told M Danielle had went back to ignoring them too. This time, she said, they weren't going to allow it. They planned on going to her house to find out what was going on. Rashida told Malik she would report back. M really came through.

It's the following week and I'm feeling good about this plan they've updated me on, knowing I'll be closer to getting some answers, until fourth period, when a note falls out of my locker. It's folded and taped shut, and simply says, *read this when you're alone.* I know what that means. Heartache.

That afternoon I'm nowhere *near* being on my A-game during my show. I excuse it as cold and flu season and sit there anxiously playing song after song, trying to fill the space of when I'd usually give advice, until my hour is up. I rush home, tell my mom I'm not feeling a hundred, and go downstairs. I know even before I pry it open, I'm gonna be a wreck.

Dear Prince,

I am sorry. Sorry it took this long to say something I didn't have the courage to say in person. Communication has been hard for me lately. Shutting everyone out has been the way I don't have to deal with my problems. But it's not fair to you. You've been kind and sweet and a gentleman and everything I assumed boys our age couldn't be. Which is why I have to end this.

You're a good person. It's not an easy thing to say, because there are so many people in this world who aren't. But you are; you care about your family so deeply, you love to help people find joy through love, and you have a knack for something that can truly make the lives of others around you happy. You're so generous and noble with your time. I want you to use your time wisely, and I don't want you wasting it on feelings about me.

Now the truth. Last summer, I was assaulted by a college guy. That's why Destiny and I aren't friends anymore. And that was the compromising situation she put me in that I alluded to in the car. I felt stupid in so many ways – in letting her trick me into thinking it was okay to go in there, in staying when there were way more boys in there than girls, and being loyal when she went in the back room and left me by myself. While I was waiting for her, I started talking to a guy who initially made me feel more comfortable. We were talking and getting to know each other and things were good…until they weren't. It ended with me fighting him off, running out of the apartment with a ripped sundress and leaving Destiny behind.

So last weekend wasn't your fault. I am so attracted to you, Prince. You're everything I would want in a boyfriend, and for that reason I tried to force it. But I just wasn't ready. And it made me realize that overall, I'm not ready to be serious with someone. Whatever fear is holding me back, I need to take time to figure it out. But thank you. For being patient with me, for being so good at reading me. Rashida told me once that she feels like you were the reason me and her rekindled things, and I didn't want to believe it at first, but I believe it now. I felt so much fear of being judged, of wondering if I had good people in my life. And being around you showed me I do attract good people, and I do know the difference. I have to get better at trusting my own judgement. I'm a better person for having known you. Right now, I just need to work on being the best person I can be. And you deserve the best, P. Be well, Prince.

Dani

I read the note repeatedly. Trying to make sense of it all. A college guy attacked her. I am shell-shocked. Of course. Her fear of trusting. The way she can disconnect so easily. She's terrified.

Then I immediately become enraged. The thought of some man trying to hurt her makes me want to punch a wall. This is heavy, even for me. I want so badly to call her, to tell her things will be okay, to take as much time as she needs and I'm here when she's ready. That she's made so much progress that I know three more dates could help even more. But even I am experiencing all these emotions at once, so who am I to even attempt to understand what she's going through? I just can't. With all the articles and books I'd be willing to check out of the library, what Dani truly needs is a professional. Someone who could help her way past my basic-ass knowledge of what she's been through. So instead, I respond with a brief, simple text.

ME: I'm so sorry you went through what you went
through. I'm around if you ever want to talk about it
or just hang again. But for now, be well, Dani.
We'll always have the three dates.

She responds instantaneously.

DANI: Always.

The following day I call in sick at the station, so even Uncle Jerome knows this is serious and takes Mook and Ma out for dinner, giving me some much-needed space. With a little time to myself, I do the one thing I always do when I need to clear my head. I pull out my crates and listen to some music, 'cause…this one hurts, man. And it requires the old stuff. You know, the heartbreak singing from back in the day. The begging and pleading, the Jodeci and Boyz II Men and all those joints that make you feel like losing the love of your life is the hardest thing ever. I used to laugh at my uncle anytime he was getting over his girlfriend of the moment, belting these songs out like his world ended. I always appreciated the vocals but felt the lyrics were extra as hell. Now that my heart has been torn into smithereens, the music hits different.

I hear my back door open and grab my bat. "Ayo, Prince, where you at!?" I heave a deep sigh of relief.

"I'm down here!" I yell up, and hear multiple footsteps coming downstairs. So, I guess the whole crew found out.

"Prince, you down here listening to this sad-ass music—"

"Malik, man, *not tonight*." I pout, sitting on my futon in nothing but my boxers and a tee.

"Aww, P. You sitting here sulking in yo draws, man?" He's giggling a little. "I know you hurtin'."

Yasin throws my sweats from across the room and they come out of their coats, hats and gloves.

"It's so damn cold in the D," Malik says, still rubbing his hands together. Then he looks at me. "Aye, I'm sorry, man."

"It's all right," I reply, and my shoulders droop. "Maybe it was dumb of me to pursue her."

"I know I said that, but I don't mean it," Malik says, and I'm stunned. "She's a good chick…she's been through some shit."

I finish putting on my sweats and hold up her letter. "Yeah, she told me. It's some difficult shit. She needs her space and I need to respect it."

Malik pauses. "Not long after they started hanging out again, I was tryna talk mess about Danielle to Rashida. 'Cause it was pissin' me off that Danielle was so flaky to you and to Rashida. And Shida didn't tell me much, but she put me in my place real fast."

"Whaaaaat?" Yaz replies, and we laugh.

"Whatever," Malik says. "I guess I deserved it. I need to be better about how I talk about these girls—" I clear my throat. "About women."

"Well, thank god someone got to you. Keep her," Ant says, then points to me. "What we gonna do about this one, though?"

"Y'all don't have to worry about me. I'll figure this out."

"I know you the love coach or marriage counsellor or whatever you call yourself these days," Malik says, "but you gotta learn how to ask for help, P. We want you happy. You taught me to stop being such a hypocrite. And even when you're not around, you still forced me to step my game up, 'cause every time I was around Shida she was telling me how good you were treating Danielle and how I need to do better."

"And you helped me get over my fears and ask Jordan out," Yasin chimes in.

So this is what people mean when they say chip off the old block. This conversation sounds like a mirror image of what I've told my mom all school year, about learning how to trust those around you. These guys are the closest things to fam I got outside of Ma, Mook and Jerome, and I'm not allowing them the opportunity to help. They're right.

We all look at Ant.

"Please! I tried love and it got me a baby. I got enough love from Kisha to last me for a good while. Right now, no woman could even come close to competing for daddy-daughter time."

"No one can compete with those chubby legs," I cut in.

"No one. Little rotisserie chicken." We all chuckle. Anthony goes over to my player and pulls out Bruno Mars. "Aww shit!" he says. "A classic."

"That's a stretch," I say. "That's not even old-school."

"It don't have to be old-school to be a classic, P," Ant says. I shrug. He has a point. Bruno's range puts him in that category.

"Put that record on," Malik says, walking over to him. "Come on, Yaz." Yasin looks at me like, *What's about to happen?* and I shrug.

Anthony adds the record and they huddle together, until Ant spins around like he's an R & B singer, mouthing Bruno's lyrics. I can't help but chuckle.

"What the *hell* are you doing?" I say, watching them attempt to coordinate moves. Ant is the lead vocalist, using my wave brush to fake belt the lyrics, Yasin is barely able to keep up (poor guy), Malik is once again doing the *most*, trying to moonwalk and almost falling flat on his ass. At the end of it all we are crying. And I'm grateful. Sometimes just being around your homies is the perfect remedy for a heartbreak.

Chapter Eighteen

Time to Face the Music

Danielle

I come downstairs to my dad chilling in his office, headphones in, and my heart comes out my chest a little. It reminds me of me and Prince. I want to turn around and go back upstairs to my safe space, but that's a cop-out. And I'm tired of doing that. I pretty much shove the paper in my dad's face before he's off again, this time to Germany for four weeks. Then R and R, then back over to close out. I'll miss him terribly, and I'm ready to tell my family what happened. This isn't a conversation I want to have on the phone.

My dad begins to read, and I slowly see his face change – he frowns, then scowls. Then I notice his hands are starting to shake, his massive, calloused hands that have seen the world. Seen things I couldn't imagine.

He recites the sentence out loud, like reading it with his voice will change his reaction. "'I went to a college party and a guy I thought I could trust tried to do me harm…'" His voice melts away, unable to read the rest. He slaps the essay on his lap, his eyes near tears. "Dani, baby. Why didn't you tell me?" he says, his voice so small. I entrusted him with this essay first, feeling like the things he's witnessed that he would never share with me hardened him, made him equipped for something like this. But maybe I was wrong to make that assumption. He still loves me, after all. I'm his babygirl.

"I'm sorry, Daddy, I just didn't know what to tell you, or how. I just felt like people might say what I experienced is easy to move past. Or be okay with. But I just wasn't that person. It bothered me to no end that someone violated me without my permission. That someone felt they had a right even after I made it clear that's not what I wanted. That someone touched—" I feel the biggest lump in my throat.

My dad gets up to hold me, but before he does, I urge him to keep reading. He starts reading again silently, too afraid to let the rest of the words come out his mouth, and then I see his jaw relax, his calm beginning to come back.

He reads out loud again. "'One of the healthiest things I did during this time was read and write letters to authors who have kept me alive. Authors who are long gone, who've endured things unimaginable – racism, disappointment, pain, financial hardship, being harshly critiqued for telling their stories and so much more – and who stood in the face of their adversaries with defiance, with grace and intention. They gave so much of themselves to their work, realizing the importance of showing other Black women a mirror image of themselves. They showed me and girls like me that we are not alone in our struggles, that storytelling is a way to connect us all, and their truths will inspire and heal so many women like them. Their work helped me to work on myself and ultimately take my power back, and it's why I want to go to a school like NYU…'"

My dad stands up and folds me into his arms.

"I couldn't protect you. I'm so sorry. I couldn't make you feel safe." I hear his sniffles in my ear as I nuzzle into his strong, protective arms, which have always felt like home.

"I feel safe now," I respond, my tears dropping down to the corners of my smile. I look up at him. "I'm doing what I have to do to make sure I'm okay. I found some resources online for a few local support groups, and I even made an appointment with our school counsellor." I pause, lowering my voice. "But I shared this with you first, because I wouldn't have been able to go from a victim to a survivor without you fostering my love for reading. I found myself in these pages, these books."

"It looks like you're shaping up to be a writer worthy of the inscription your mom got you. Which, by the way…" he whispers, pulling back from our hug and pointing upstairs. "When you tell your mom about this, if you tell your mom about this, act like you told her first."

"Oh, I know," I say. "I'll be sure to act like she got to see it first. Plus, we all know she's my favourite parent, so it doesn't matter."

I give my dad a mischievous smile, trying to break the tension. Then I get on my tiptoes and give him a peck on his cheek, and despite him rolling his eyes, I can tell he's already forgiven me.

I think of what Prince asked me. I could never choose, but in this moment, with the weight lifted, I'm definitely a daddy's girl.

There's one more thing to do. The following week, after I have the same hard conversation with my mother, I take a small box and fill it with the printed essay I showed to my parents and the sundress I wore on that night. It's March, so I wait for a day where there's less snow on the ground and take the box, sealed tightly with as much tape as I can find, wrap it in a trash bag and take it to a nearby dumpster. I left that dress in my room as a reminder of my shortcomings in not seeing the signs, and it felt like torture. I need it away from me, out of my life for ever. I've been avoiding my healing for too long, and it's time to go through all the emotions. In some ways I was inspired by what Prince did with his ex. In order to get over her, he had to dig deeper and face all the things he didn't want to. Ask himself the hard questions and get to a space where he was able to let her go.

Prince has never been shy about tapping into his voice, and in some ways he helped me tap into mines. The confidence he has on the radio, the confidence he had with pursuing me – he didn't know if it would pan out, and he was scared half the time, but he didn't let fear silence him. We both have different fears of our own we're trying to tackle, but I hope I helped him get over his fear of following his dreams the way he's helped me get over mine of using my voice, even if I don't have it all figured out. I throw the bag into the dumpster and wipe my hands together, like I'm wiping myself clean. It's time to take my life back.

Chapter Nineteen
Go with the flow
Danielle

Tonight is the night. The spring weather is starting to break and after months of planning, Mass Tech is throwing its first hair showcase, courtesy of Esi. I've never been prouder of her. She's even convinced her parents to attend, which I know was no small feat. I'm nervous about being here, but surprisingly not for the reasons I thought I'd be. This is the first time, outside of avoiding him at school, I'll see Prince in almost two months. I haven't completely shut the world off during this time, but I have still been cautious about social functions I attend, knowing he'll likely be there. Esi even offered to find another DJ for the showcase, but Prince told her he'd still do it, and even gave her a free radio advertisement. This was big for her, and I refused to be the friend who messed that up. I told her I could be a big girl for one night.

Part of me wonders if Prince didn't cancel on her because he knew I would be there. Whatever his reasoning, I can't worry too much about it. One afternoon, while I was studying and filled with heartache, I turned on the radio just to hear that smooth baritone voice. I even thought about calling him once his airtime was done, but his ex-girlfriend beat me to it. Mercury must have been in retrograde.

"Caller eight, what's your name?"

"Hi DJ LoveJones, it's Morgan." I sat, frozen. I knew this wouldn't end well if I continued to listen, but I also couldn't *not* listen. I needed to know how this story ended.

"Wassup, Morgan. How are you?" I could tell it caught him off guard, but there was still a lovingness in his voice. That's definitely her.

"I need some advice," she said. The inflection in her voice went higher, all cute and flirtatious, and I decided I couldn't stand her.

She needed to focus on school and leave Prince alone. She didn't deserve him.

"Go ahead, sweetheart."

She was *anything* but sweet.

"How do you win someone back when you messed up?"

He paused, then cleared his throat. I could sense he was nervous about this answer. "You own up to your mistakes, you apologize, and hope the person takes you back. And if they don't, recognize it as a moment in time and learn from it. The possibility for love might be over, but there may be an opportunity for friendship."

"Prince, I miss you."

He sighed. "Morgan, you ain't gotta do this…"

"Yes, I do," she interrupted. "I was stupid for what I did and I wanted to let you and all of Detroit know." I was beyond annoyed. Like, girl, this is *not* a movie. "Tell me you'll let me take you out this weekend, just as a friend."

Prince had been so calm this whole time. I placed my ear closer to the Wi-Fi speaker on my desk, waiting to hear something in how he responded to her, something to show me the love wasn't still there. I held my breath, praying he'd say no.

But he said the words I was afraid to hear.

"Text me and we'll set something up."

My heart fell out my chest.

With my head facedown on my desk and my emotions in disrepair, I had to remind myself why I let things go. I needed to find my way but was having trouble with the how and too afraid to ask for help. My parents were concerned about me briefly, but this time, when I started to shut down again, my family and friends held me up. They held on to me and wouldn't let go, wouldn't let me fall into that deep place of folding deeper into myself. I saw how quickly I was willing to revert back to old habits when given the chance, and I didn't want to be away at college and have something trigger this type of response again.

So going to the school counsellor was the best thing I could have done.

I opened up and talked through my feelings on everything, including a boy I liked that went to Mass, without mentioning any names, of course. I was surprised at what counselling gave me – I thought he would be one to tell me when I was doing things right or wrong, but instead Mr Smith told me that his job wasn't to tell me what to do next, but to guide me to making the best decision for me.

I liked that.

During one of our sessions, I revealed to him that I felt guilty for ending things the way I did with Prince, even with writing the note. He told me I didn't owe Prince anything with regard to my own pain, but that shouldn't stop me from reconnecting. I realized that what I missed more than anything was his friendship. And if he responded coldly, then he wasn't the guy I thought he was. So that's what I decided to do. Tonight I would walk up to him and just engage. See how he's doing, because I genuinely want to know. I don't know how awkward it will be, and I'm so nervous to see him. But I still want to.

After I get the front of my hair braided and help Esi and the crew set up chairs and decor, one of the students at Mass applies my make-up. Esi was very specific about the look before running off to prepare for the show – pink lips, neutral eyeshadow and big fake lashes.

I feel like I can barely see with these eyelashes and the glue weighing down my lids, but I'm shocked at the girl staring back at me in the mirror. I look fly as hell. I feel like the make-up and the hair are a cape, and I'm ready to walk on the stage and strut my stuff. Me. Who would have thought? But it's crazy what a little self-love will do. It will make you bet on yourself each time.

"Do you like it?" the girl asks. She's two years younger than me and can apply make-up better than I ever could. But I can tell she's a little nervous about my reaction…and letting Esi down.

I suck in my cheeks and give my lips a little more pout in the mirror. "You bodied this look," I respond. "A little more blush and then we're good to go."

To kill time and fight my nerves, I decide to rush out and grab some more snacks for backstage. I head to the gymnasium with some pep in my step, feeling good about the way I look, feeling confident about the show Esi put together and my part in it, and ready to warm up to the idea of seeing Prince at some point in the night and attempt small talk. But when I open the gym doors, I must look like a deer in headlights, surprised to see Prince so soon. Of course, he has to set up his DJ booth.

"Oh!" I exclaim.

Prince stops unravelling some cords and glances at me, with an expression that's pretty unreadable. There are a few classmates setting up last-minute chairs and the balloon backdrop on the stage, looking back and forth between me and him and feeling the thick tension between us, the magnetism that wants to pull us together. I wave to them and try to play it cool as I take the long walk to his side of the stage, swinging the bag of snacks in my hand.

"Hey," Prince says as I approach him.

"Hey," I respond, smiling. Prince is usually one to fill the silence, but this time he doesn't. He continues doing what he is doing and my eyes scan the gym, thinking about what I can say next. That's when I spot some of the models go from watching us to quickly occupying themselves, acting like they haven't been nosy this whole time. The show hasn't even started yet and I already feel like I'm centre stage.

"You need help with anything?" I ask. *Ugh, Danielle. He does this all the time. This boy doesn't need my help.*

He smirks and looks back down at me. "Nah, I'm good, but thanks, though."

I hesitate before I continue. "Hey, DJ LoveJones," I say quietly, leaning on the booth. "Can I request a song?"

His manner is a bit contained, something I'm not used to. But I understand why. He cocks his head, trying to figure out what my motive is. "Sure. What do you wanna hear?"

"'Sorry,' by Justin Bieber," I respond.

Prince twists his face. "Justin Bieber!?" he proclaims, and I release a laugh, finally feeling more relaxed. He's such a music snob sometimes.

"I'm trying to apologize, Prince. And don't act like you don't like Justin."

He pauses. "He has his moments. But remind me to send you a playlist of *better* apology songs." We're silent for a moment, and I realize Prince is expecting me to continue.

"I had a lot of personal stuff going on…" I say, tapping the booth with my fingers. "And I needed time and space to deal with it."

For the first time since I got here, he catches and holds my gaze. "I'm so sorry," he says. "Your letter…it gutted me. I wanted to call you right then and there. Or come by. But I knew that was the very thing you didn't need. I'm just used to fixing things. I felt so…useless. Even now. I didn't want to come on too strong."

He's such a sweetie. I nod. "I appreciate that. I should have said something sooner. But I just didn't know what I wanted, and the last thing I wanted to do was string you along when I needed to figure me out. Make sense?"

It's his turn to nod. "It does. And are you…figuring things out?"

"Yeah, I am." He smiles and touches my hand, and that warm feeling that I feel anytime our skin comes into contact creeps back up.

"I'm glad," he says. We stand there for a moment.

"D, there you are!" We both jump, and I spin around to Esi throwing the gym doors open, her heels clicking on the hardwood floor. "They told me you went to get cups and snacks? You know I didn't want anyone seeing your look, but honestly, I'm so happy you didn't listen to me. Everyone is in the back starving and…" She stops in her tracks when she's able to take a good look at my face. "Did I…interrupt something?" My classmates don't even hide it this time; everyone in the gym is looking at us, and Prince and I clearly forgot we had an audience, lost in each other.

I shake my head. "We were just catching up."

"Yeah, it's been a while," Prince quickly chimes in,

removing his toasty hand from mines.

She smirks. "Yeah…okay." She examines my face, making sure the make-up fits the theme Esi has crafted up in her head. "She did a good job…she could have made the eyeshadow a bit more dramatic, but that's nothing a quick touch-up can't fix." Then she looks over my shoulder, in Prince's direction. "She looks beautiful, doesn't she?" Thank god my back is to Prince, 'cause the look I give Esi is the look of death. She knows her only safety is the fact that it's her night and she is completely fine taking the risk.

Prince doesn't hesitate when he says, "When doesn't she?" Esi gives me an eye as if to say *You're welcome* and takes my hand.

"Well, if you don't mind. We have a show to do, so I need to take my prettiest model."

"Be my guest," Prince replies. And as Esi leads me out the gym, I sneak a stare at Prince. He's back to setting up, but he quickly looks up, returning my gaze. My stomach takes a flip. Nothing about my feelings has changed the least bit.

The backstage is electric. The designated area is set up on the other side of the gym behind a partition, with a few rows of black curtains up to act as dressing rooms, and long tables lined with plastic red tablecloths. Earlier we brought in a few platters from the grocery store, but it's already picked on, everyone scarfing down the cheese-and-cracker platters like they haven't eaten in days. I take my matching red cups and chips out the bag, as well as a few boxes of tea and some energy drinks I bought in case anyone needs caffeine. Esi doesn't seem like she's slept all week, so if anyone needs it, it's her. A few people rush to the table, trying to snack on the few items I brought.

The tables on the other side are filled with hair supplies – silk scarves and curlers, Blue Magic and Eco Styler gel. Bobby pins are scattered everywhere, along with random weave packets and toothbrushes to slick down baby hairs. And there's a fine mist of hairspray residue in the air. Some of the models are getting last-minute tweaks done by a few of the stylists, others are beginning to put on their pieces, but the hairstylists backstage are all acting as artisans, teasing and curling and twisting hair with precision and quality. This is our Paris Fashion Week right here.

Esi sits me down and puts some finishing touches on my hair, which is currently braided at my scalp with my natural hair flowing loose in the back, and she begins to attach more colourful hairpieces so that it hangs even longer and looks grander. Rashida pops out from one of the dressing rooms and yells, "Anyone got some safety pins?!" One of the girls rushes over to her and she grabs a few and closes the curtain. She emerges sometime later with another model, fiddling with the model's dress strap, which I assume broke sometime today. The chaos back here is insane and exhilarating. Finally Rashida comes over to us. "You need help?" she asks Esi.

"Yesss! Can you take this glue and add a few more rhinestones on that side? I'll attach the rest of her hair and add the flower pieces after my introduction."

"I'm gonna look like a bouquet," I tell her, and we all laugh.

"Well, you are our flower child," Esi replies, "and I'm putting you to work too. Put some more baby oil on those legs of yours."

"If I put any more on my body, I promise you I'll start a grease fire," I whine, and a few people giggle.

"Have you seen Christian?" Christian is one of our star athletes – a point guard on our basketball team, who recently got a full ride to Kentucky. I don't even watch sports like that and I know exactly who he is. Just like everyone else, because the school never lets us forget. "He had two girls wipe him down with a whole bottle." I shake my head. What a diva.

"How are you doing?" I ask Esi, as she begins separating fake pieces of wildflowers and orchids and places them on the table to stick between my curls. She's masking it pretty well, but I'm sure she's slightly freaked out.

"Stressed, but in my element," she says, squeezing my shoulder. And I squeeze her hands back.

"Well, if we haven't said it yet tonight, we're proud of you, Esi."

"Yes," Rashida responds, looking around. "You got people from the neighbourhood all here to show us their talent. It's amazing."

Esi beams. "I couldn't have done any of this without you both." She kisses my cheek. "Thank you, Dani, for being my model. You look exactly how I wanted you to." It was my turn to smile. She's finally forgiven me.

"What am I doing here?" Rashida huffs, and we laugh.

"Shida, don't make this about you right now. We got our Dani back."

"Fine," Rashida responds jokingly. "I love y'all." We all come in for a bear hug, but Esi quickly reminds us why we're here.

"Be careful with that side, Shida," she says.

Rashida rolls her eyes. "Way to ruin the moment." She looks at her watch. "Esi, twenty minutes before showtime, girl. You need to go prep." Esi's eyes perk up and she rushes off, to do whatever it is she needs to.

"Rashida, you are the queen of schedules, huh?"

Rashida nods. "It's a perk of being the oldest, I guess. I'm always helping someone get ready or get their day started. Or now, planning a hair show."

"Mass Tech…how we doing toniiiight!" I hear that sexy voice yell into the microphone as I'm backstage preparing, and I shudder. *Dani, you gotta do better,* I tell myself. Rashida and I rush to the side of the stage to watch the intro. "Welcome to Mass's first-ever Hair Wars, a tradition as old as time in the Motor City. My name is DJ LoveJones…" The crowd roars, and he waits for them to settle before he continues, "And I'll be your emcee for the night. If you haven't been to a hair show before, I don't know what rock you've been living under, but Detroit is the mecca of shows, the place where hairstylists go *off*. So first, we gotta give credit where credit is due. Shout-out to the original don himself, Hump the Grinder, who started Hair Wars as a DJ and created a space for us to be Black and beautiful. A space that we're honouring tonight." The crowd claps. "Okay, next I want to bring out tonight's true superstar, the mastermind behind all this. Everyone give it up for Esi Adu!"

Esi glides across the stage wearing a gorgeous corset, with a long, mermaid-style skirt adorned in kente cloth. Her hair is twisted up in Bantu knots, to which she's added lilac hairpieces to tie around the knots, and a few loose ends to frame her face. She looks like a true African queen.

"Thank you, DJ LoveJones, and everyone, give it up for him for taking time out of his busy schedule to emcee for the night!" The crowd cheers and Esi claps with such grace. Prince bows and is back to adjusting his system.

Esi goes on, "There is a saying in Black culture – a Black woman's hair is her crown and glory. I'm sure that rings true for a lot of you here tonight, and for me, too. My parents immigrated here from Ghana when I was only one year old – my dad brought my mother, me and my older brother to the land of the free. Give it up for my parents, Dr and Mrs Adu!" The audience claps and Esi's dad immediately stands up and waves to the crowd, basking in the recognition. Which has me and Shida dead. Her mom is sitting there quietly, shy at the attention, but gives the people around her a quick smile. "He was a PhD student, and hair is what kept our lights on. I'd escort my mom to houses around the D, watching her braid hair in people's living rooms and kitchens. And I watched her fingers twist and turn with exquisite detail, how she was able to make masterpieces out of our manes. I, like many Black girls, experienced some insecurities when I was younger, getting teased for not having 'enough' hair." She gestures with air quotes. "It was considered too kinky. Too unruly. But by seven, I was doing my own hair, and when I discovered Hair Wars, my life changed. I remember stealing my dad's laptop (sorry, Papa) and watching YouTube video after YouTube video, being mesmerized by Hair Wars. The ferocity, the sass, the poise. The show was unapologetic, the confidence was thrilling, and it was just for us." A few people hum and holler.

"Recently, I kept seeing White people pop on my phone, taking the very thing that came from us and making it trendy. Making it profitable. And it just…pissed me off. Because this 'trend' didn't apply to us growing up. It didn't apply when a White mother touched my hair randomly in a supermarket. It didn't apply when a clothing store I worked at told me my hair was too distracting to customers. Or when a seven-year-old comes home to their dad with their hair chopped off from a teacher at school. Or when a teenage boy has to cut his locs in order to participate in a wrestling match. Society has been policing our hair for decades, but now it's in. Like we didn't start this. Like Detroit isn't the hair capital of the world." She pauses as more people clap. "So, tonight is us giving us our flowers. Welcome to Mass Tech's Hair Wars. I hope you enjoy the show as much as I enjoyed putting it together. Let's honour the great stylists who changed the culture." People stand and cheer as Esi does a slight bow and descends from the stage. She knows she killed it.

Our high-school majorettes hit the stage first, getting the crowd hyped like a pep rally. Prince cuts and spins the set like he was born to do this, and I don't know what is making the crowd more pumped, his music or the dancing. It seems like both he and the majorettes are competing for the crowd's attention. Either way, everyone is up out of their seats by the end of the performance, decked out in only the way Black people can be – decadent, overdressed and flawless. In the audience I see heels and miniskirts, glitter and all types of natural hairstyles (you would think they were participating in the hair show), head wraps and sequins. Suddenly Mook pops out of his seat, into the aisle, and starts dancing, and the crowd goes nuts. I'm hurting from laughing so hard, watching his locs shake while the crowd hypes him up. I catch Prince chuckling himself, then motioning toward his boys to help him out, knowing his brother is vibing off everyone's energy.

"Everyone give it up for my lil bro, the constant life of the party!" Mook isn't ready to take his seat yet, so Ant snatches him up, tickling his stomach while he carries Mook back to his mom.

The majorettes begin to make their way offstage and on cue, the lights in the gym shut off, and the spotlights from the side of the stage turn on, lighting up the runway with shades of red. A fog emerges and from the other side of the stage, two girls from my Spanish class stand side by side with

Christian, whose muscles have been oiled down to the point of blinding the audience. I giggle, thinking about Rashida's comment.

"Aight, ladies and gents," Prince bellows, transitioning into the next song, "introducing styles by Mia the mixologist. Known for making the perfect colour cocktail!" They all walk to the middle of the runway, and the two girls release themselves from Christian's grasp, strutting their stuff to the end of the runway. The girl to the left of our beloved point guard has her hair down in curls and does a little tease with her hair, shaking it to and fro for everyone to see, her hair colour changing with each shake and flip of her hand. Her hair looks almost psychedelic and the audience claps. Girl number one walks back to Christian and now it's girl number two's turn, her walk a bit more contained, as she's sporting a yellow curly fauxhawk on her head. "Don't hurt 'em!" Prince yells into the mic. That statement gives her a jolt of confidence, and she gets down on one knee and throws up the hand-horn sign and rocks her head up and back like she's in a rock band. More hoots from the crowd.

Finally, it's Christian's turn. He walks, and rather stiffly I might add, down the runway and blows a kiss at the audience. What they can't see that I can from backstage is that his stylist is also a barber and etched a full basketball hoop and rim in the back of his head, which is also embellished with orange and beige colour. He turns around and points to it, and the audience hoots. The models walk offstage and the beat picks up, Prince scratching Detroit techno music next. Some people from the crowd get up out of their seats and start bouncing to the rhythm.

"Next we got Jaylen, aka the Hair Doctor, who says their job is to bring that tired hair back to life!" Out walks Jaylen in six-inch stiletto boots and a mink coat, pounding the runway like they just stepped out of Milan Fashion Week. They prance to the front of the stage, rip their jacket off, and throw it into the crowd (to a friend, of course), shake their imaginary hair, and extend their hands out to summon their models like a band director summons their troupe, and the models emerge from the back of the crowd. The audience loses it.

The models walk up to the stage, surrounding Jaylen while they vogue. With each move they spritz a little hairspray on one model, or fix a piece with another, or, cutting and spinning scissors in their hands, create masterpieces through their movements. "We just getting started, and these stylists ain't come here to play!" Prince yells on the mic.

"There you are! I've been looking for you!" Esi says, catching me peeking out from behind the curtain. "Let's finish you up." I take one last peek, the next act opening with a tightly choreographed routine as the audience explodes with noise.

Just when I thought I was ready to hit the stage, my nerves pick right back up. My mom is in the audience, and so is my school counsellor, Mr Smith. I got my girls backstage cheering me on (Rashida said she'll even slip out so I can look in her direction if I get nervous), but I haven't done anything this daring since I began my high-school journey, to be honest.

I'm sitting in the chair while Esi and Rashida finish up the last bit of it. The pieces are all different colours, but once Esi teases out my curls and makes my 'fro bigger, it blends into my hair quite nicely, making it look like an arrangement ready for a bride.

"Esi, I'm speechless," I say, looking in one of the few mirrors available backstage. She's standing behind me, putting last-minute touches on the look. I'm wearing a long, sheer lace dress with a white midi dress underneath. The dress is lined with frills and matching fingerless gloves, my nails done up with a gold shimmer, rhinestones and a cutout heart at the centre. I have to admit, Esi's nail tech is the best in the city.

"I wanted this look to be as old as time," she says.

"I know I act like an old woman sometimes, but screw you," I respond, chuckling.

She grabs my shoulders. "Girl, please. Like Diana Ross. I was inspired by a picture of her where she's sitting down and her tresses are cascading around her face and body, and flowers are placed all around her hair. A classic beauty."

Okay, I'll allow that.

"It works," I respond.

"Of course it does. Now you see why I needed my girl to do this."

I nod. "I won't let you down, but hopefully I don't trip on this hair," I add. "It's heavy." She playfully slaps my arm.

*   *   *

"And last, but certainly not least, is Esi Adu's main attraction. Her love letter to Hair Wars, to hair shows across the country, to Black womanhood throughout the decades. Everyone, Bow Down, modelled by the incomparable Danielle Ford." I feel like the last part of that wasn't in the script, but it puts a smile on my face. Prince still knows how to ease my nerves, even when he doesn't realize it. The LED lights dazzle, and I know that's my signal. Esi's instructions were to move slowly – to lure the audience in with steady movements and a fierce face. To let the piece speak for itself.

At first I thought it was Esi's nice way of saying, *Be boring, Dani*, but now that I see everything in its place, she really made me the showstopper. *A classic beauty* keeps ringing in my head as I descend the runway, Riri blaring behind me. I'm not even joking when I tell you I can hear gasps as I approach the end of the stage, onlookers even more impressed when they see the intricate detail of the back of my hair. I freeze in a pose at the edge of the runway, my hands on my hips, then look this way and that. I catch Rashida in the crowd and she's smiling so hard I can almost feel it, both of her thumbs up, cheering me on to greatness. Remembering the Motown images I saw at the museum and channelling my inner Supreme pose, I suck in my midsection and lift my head.

I slowly do a half spin and turn on my toes, thanking the universe I didn't trip in these heels, and walk to the back of the stage. I hear more praise behind me and I do one last thing: I sneak a glance at Prince. His headphones are halfway off his ears, and he looks like he hasn't moved since I hit the runway, transfixed. I give him a smile, and even with the stage lights blinding me, I see his dimple form. I'm floating.

After the show, Rashida and some other models help me take the pieces and flowers out of my hair while Esi gets interviewed by the *Free Press* and a few local sites and influencers. Me, Rashida and a few of the other stylists and models plan to take Esi to a Coney Island to celebrate, and I told Rashida it might be nice to invite Prince. So now she's frantically trying to take as much out of my hair as possible so that I can extend the invitation.

"Ouch! Don't rip it out!" I tell Rashida. "I'm still tender-headed."

"I'm sorry," she says. "I don't want you to miss him."

"Miss who?" one of the models asks, and I give Rashida a death glare. She shrugs, unbothered. When I don't say anything, the model figures it out. "Well, if it's a certain DJ, you might want to go out now. He's almost finished packing up." I can't contain myself any longer and rush to put my heels back on while Rashida works faster.

"Last one," she chimes as I buckle the last of my strap.

I rush back over to the DJ booth, spotting another girl already there talking to Prince. He doesn't seem that engaged, so I assume it's a fan. I lift a hand to wave in his direction and he freezes. Something…isn't right. The girl turns around.

"Hi," she says, her voice short. "I'm Morgan."

Of course. My heart sinks. But this time, I play it off.

"I'm Danielle," I say, and wave.

Prince jumps in. "Morgan was just stopping by—"

"Actually," Morgan interrupts, "I was seeing if we could grab some food after this. You *still* owe me a date."

"Morgan, look. I…"

I need to *go*.

I can't let this ruin Esi's night, and hearing him say yes will absolutely ruin me. "I'm going to leave you two. Prince, it was nice seeing you," I say. "I just wanted to say thank you for doing this. Really, the night was so special to Esi and it wouldn't be complete without you."

"Of course, Dani, but can we—"

"I gotta go! Going to celebrate. But see you around?"

His shoulders sink and he nods. "See you around."

"Nice to meet you, Morgan," I add, my eyes sliding through her. She doesn't say anything, and I don't expect her to. But I continue to channel my Diana Ross as I walk off with the class and grace Esi bestowed upon me for the night. Rashida is waiting for me at the gym doors, her mouth practically in a snarl.

"Down, girl," I say, masking my pain with a smirk.

"Dani—"

"Nope. Esi put together a show for the ages. This is a time of celebration, right?" Rashida snaps back into it.

"You're right." She intertwines her arm with mines. "Let's go enjoy our girl's win."

* * *

I'm brushing my teeth after our celebration and am about to head to bed when I open my emails. I've been avoiding them for the last few days, too tired from last-minute preparations for the show to even open them up, and almost hyperventilate when I scroll through my inbox. An email from NYU. I rush into my mom's room, frantic and barely able to form coherent sentences.

"What, baby, what?" my mom asks, worried.

I still can't talk, so I show Mom my phone screen and she swaddles me in her arms like a baby, sitting me on her lap.

"Whatever happens, Dani, you are worthy of everything your heart desires. Remember our line of strong women." I nod, ready to face whatever decision life has given me.

My mom rocks me as I log into my account and open up my application. I'm unable to breathe suddenly.

"What?!" my mom exclaims. I look up at her, my eyes filled with tears.

"It says congratulations," I murmur. My mom screams and we fall out on my parents' bed, our laughs boisterous and unrestrained and full of relief.

Chapter Twenty
Strike a Chord
PRINCE

"Can we talk?" I ask my mom, watching her watching TV. I put Mook down for bed a little earlier than usual to give us this moment. Which was perfect, because he was still cranky from being out at the hair show the night before. If I don't do this now, I never will.

"Of course," my mom says, patting the couch cushion for me to sit next to her. I drop down and lay my head on her lap, a thing I used to do as a kid, when she was hurting too much to get out of bed. We'd sit in her room, watching TV or listening to music, me entertaining my mom with every detail of my middle-school drama – who was suspended, what girl I thought was cute that week (which included Dani more times than she realized), my short-lived basketball career and the moment I recognized that even though I was tall, I couldn't ball to save my life, our suspicion that the principal and our gym teacher were having an affair –

anything to take my mom's mind off the physical pain of her sickness, and the emotional pain of losing the love of her life. Anything to see her face light up with laughter. She immediately rubs my mane like she did back in the day.

"I miss doing this," she says. "You're too busy for me now."

"I'm sorry," I say, patting her knee.

She chuckles. "Prince, why are you apologizing, baby?" She looks down at me, realizing it's not being busy that I'm apologizing for. "Something is up. Out with it."

I'm too afraid to look her in the eyes when I say it, so I lie there still, like a kid admitting they broke their mom's favourite keepsake. Trust me, I have experience in that department too.

"My grades aren't the best this semester, Ma."

I feel her body stiffen. "Like how bad?" she asks.

My voice goes solemn. "I'm not failing…" No, Prince. Don't do the same thing you did to Mr Smith. Be honest. You're about to be eighteen in a few weeks – show your mom you can be a man who can own up to his faults. I slowly sit up and look my mom in the eye. That's what she deserves. I clear my throat. "I got a couple Ds. And I didn't apply to any schools like I told you I did."

"Prince!" my mom barks.

"I know, I know," I say, putting my hands up in defeat. "But I am going to community college, and Mr Smith has offered to help me get into a university sophomore year."

"And will that university be in New York?" I freeze. *Where is this coming from?* I've never told her I wanted to go. It's as if she reads my mind. "Prince, I've seen your search history."

"Dang, Ma, you snooping on me?"

She smacks her lips. "It's *my* computer. I was trying to find something I looked up a few days before. You know I can be forgetful." She's right. Her falls have caused her memory to lapse some. I feel guilty even letting that come out my mouth. "Anyway, I saw multiple searches of you looking at a music programme there. I was just waiting...maybe hoping...you'd come to me with good news about you getting in. I didn't want to press it if you weren't ready to tell me. I definitely didn't want to admit what I saw."

I go silent. At a true loss for words. "I...I just don't want you to think I'm abandoning you..."

My mom shakes her head. "Boy, I was taking care of myself before you were even born."

"But Ma, that's different, that was before..."

"MS?" she sighs. "Prince, I know I lean on you a lot. But a lot of it is convenience. I trust you. You *want* to help me. But you have to understand, sometimes you take on too much and cause yourself to burn out too."

I sit there, perplexed. "What do you mean?"

"When I ask you to do something for me and then I find out later from your uncle that you had a project, and a radio side gig, and doing the station every day *and* school...do you know how bad I feel? I would have never asked you to do those things if I had known you had all that on your plate."

"But I *want* to do those things."

"I know. I can tell. But you can't be everything to everybody. Guess what? If I ask you to remind your uncle to come over and fix something? It's 'cause I know you'll run into him at the studio and it's another reminder. But if you would have said, 'Ma, text me to remind me,' or, 'I won't see him at the station today,' or, 'I have so many things on my plate I won't remember,' then guess what I would have done? I would have called him every day until he came over. 'Cause remember, he's my brother. We grew up together. I know how to get something out of him if I need to. Or I would have found another way to get it done.

"Because that's what you do. You find a way to get it done. Being tight with money has never defined me. Having MS has never defined me. But you know what has? Being a mother. I've been fortunate to be raising two of the smartest, most handsome, most amazing Black boys on this planet."

She begins to cry. "You and Mook both have such good hearts. And I feel so blessed to say I created you." I have no time to collect myself and my tears fall quickly. "You have so much potential. And all I gotta do is let you go off for a few years to find yourself so you come back to me a better person to the world. I would do that in a heartbeat." She sighs heavily, and then says the things I've been needing to hear. "I know your grades need some work and you're going to community college. So let's use this as a transitional year for us all. We'll work together so we can slowly help each other become more self-sufficient. We'll work on a plan to have my closest people help me whenever I need it. And you'll show me how you do certain things so I can learn on my own, or ask someone else to help me.

"I'm sorry I scared you in the beginning of all this. I know it scarred you finding your mom like that, and this thing was so new to me I probably shared too much with you. But you were all I had to talk to. I didn't know how to manage the newness of MS and raise two kids as a single mom, and I probably traumatized you. And you..." Her voice cracks. "You just helped me so much, Prince. I will never ever be able to repay you for that."

She grabs my chin. "But I've lived with this thing for a long time now. I can do this, Prince. I need you to believe I can do this. Do you?"

The last thing I ever wanted to do was make my mom feel like I didn't believe she could do it. I was young and afraid when she was diagnosed, but I also saw how quickly she went into fight-or-flight mode. My mom set an example of what happens when life throws a curveball at you and you crawl and scratch your way out to survive. She fought for herself. And to me, that makes her one of the most powerful people in the world. I know she can.

I hug my mama as tightly as I can, resting my chin on the top of her head. Watching my tears splatter onto her coils. "You give me and Mook way too much credit. We are who we are because of you. I always tell you to stop being superwoman, 'cause that's the way I see you. A force too big for this world. I never want to lose you. Ever," I whisper. My mom's body is trembling as I hold her tight and she bawls. "There's no one I believe in more."

Chapter Twenty-One

In Tune

PRINCE

YASIN: It's done. I dropped the note off.

PRINCE: Ok thanks man. I owe you.

YASIN: No sweat. I hope things work out, but you did the best you could. No regrets.

I smile.

PRINCE: Yeah man, no regrets.

I'm sitting on my porch, letting the warm air recharge me. Outside, the neighbourhood is calm, yet vibrant. The suffocating winter has had everyone itching to go outside, and May is here to deliver the perfect mix of afternoon breezes combined with longer hours of daylight. That's what

I see right now. Kids digging in the dirt, a group of friends who came to visit saying goodbye to each other for what feels like hours, my city happy to just be out in the sunlight.

That's what I keep telling myself. I did all I could. And whatever happens, I'm proud of myself and proud of Danielle. When we started dating, she was timid, she was angry, but most importantly, she was hurt. The girl I saw at the hair show was more bold, more confident, more secure. I wish I could take the credit for that, but I can't – it was all her. And I'd also like to think it was thanks to the people who love her most: the friends who wouldn't let her go, the devotion of her parents who adore her, and maybe…just maybe…a little bit of me to show her that not all guys are bad guys.

And what Danielle brought to my life, man. She never gave up on me. She never accepted my impulse to settle. She saw beneath my complacency and called out my jitters. She told me to read more, and I did. Which helped me get over my own issues. She helped me understand it's okay not to be so heroic all the damn time, and that showing your faults is okay, it only makes you human. Everything about her, everything about this, changed me. If I wanted a girl like Dani, I needed to be a better human myself. She made me grow the hell up.

I decided this time around to keep things simple. No elaborate date. No crazy new location. Just this. Just us. Because even with the dramatic shit I was planning, when me and Danielle got lost in the moment, we were lost in just each other. When we drowned out all the noise and chaos around us was when I felt the most in tune with her. For this occasion, a grand gesture didn't feel right. I had been watching everyone at school, giving ridiculous-ass promposals, decking out red carpets in front of their homes, and while I thought it was beautiful, I also realized that wasn't us. That wasn't Danielle. She would never want me to ask her out like that. It was the intimate ways I connected with her – us alone in her basement, me silently sneaking skates into her locker, us sitting together at a bookstore – where I saw her fall for me. I came in trying to win her over, and she came in and changed my entire path. The best love I could possibly give her is selfless love – to let her go on whatever journey she needs to go on to find love within herself and hope one day she comes back to me. She is the type of love songwriters like Smokey Robinson were inspired by.

After Danielle rushed off at the hair show, I did something I should have done a long time ago. I took Morgan out. She talked about working things out and being my date to prom, and I told her I didn't plan on going, just emceeing. Truth is, if I wasn't attending prom with Danielle, it just wasn't worth it to me.

We hashed it out. I was honest with Morgan about what we had, and how we'd grown apart. Honest about why I thought she wanted me in the first place. And she admitted she kept reaching out because she was lonely. I explained to her why I couldn't be her back-up plan, her go-to when things went south with whoever she was dating at the moment. I confessed to Morgan that I loved Danielle, and that whatever happened between me and her, it wouldn't be fair to try to work things out with Morgan.

My heart was somewhere else completely.

She wasn't thrilled, but it was clear it was done between us. And when I finally admitted to Morgan my feelings for Danielle, when I said it out loud for the first time ever, I knew I had to give it one more shot.

My phone buzzes, and I feel like luck is on my side, because Danielle Ford's stunning face pops up on my screen. I hit accept. "Can you come over?" is all she asks me, and I tell her I'm on my way.

Chapter Twenty-Two

Love Notes

Danielle

I meet Prince on my front porch. He comes out of the car, just as timid as I am about what needs to be done. He wrote me my first love letter, the best letter. His words were so raw, so authentic. He could be a writer if he wanted to.

Dear Danielle,

I picked up one of the books I saw you holding in the library and read the dedication. And you right, them joints are fire.

"Bicycles: because love requires trust and balance."

First, you need to trust me. So here's the truth. Morgan and I are done…well, let's be clear, we BEEN done, but I needed to be man enough to tell her. And honest enough to tell her why.

With balance, I had to work out everything with my family, and my grades. Mr Smith is helping me to transfer my sophomore year out of state to whoever will have me (but my heart is in New York…for a lot of reasons), and I signed up for the summer programme at the museum and got in! All thanks to you. I see now why you needed space to heal. I needed space to get my shit together. To be a better man for myself, and hopefully one day a better man for you.

I love you, Danielle. You probably knew that, but you've made me recognize the power of words, how they matter, so I'm telling you now. Here, so that this is a love note you can hold close to you. Whatever happens between us, whatever man you end up settling down with (although I promise he'll suck in comparison to me), keep this note. Write about me in one of your books, write about us. That will be your love note to me. A way to subtly let me know you never forgot about me. This memory. This moment in time when the world was so confusing and we had to grow up, and we grew up in one another. That our time together was boundless, that affection and appreciation and fondness and emotion are all the things we felt together (and yes, I looked at a thesaurus for words to describe love, so what). Because I love you. Did I say that? I love you enough to lose you, to be thankful to have had you, to want you to be the happiest version of Danielle you can be. And whether that's with me or without, your mom is right. If anyone deserves a true love story, it's you.

Your Prince

Love Notes Mixtape, Volume ∞

I step off the porch and approach him. He's standing there with his hands in his pockets. Waiting for me to say something, so we make small talk, too nervous to broach the subject at hand.

"So, how did that essay turn out?" he asks.

"Good enough to get into NYU," I respond with the hugest grin, unable to contain my excitement.

"Yooooooo!" he says. "That's incredible, Dani!" He gives me the same look my dad gave me on FaceTime, the same look my mom gave me as we collapsed on the bed – their faces beaming with pride. I know he's for real happy for me, and it makes me giddy.

"Yeah, me and Esi both got in. We're going to be roommates, too. And Shida is coming to help us move in. Me and Esi's parents chipped in on this Airbnb in the West Village so all the families can stay there while we do our freshman move-in this August. I think this trip is for them more than us, but I can't wait."

"You deserve all that and more, Danielle Ford," he says, hands still in his khaki shorts pockets, his gorgeous calves peeking between his shorts and socks.

"Thank you. So…what about you? You feel okay about going local?" I respond, afraid to ask but also needing to know.

"Yeah, it'll be me and Ant at Wayne, which is cool. We're going to take most of the same classes, and he and I are going to be on each other. He wants to transfer to State and I want to…" My eyes go wide and I keep my lips tight with such velocity, forcing myself not to finish this sentence and be disappointed. He shoots me a cynical look and smiles.

"For real, P?!" I pout. He laughs.

"You're so easy to get riled up. I missed it." I blush. "It's still CUNY. That's my goal."

I let go of the hugest sigh. He's still dreaming big. "I love that," I respond with almost a whisper. "What about Malik and Yasin?"

"M is going to Western…" And he raises his eyebrow, which causes me to almost snort-laugh.

"With Rashida?" I respond. He nods.

"Yep, how convenient," he says with a smirk. "For someone who has been denying his feelings, he sure went all in. And Yasin got into Howard's architecture program, so he's going there."

"Wait…HOWARD?" *The* Howard. I love that for him.

Prince chuckles. "I guess he couldn't get enough of me, Malik and Ant. I'm excited to go cut up with him for homecoming."

"That's cool," I say. "I knew he could draw, but I didn't know he wanted to be an architect."

"I bet he'll shift majors to animation or become a picture book illustrator. Reading all those books to Mook made me realize Yaz could easily do that." He shrugs. "I could be wrong, though."

"When he comes to visit you, we'll take him to some author signings or Comic Con. Open himself up to the idea."

His smile glares as bright as the sunrays reflecting off his retro patent-leather Jordans. "We?"

It was time to acknowledge why he was here. "I got the Bluetooth radio you had Yasin drop off. I love that you wrote *and* recorded the letter," I say. "Felt like I was following along while listening to an audiobook. You *do* have the best radio voice. You know that, right?"

His cheeks go red. "You're the writer, I'm the speaker. I wanted you to hear those words out my mouth. I figured this was the best of both worlds." He shrugs again. "And who knows? Maybe audiobook recordings are in my future. Anything to make some extra cash, right?"

"Right."

We stand there, his eyes connected to mines, and I feel whole.

"I read somewhere that the best lovers are best friends first. And Prince, you've become my very best friend. That's what I missed the most. I missed our laughs, and our talks... and your clumsy ass."

"I missed everything about you, too," he chimes. "I never thought I could miss someone so badly."

Afraid of what to do next, we don't move, still lost in each other's eyes, until we hear a *click-click-click* noise, our eyes widening at the same time. Uh-oh. Before we have a chance to sprint off, the lawn sprinklers cut on.

Right.

On.

My.

Silk.

Press.

I'm pissed. I purposely got this done before I called Prince over, trying to be extra cute when I admitted my feelings for him. Prince's eyes are so big I can't help but howl with laughter. "You look like you've seen a ghost!" I say.

"The ghost of straight hair past," he responds. I shake my head. *And I'm supposed to be the dork.* He takes hold of my waist, pulling me back into the sprinklers.

"What are you doing? We're getting even more wet!"

"Teach me how to ballroom dance," he says.

"But we don't have any music!"

"Shh, just trust me."

"Okay," is all I say as I smile and take his hands. Prince purses his lips and uses his voice and air to create sound, to create a rhythm to step to, and I chuckle.

"Let my voice guide you," I say, and whisper in his ear where to step. I take the lead this time, and we step forward and back, make our half turns, and do it all over again. He's stumbling a little bit but finally, when he is getting the hang of it, I say, "I thought you wouldn't let me teach you until I said those words."

He stops beatboxing.

"Then say it," he says silkily.

"Say what?" I reply teasingly.

"Say the words I've been dying to hear."

I pause. "'Don't ever think I fell for you or fell over you. I didn't fall in love, I rose in it. I saw you and made up my mind. *My* mind. And I made up my mind to follow you too,'" I recite.

He pulls away and looks at me, grinning super hard, his eyes squinting from the water droplets cascading from his face. "I liiiike that. You pen those bars?"

"I wish," I reply. "Maybe one day I'll write something half as good as that. It's Toni Morrison."

"Toni be knowing," is all he says as he pulls me closer again, our lips locking into a soft, tender rhythm. It's as if the sprinklers washed away any doubts we had about our love for one another, for the crazy year ahead – him in Detroit and me in New York City. This time, we let the whistle of the trees and the humming of birds be our melody as we lock lips and dance. Our clothes drenched, my hair soaked, our faces dripping. Us in each other's arms, never letting go.

He's right. She does.

Acknowledgements

To think when I set out to write this story in 2019, it would become all of this and more. I'm incredibly grateful for the people in my life who have ridden with me since day one, who helped me build this imaginary love story in my head into a piece of work I'm proud of.

Working in the publishing biz for so long, I knew the one thing I refused to do was compromise the vision for my work, and was willing to forgo writing if I wasn't able to write it my way. But that didn't mean standing in my truth wasn't scary. Dhonielle, thank you for never making me feel like I had to water down anything. The best teachers are the ones who pull the best work out of their students, and you are that. I am so lucky to have had you to usher in my first piece of literature.

To Jo and Suzie, thank you for your support and help with guiding through the other side of the publishing process. Patrice, I love that you are always a voice of reason and one of the rare people who understand my struggle as both a publishing professional and author. I'm beholden. And a big thank-you to the rest of the Cake and New Leaf team – Margo, Clay, Miranda, Sophia, and others who have helped me in each stage of the process.

Thank you to the team at Usborne: Rebecca Hill, Sarah Stewart, Will Steele, Sarah Cronin, Jo Olney, Alice Moloney, and anyone else I didn't call by name but has been instrumental in helping me publish *Love Radio* in the UK. Noa Denmon and Krista Vossen, my cover is a dream brought to life and it's all because of you two.

There are a lot of people in the industry who I've worked with who really believe in me, and I'd be remiss if I didn't acknowledge them now.

Howard University Bookstore – the place that showed me a job in publishing even existed. To my Howard University Bookstore fam and my work study boss, Monique Mozee. You were the first example of a Black female publishing professional that I wanted to be like. You were charming and passionate and open and kind. You poured so much into my career, and you helped me get into this industry, when I was ready to give up and move out of NYC. You were the big sister I never had and saved me in many ways while I was in DC.

Saraciea, what can I say that I haven't already said to you? My first real publishing friend. Who knew all parts of my life, including the parts

I kept hidden from the rest of the industry. I truly value your realness, the way you calm my fears, and how you always have my back.

Jane Lee and Kamilah "Hype Queen" Cole, thank you for championing me from the beginning. I knew having you read this would give me the confidence I needed to do this thing right. The fact that you both sent me texts, pictures, audio notes, and displayed real tears over my little story, was enough to let me know if you two loved *Love Radio*, then I did my best. Thanks for helping me deal with my newly formed anxiety, for calling me out and telling me to stfu and accept the goodness coming to me. And to Jane – we bonded at work in a way that I'm amazed by to this day. You are a sweet, sweet human, who cares about mentorship and people in a way that's so incredibly rare. We've had each other's backs over the years, and you are one of the few people to understand my random-ass ideas, just as I understand yours. Thank you for always lending an ear and for forcing me to do all the things for my book that I tell other authors to do every single day but was too afraid to do myself. Love you, kiddo.

Vintage S&S fam – Anthony, Bernadette, Lydia, Nick, and Sooji, thank you for your advice and support in making this decision. While there are not many of y'all still in publishing (lol), it's nice to know I always have you for guidance and friendship. And a special shout-out to you, Sooji, who were with me the day I signed my book deal and sat outside with me in the freezing cold to have a drink in Brooklyn and CELEBRATE such a whirlwind week.

To Carla, Nicole, and Rio; I'll never forget the night I won Indies Introduce and how the chat blew up. You all gave me my flowers, your contacts, your love, and you didn't even read the book. The kinship I feel for you all is real; thank you for your writing advice and being examples of phenomenal writers I look up to. A group to bond over losing our beloved bell hooks/sending poetry or art to one another to brighten our day/hyping each other up to remind ourselves of who tf we are/talking ish about anything and everything Black women talk smack about/and everything in between. Just being in your presence as you are shaping your own stories is an MFA program in itself. Our bond is real and I'm so grateful to have y'all.

Michael, my first beta reader of my first two chapters. When I was deathly afraid to pass this first iteration your way, but I also knew that whatever feedback you gave would be brutally honest and help me press on, and it was. Your honesty and love was what made me realize I could actually do this. Luana, I love you for putting me in my place as a newbie author; you are a shining light girl, and already killing the game. Baby genius Tyler (lol), thank you for tweaking my marketing copy in a way only your smart behind could and always sharing memes you created of me even though I secretly hate it. The rest of my Harper crew – Sabrina, Shannon, Valerie, Lisa, Katie, Mabel, Emily, Seoling – and everyone else at Harper I can't name but had the pleasure working with, thank you all for your unique insights and teaching me a few things; Harper was the place where I blossomed in my marketing career, and its due in large part to working with some incredible teachers, most of whom were younger than me.

Jasmine, thank you for giving me my first blurb. You have been nothing but supportive and passionate and coming from the biggest Black romance writer in the game, it means everything. I will never forget it. To Liz for my second blurb. I got to work with you from day one, so to have your support is monumental. Thank you for the realness you brought to my blurb and your work. Karah, Paige, Caroline, Venessa, Namrata, Jenn, Booki, Kris, Georgia, Milena, Maudee, Candace, Jackie, Yona, Malaika, Gilda, Uli, Linda, Natalie, Richard, Dana, Elizabeth, Amani – I can't possibly name the ways you've helped me navigate this industry, but you all know and deserve to be recognized. Glory, thank you for revealing my cover and giving me my first real community of readers who GOT me. Those old WRBG Brooklyn meetups were soul food. I would have left publishing long ago if it wasn't for them.

Phebe and Arti: thank you for having long discussions and being open and honest about your disabilities, long before I even wrote this story. I've learned so much from you both about being honest with yourself and your body. About learning to rest and refusing to buy into ableism in a way that society tries to force upon you. I'm grateful to you both for offering to read *Love Radio* and make sure I did Lori justice. Thank you, Jonathan, for your musical feedback.

To my girls' trip group chat crew: I said this on our girls' trip, but you all were truly the reason I was able to go through this process. You kept me sane, confident, and with all the discipline and work that went into this project, you all helped me let my hair down. I'm thankful to have a friend turned sister in Shanelle, who I've known way too long and love as true blood – it is a rare treat to know someone who will have your back and give you all they have. Thank you for all that you bring to our friendship. Kiah, I hope I honoured you and your family with date number two; we're all just waiting for you to reopen that record shop, sis. Gelila, my music soul mate, I can't envision my twenties without running through NYC listening to musicians in tiny concert venues before they hit it big. You showed me the best parts of the city. Lola, I talk to you way too much, and I couldn't see it any other way. Thank you for understanding me in a way most people don't.

My childhood homies from Detroit who I still feel so close with to this day – Crystal and Shari. I love how we can still reminisce, unpack, and how we can link and pick up right where we left off. Both of you ladies were always true to yourselves, and I truly believe it's why we still ride for each other all these years. Appreciate your brainstorming sessions with me and support as I was crafting *Love Radio*.

To writers that I've had the pleasure to work with or be around like Wayétu M., Ibi Z., Angie T., Tiffany J., Liara T., Abigail W., Victoria A., Tahereh M., Adam S., Lamar G., Julie M., Becky A., Jasmin K., Jason R., Nic S., Nicola Y., Ashley W., Ben P., and other authors who I've worked with directly or indirectly or just had the pleasure of your warmth and company; your trust and faith in my ability to talk about your book in the right way or appease my wild marketing ideas have meant everything. Thanks for entrusting me with your work.

And to my girl Nesha. You're not physically here with us, but your love still is infectious. You showed me the meaning of loving someone with no family attachment, no blood; that you can still love as purely and wholly as you loved me. I wish osteosarcoma didn't take you away from us, but I'm thankful to have known you and experience a sisterfriend-soulmate-kinda-love. You helped me realize I can be with someone who will love all my imperfections and love me in spite of. What a gift. Tiffany and Chardai, I'm so thankful that I've been able to witness this friendship with you both, and to continue our versions of it to this day. To Angie, Ren, Rhonda, Shanice, and the rest of my extended family – our bond is unshakable.

To my mommy, the first artist I ever met – I've learned to become an artist because of you and have been so grateful to grow up watching you create. Whether it was through your paintings, listening to your angelic voice, or watching you act your ass off in a local production, I got to witness it all. I am the Black woman I am because of you. I love you. To my first prince, my papa, the first man I ever loved. Thank you for always pushing me to do better, for believing in my ambition before I did. You've made me feel like the luckiest daughter in the world. Chevella, I wish there was a better word for stepmom, because it just doesn't suit you. You've been an integral part of my life and loved me just because, and I'm incredibly appreciative. To Blaire and Chelsea, my sisters. I held each of you in my arms and knew at seven and eleven I had partners for life. Our bond is ours to cherish forever, and I love that I have it with you two crazy women. I couldn't ask for a better village.

Saving the best for last, I cannot forget about you, baby. To Ajit, my forever muse – I feel like I've lived a thousand lives with you, and ready to live a thousand more. There's so much I could say, but the thing that always comes back to me is how you enrich my life with joy. Thank you for making your daily goal to make me deep belly laugh. In a world that's so cruel to Black women, you always know the ways to restore me. The Maya quote at the end is dedicated to you. I rose in love with you, and life has never been the same. Thank you for making me happy.

And to that reader who has been looking for this type of story. I hope I did it justice, and I cannot wait to meet you.